i

Kelvin Robertson

Fishing for Fish

For the crew of Little Jeannie, for all the fun we've had over the years, and especially to Neil for the illustration.

Chapter 1

Charles had not realised before that he could summon up such determination. His heart felt as if it were beating like that of a hummingbird, and he was struggling to take in enough breath to propel him towards the lady in the high-visibility jacket who was beginning to close the barrier. He had not broken into a run in years, but somehow, with an awkward gait he was nearly there.

'Wait, wait,' he managed to blurt, attracting her attention just as she was about to close off his only escape route.

'Hurry up, the train is about to leave,' she said, taking pity on him, leaving just enough room for him to squeeze through. 'There, look, the train guard,' she said, pointing to the last carriage door.

With just seconds to spare, he reached for its handle.

'Steady on. You've cut it fine, haven't you?'

With his lungs about to burst Charles looked up to see the guard grinning down, his peaked hat square on his head, looking authoritative.

'Yes, I must catch this train.'

'You have. This is the last resort for late passengers, up here. No luggage?'

'No, I had to leave in a hurry.'

'I can see that. Come on, get aboard. We're leaving in about twenty seconds according to my watch.'

Gratefully, Charles pulled himself into the carriage as the shrill blast of the platform guard's whistle reminded him of just how close he had come to disaster. Mumbling a few words of gratitude, he made his way past the guard and into the carriage. He did not have a seat reservation; in fact, he did not even have a ticket, but at that moment it was of little consequence. The fact that he was leaving London was all that mattered. Shuffling down the aisle, he made his way towards the nearest vacant seat, landing heavily upon it, reassured that he was unnoticed. The man in the window seat did not even look up from his newspaper and those on the far side of the aisle were too preoccupied to take any notice. Recovering some faculties, Charles took deep breaths and stared involuntarily at the maker's name on the seat in front of him, a focus point amidst the blur, an oasis of calm removed from the violence.

The train began to move and he was able to relax a little. He had made it, escaped, and now he dared look around the carriage. Too early for the commuters, the passengers looked a mixed bag – older people, mostly, and he felt some relief to see them all seated. It meant he was the last to enter the carriage. If anyone had followed him, boarded another carriage, then at least he could watch the connecting door for danger.

Were the men dead? Without their intervention he might have suffered the same fate, or at least be a prisoner of... Andrei Potanin? To his mind there was no other explanation. His employer was a powerful man with connections to the Kremlin itself, and he was sure from the letter that had come into his possession just a few hours earlier that it was more than a simple and fleeting acquaintance.

The train began to pick up speed. People, seats,

kiosks, they all became a blur and then there was nothing, just a plethora of railway signals, overhead wires, and Victorian brick structures. Oh, what a relief... and then the thought occurred. Where was the train travelling to? He had bought a platform ticket, the quickest and easiest way to pass through the barrier, but had no idea which train he had boarded. Having summoned every drop of strength to get this far, he was just grateful to be moving. He had taken the first train he could see, aware that Kings Cross served the north of the country. Newcastle, perhaps? He could hide for a while or cross the border into Scotland, hide out for a week, maybe longer, but at that moment he didn't really care where the train was going just so long as it was away from London.

Turning his head, he glanced briefly at his fellow passenger, glad to see the man was more interested in his newspaper than the panic-stricken individual sitting in the adjacent seat. Charles was becoming paranoid but with good reason, and settling back in his seat, he suddenly became aware of a throbbing pain in his left hand. Looking down, he noticed congealed blood on his fingers and turned his palm face up to reveal the source: a gash no more than a few centimetres long. Not serious, he reasoned. Most of the blood had already dried and yet it was a reminder of how close he had come to catastrophe.

'Are you alright? That looks nasty,' said the man in the window seat, who had finally taken his eyes off his newspaper.

'Er, yes, nothing really. I caught it on something sharp on my way to the station. No idea what.'

The man grunted and returned to his newspaper, leaving Charles to his wound. Slowly squeezing his fingers together, he grimaced in pain and tried to think about his destination. He had no clear idea of where he should go, and with nowhere to stay, no spare clothes, not even a toothbrush, he had a problem. But before he could consider his position a voice close behind interrupted his thoughts.

'Tickets, please.'

He turned his head to see the same guard who had rescued him inspecting tickets and moving ever closer, his fellow passenger folded his newspaper, began to fumble in his jacket pocket for his own ticket and Charles began to fret that he didn't have one. Perhaps he could buy a ticket, but having no idea of what it might cost or the funds he possessed, he was at a loss. He had his credit cards, of course, but the thought occurred that anyone with the right resources might be able to view his account and there was the distinct possibility that they would see he was heading north on the three o'clock train to... Where was the train heading? He still had little idea.

'Tickets, please.'

Charles's neighbour produced his ticket and then the inspector turned to him.

'Ticket, please, sir.'

'Ah, I don't have one, can I purchase one off you?'

'Certainly, sir, but it will be a lot more expensive.'

'No matter, er... Where are we headed?'

The ticket collector frowned. 'Edinburgh.'

'Kings Cross to Edinburgh, please.'

'That will be one hundred and twenty-seven pounds.'

'How much?'

'This is a first-class coach, sir.'

'Oh, of course.'

'Do you take cash?'

'Yes, sir.'

Charles fumbled in his pocket, retrieving some loose change and a twenty-pound note, obviously not enough to cover the fare.

'Drat, it will have to be a credit card,' he said, swapping the cash for his card and thinking, So much for not leaving a trail... 'What time is the last train from Edinburgh back to London?'

'Nineteen thirty-six, platform six. Tomorrow, is it, sir?'

'Er, yes – or maybe Friday, I haven't decided. Thank you,' he said, swiping his credit card across the ticket inspector's reader and wondering if he might take the late train back to Newcastle and stay there.

'Your ticket, sir. Have a pleasant journey,' said the inspector, turning to the seats opposite and leaving Charles with an overwhelming feeling of apoplexy.

Screwing his eyes tight shut, he tried to make sense of his situation. He was on a train to Edinburgh, a city he had never visited and dressed in nothing but his business suit – hardly the right attire for the Scottish weather he mused.

The blue light flashed its circular path, illuminating the two body bags and three men standing beside the ambulance. One, hands in his pockets, took a step back and turned to his colleague, a taller and older man. With a grim look on his face he said, 'Funny do, Graham, what do you think happened?'

'Blimey, well, it wasn't robbery, I'm sure. The pair are braan bread and still have money and cards on them, and both are in possession of their mobile phones. It seems no one saw anything, nor heard anything. I wonder if they came from the Queens Head over there, an altercation maybe, or some sort of vendetta? Who knows, but it's a starting point,' said the sergeant, pointing to the public house at the far end of the street. 'It's possible they came from there.'

'Right, let's do some old-fashioned policing, get a few uniforms knocking on doors and asking questions, see if there are any security cameras in the area. In the meantime, I suggest we take a walk to that pub,' he said, making way for the medics who were ready to lift the first of the bodies onto a stretcher. He turned to the third man, who was dressed in a white coat and wearing a medical mask.

'We are going for a look in that pub, Henderson. Let me have anything you can as soon as. There is more to this double murder than meets the eye, I am sure.'

The forensic pathologist nodded, finished writing and looked up at Inspector Mills.

'We've collected about as much evidence as we can for now Eddie. I will determine the cause of death back in the morgue, though it appears both died of stab wounds. Apart from knowing exactly what murder weapon the killer used, all I can say is that I think one man killed both of them.'

'How so?'

'They were in identical positions. Must have happened very quickly, neither victim seemed to have moved far. I will know better when I have had a closer look at the stab wounds.'

The inspector pursed his lips and nodded. Henderson knew his job, he would give him that. His report would at least clear up the cause of death and maybe furnish a few more clues for the detectives to work on.

'Come on, Graham, let's have a look in the pub,' said the Inspector

The Queens Head had seen better days, one of just a small number of old-fashioned drinking pubs left in Islington. As the two policemen walked in they noticed workers calling in on their way home beginning to congregate in the bar.

'Have a wander round, Sergeant, see if there is anyone you know while I tackle the landlord.'

Inspector Mills cast his eye over the assembly. A few tradesmen, a group of city types in suits chatting and laughing, and seated in a corner three hardened drinkers, their faces worn down by neglect. A heavily built man emerged from a doorway behind the bar and the inspector guessed he was the landlord.

'Can I have a word?'

The man looked up, his eyes narrowing slightly.

'What about, who are you?'

'Police, there's been some trouble down towards the junction. Are you the landlord?'

'Yes. What kind of trouble?' Not all visitors to his establishment were law-abiding citizens and the last thing he needed was the police snooping round. 'In there,' he said, pointing. 'The pump room, we can talk privately in there.'

He instructed the young barman to hold the fort. 'This man is from the brewery and wants to inspect our pumps,' he said, and then to the inspector, 'What's this about? My pub is honest. The problem I had with those thieving bastards doing their fencing in here, I put a stop to weeks ago.'

'No, it's nothing like that. A murder, a double murder just hours ago. We think the victims might have spent time in here before they were attacked.'

The publican's jaw dropped. 'I heard something was

happening. How can I help?'

'Do you have CCTV?'

'Back of the bar and near the entrance, and there is another camera outside.'

'Good, that's a start.'

'Who were they?'

'That's what we are trying to find out. Two men in their mid- to late twenties, we think, though it's too early to be sure. One has a well-trimmed dark beard and hair colour to match, the other had lighter hair. Both Caucasian. Any idea?'

The publican stroked the growth on his own chin, his eyes looking inward. Hundreds of people visited his pub. He could not recall all of them, yet a picture was forming and he did remember two men who fitted the description.

'Maybe. There were two men in here for a short time this afternoon, looked as if they were waiting for someone, but other than that I can't say.'

'That is helpful, it could save us time – particularly if you can let us have the recordings from your surveillance cameras. I'll get someone over here to take care of that.'

'Do you think it's gang-related? We've seen an increase in gangs around here.'

'Too early to say. First step is to identify them.'

'There is something...'

'What?'

'They only drank a couple of soft drinks, orange juice, if I remember correctly. No chance of retiring early if all my customers drink nothing but orange juice.'

The clickity-click of steel wheels on steel rails had a different sound to the one Charles remembered from his youth. Modern trains were soundproofed and the rails laid better, but even so, a methodical metallic rhythm did percolate into the carriage. Sitting and staring into space, he felt almost hypnotised by the sound and just as he was beginning to doze off an announcement over the communication system alerted him.

York would be the first stop, then on to Edinburgh via Northallerton, Newcastle and Berwick-upon-Tweed. Should he travel all the way to Edinburgh, he wondered, find a cash machine, draw out as much cash as he could and use some to purchase a ticket back to Newcastle? If he did that he might throw off any pursuit, untraceable, the beginnings of a plan, he felt, and he needed one.

Entering a search term into his mobile phone, he looked for accommodation for the night. Newcastle's Royal Station Hotel looked a good bet, not far from the station and probably easy to book a room for just one night. With luck, anybody following him would be on a wild goose chase north of the border while he made his escape.

That's it, he almost said out loud, before an attendant passing by with a trolley cut short his thoughts. He had not eaten nor had a drink since earlier that morning. Coffee and a chocolate bar were tempting, and after a glance along the corridor he purchased his refreshments. There were unoccupied window seats on the opposite side of the carriage, so he got up and moved across the aisle, took the window seat, and with the row to himself he sipped his hot drink, though he could not help worrying.

'What a mess, what am I going to do?' he said to himself, sinking back in his seat and finishing his snack. At least the sugar rush was lifting his spirits, but before he could further consider his predicament the speaker system burst into life.

'Ladies and gentlemen,' said the announcer, 'owing to snow on the line this train will terminate at York. Passengers travelling on to Newcastle and Edinburgh will find coaches waiting on the forecourt to take them to Northallerton to connect with a train to complete your journey. East Coast Main Line services apologise for the delay and we wish you a safe onward journey.'

Confused, Charles found the information too much to take in. Shifting his position, he looked along the corridor between the rows of seats to see the same message repeated on the scrolling messageboard.

'York, why not?' he said to himself as he recovered his faculties. No one would know he hadn't completed the journey if they discovered he had bought a ticket to Edinburgh. Surely they would go there to look for him – and York was further from Edinburgh than Newcastle. On the surface it was a much better idea; he would have more time to pull himself together, but the mention of snow reminded him that he was not wearing the warmest of clothes.

The surveillance cameras of the Queens Head public house were not the most modern and the CCTV footage was grainy.

'What do you think, Tabz, can you work with this?' asked the inspector.

The young Afro-Caribbean woman tapped several keys on her computer, sharpening the image, and after a further adjustment looked up at her superior.

'I fink I can do somefing with dis. Do you want to stay while I run frough the tape? You said the murder took place between two and free, so I can speed the recording up to look for likely suspects.'

'Okay, but let's find our victims first, establish their movements, and then you can trawl through the rest to see what you come up with,' said Inspector Mills.

An experienced officer with twenty years in the force, he would normally know what to look for but there was something strange about this case. Pulling up a chair, he spent the next half an hour watching as the young woman ran the recording at twice normal speed.

'That looks like them,' he said. 'Can you zoom in, make the image a bit clearer?'

'Yep, no problem. How's that?' she said, clicking on several icons.

'Brilliant, Tabz. Now we need to find a match, find out their names and try to understand what went on. Can you run some prints off and pass them to Sergeant Fox? He is working with the uniformed team going door to door, and a decent image could do wonders for a potential witness's memory.'

'Leave it wiv me, sir. I will run off some prints and then check databases to see if I can find a match. If I do, I'll call you straight away like.'

Inspector Mills did not reply directly, he simply sat quietly, examining the two faces on the screen. The pathologist had inferred that the killer – or killers – knew exactly what he was doing, a professional, and that was beginning to bother him.

'Okay,' he said finally. 'I have a meeting with the chief in a few minutes. I can at least tell him we believe we are on the way to identifying the victims, and hopefully you will be able to tell me soon enough who they were. Then it will be a case of finding the murderer or murderers.'

'I'll look again, see if anyfing shows up.'

'Thanks, Tabz.'

He would need to present something to his boss,

because the media had already latched onto the story and the superintendent would need something to keep them at bay. Thinking how to handle the problem, he entered his boss's office.

'Take a seat. What have you got for me, Eddie?'

'Not a lot, sir. We have some CCTV showing the victims leaving the Queens Head, but no info yet on who they were. I have the intelligence team conducting a search for a positive ID and DS Fox is organising a house to house. I'm hopeful we'll turn something up soon.'

'Hmm, I have agreed to a press conference at ten in the morning. I need to show we are making progress even if we must pad it out for public consumption.'

'Henderson thinks it was a professional job. I don't know what makes him think that, but he's the expert and he seemed certain it wasn't just a random stabbing or something gang-related.'

'Professional? What does that mean?'

'Maybe organised crime, maybe a foreign player is involved. I don't know.'

'A foreign player? That could prove difficult. Let's hope your analyst can eliminate that scenario, because I don't want the security agencies breathing down my neck.'

After an interminable delay the train finally moved through the January afternoon mist, passing the smudged green 'go' signal hanging over the rails. In his imagination, Charles believed for a moment that the Cyclops had come to take him.

'Silly fool,' he said to himself, peering further into the gloom and wondering how near to York they were.

The surroundings were unfamiliar, the name of the one small station they passed through unknown to him, then lights began appearing and the train slowed dramatically. Some of the other passengers knew the routine, standing and reaching for their possessions, and then the platform came into view. A squeal of brakes and the train came to a halt, the carriage doors opened and the passengers streamed onto the platform.

Charles hung back, following only once the crush had subsided. The question then arose as to whether he should join those travelling on, take the coach to Northallerton, or remain in York? Northallerton did not sound very inviting and it was probably not a large town, the choice had been between Newcastle and Edinburgh but now York became a possibility.

Mulling his options, time implications, he believed that obtaining cash from a machine in Edinburgh and then retracing his journey back to Newcastle was a sound enough plan, but this added complication was causing him to re-think. Why not York? It did appear a more inviting prospect.

If the people pursuing him were Andrei Potanin's men, he knew how ruthless they could be. On more than one occasion he had witnessed their thuggish ways. He was simply an accountant, no threat to anyone, a fly-on-the-wall that no one seemed to pay much attention to, and yet he knew he was a central figure of the organisation – one who contributed more than his fair share to its success. In exercising a wide-ranging control over the money passing through his employer's business, he knew what made it tick and that had given him the opportunity to siphon off a tiny percentage for himself.

But that was the problem. If Potanin or even Sergei found out what he had done, he would be toast. But he had a plan, take as much as he could without raising suspicion and then disappear into a life of modest luxury, and to that end, he had covertly created a new persona. When the time came, he would have a passport in the name of Chris Kent, a bank account in that name and a Bitcoin wallet. His new persona was not quite Superman, but then he never aspired to be super. All he ever wanted was a comfortable, trouble-free life and if he remained in the shadows, he could realise that ambition. There was no woman in his life to complicate matters, and provided he could disappear unnoticed, a happy and comfortable future awaited.

There had been a woman in his life, Jenny, but she had left ten years earlier – bored, she said, tired of his long hours away from her. In the end, the temptation of their daughter's secondary-school teacher had proved too much for her. He had given up their shared home and moved to a rented flat in Islington close to his work, rarely seeing his ex-wife and their daughter, but he made sure Sally had enough money to complete her education and they kept in touch. She would ask his advice as she studied to become an accountant like him, and on completing her training, he had helped her find a position with a top London firm.

Their collaboration paid off. Sally was well-qualified and good at her job, and after a year working in London she went to work for an American company in Dubai. Although he did miss her, he was glad she was doing well. When he could make time he liked to visit her in Dubai, and it was on such a visit a so-called 'friend of his daughter' invited him for a drink at the Windows Bar on the 51st floor of the Voco hotel.

'This is Jake, Dad,' Sally said, making the introductions. 'Jake, my dad, Charles.'

'Pleased to meet you,' said the American, offering his

hand. 'Let me order drinks. Sally, what about those seats over there? The view is spectacular. What d'you say, Charles?'

'Of course, whatever.'

Jake ordered the drinks and led the way towards some large comfortable armchairs.

'Sally here says you are an accountant, Charles. It obviously runs in the family.'

'I suppose it does. I must say, Sally surprised me in taking up the profession. I thought she would opt for a career in retail. You should see her wardrobe.'

'Don't be silly, Dad. Retail is okay if you don't mind being on your feet all day. I had enough of that with my Saturday job when I was a school. Teaching, maybe. I could handle maths.'

'So why accountancy?' asked Jake.

'Because of Dad. He always seemed to have plenty of money and never seemed rushed off his feet. It looked a no-brainer if I could pass the exams.'

'And is it a no-brainer, Sally?' asked Charles.

'Hardly, it's hard work but the rewards are there. I have a good life out here, everything I need, friends, a flat and a Ferrari.'

'The three Fs,' laughed Jake.

Sally just smiled. She was doing well and she knew it, and as the drinks arrived, she stood.

'I'm just off to powder my nose, if you will excuse me for a few minutes. I'm sure you both have plenty to talk about.'

Charles watched her go, a proud father. Sure, he had regrets, but she was her own woman and at least he managed to spend some time with her. He raised his glass, took a sip of whisky, and turned towards Jake, smiling – but not for long.

'Do you know your employer is involved in the drug trade?' Jake said.

'No... No, I don't,' stuttered Charles, almost choking, the smile wiped from his face.

'Come now, Charles. You must know, or at least suspect?'

Flabbergasted, wrong-footed and unsure of what to say, he simply looked at his glass. He was aware that a portion of his employer's dealings were not exactly honest, and he half suspected drugs were involved, but he had the sense to steer clear of any involvement.

'Charles, you are an interesting individual,' Jake continued. 'Let me tell you that it has come to the attention of the United States Office of Foreign Assets Control that you have been moving money for your employer, undertaking illegal and proscribed transactions. Financing the acquisition of Iranian oil, for example, a secondary buyer of Russian oil. There are other transactions of which I am sure you are aware, and I am also sure you realise the severity of any penalties we might impose.'

'We?' said a shocked Charles Clark.

'The Government of the United States of America. There are sanctions in place, you know. I work for an accountancy firm, Tanner Williamson, here in Dubai, but part of my brief is to work with the United States Financial Crimes Enforcement Network.'

'Jake' – highly unlikely that was his real name – was convincing. He knew a lot about Andrei Potanin and his connections, and said he knew of a money laundering operation involving his companies.

'You realise you're up to your neck in it, don't you, Charles?'

Charles was speechless, finally managing to stutter,

'M-money laundering? I know nothing about that.'

'Maybe, but you work for an organisation that pursues such activities and you're looking at a twenty-year stretch if you are implicated, buddy. How does that read?'

'Not very well.'

'So, what can we do about it?'

'I have no idea, except remaining here in Dubai might be a possibility.'

'How come?'

'As far as I am aware, the United States does not have an extradition treaty with any of the Gulf states.'

'You certainly know your stuff, Charles. Okay. Suppose you remain here, out of our reach. For how long – two years, ten years? Do you really want to live here for that length of time, no friends, no chance to visit the UK for fear of the authorities picking you up? I don't think so. We have a long memory and a longer arm. Here's what you are going to do,' Jake said in a matter-of-fact tone, as if he was simply describing a shirt or a bottle of sauce. But he was convincing, and after hearing more of the consequences, Charles felt obliged to accept his offer.

'You don't need to do a lot or take much of a risk, Charles. What we want are names, places, anything related to deals under the counter, so to speak.'

'I've never laundered any money.'

'You've transferred millions for your employer, Potanin. You're implicated by association, believe me. Okay, here comes Sally... We'll talk again.'

Charles remembered sitting back in his seat, a player in a drama, a man who had just sold his soul. He could not refuse, and since that day he had become a spy. It was a low-key drama, meeting in obscure surroundings to pass on some snippet of information – not much in the scheme of things, but enough to keep him out of the hands of American law enforcement and that was when he began to apply some forethought.

Bloody hell, what have I got myself into? he thought as he returned to the present. The last passenger was leaving the carriage and outside a loudspeaker burst into life, repeating the arrangements for the next part of the journey. In that moment, Charles Clark faded from view and was replaced by Chris Kent, not quite Superman.

Stepping onto the platform, he shivered. The cold winter's air sliced through his lightweight business suit and he wondered if perhaps he might find a shop, buy some thermal underwear and a decent jacket or a coat. It sounded a good idea as he stuck his hands into his trouser pockets and followed the crowd towards the gate, where an employee of the train company was ushering them towards a line of waiting coaches. Some broke away and stood looking up at the announcement board. Chris, as he now was, decided that York would be his destination.

'Leave him alone,' one had said.

His attackers had reacted, momentarily releasing the pressure on his arms. He remembered daring to glance at them, remembered their expressionless, pale faces. He did not know them, yet felt he should, and then the grip in his arms slackened completely as violence erupted. At last, he was able to stand free, only to watch in horror as two men fell dying onto the London pavement. A trigger, an action that blew away all conscious fear, replaced instead by a primeval desire to live.

Without realising it he was running, his heart

pounding, his surroundings a blur. Turning the first corner he came to, he darted along the street. A flashing yellow light, a beacon of hope: a dust lorry. Jumping up beside the operative, he used him as a shield. Astonishingly the man seemed unsurprised, simply grinning as if it were a regular occurrence.

'Watch out, this thing can kill you,' he said, and Charles nodded nervously.

If the mechanisms on the back of the lorry didn't kill him, someone would. But his luck held and although the killers were on his tail, in their haste they dashed past the end of the street without so much as a glance in his direction. Charles took the opportunity to jump from the small working platform and resume his flight.

'Now where are you going?' asked the operative, as the stranger ran between the vehicle and the row of terraced houses, unaware of the sarcasm.

Finally, Charles emerged in a breathless state onto a busy thoroughfare. Unsure of exactly where he was, he paused to look around. Where were they? A London cab pulled up just a few metres away to disgorge its fare and Charles took the opportunity to jump in.

'Kings Cross,' he voiced.

'Underground or rail?'

'Er... railway station.'

Why he'd said Kings Cross he had no idea. Perhaps he believed it to be the furthermost station from the killings, or perhaps he had some deep psychological desire to visit the north. Doubtful. The reason was more to do with blind panic rather than any rational decision, and now he found himself in York with no idea of what to do next.

He followed the crowd of passengers towards the exit

gate. They passed the large black noticeboard with its ever-changing catalogue and he spotted one train that would be leaving in just five minutes. He noted the platform number, he had just passed it, and the destination, Scarborough. He had heard of it, on the coast somewhere he thought.

'Bugger it,' he swore under his breath. 'A holiday beside the sea, I haven't done that since childhood. Twenty quid should get me there.'

Detective Sergeant Forrest took a sip of coffee from his plastic cup and stared at the image of two bodies lying side by side on the pavement. They seemed to have peaceful looks on their faces but he knew their deaths were anything but. It had been a particularly horrific killing. In twenty years as a serving policeman, it was one of the worst he had seen. Taking another sip, he wondered about the killers. His team had taken a sanitised version of the image from door to door and spoken to residents, asked if they had seen or heard anything and had they any security cameras.

'Detective Sergeant Forrest?' said a voice, interrupting his thoughts.

He looked up to see Tabz, the department's senior analyst, holding a sheet of paper.

'I have been conducting a search of all the databases. The inspector told me to bring anyfing I could find out about yesterday's double murder to you and you will pass it on like.'

'Yeah, that's right. What 'ave you got?'

'Not much. In fact, nofing. The fingerprints and DNA of the victims do not show up anywhere on the databases I have access to, but one of the uniforms has turned up some video from one of those fancy doorbells.

What caused it to start recording I don't know, but it caught two men accosting a third and I thought it might be relevant,' she said, handing over the print.

'Clear enough. Any idea who 'e is?'

'I don't, sir. Do you want me to keep looking to see if I can identify him?'

'Of course. Thanks, Tabz, I'll talk to the inspector right away.'

In the basement of the large Victorian building halfway along Packington Street, two men watched a large-screen television. The main story on the local news was about the murders, and a male reporter with his back to the crime scene was relating what he knew.

'It seems the double murder that took place here this afternoon is not gang-related. From what we have learned, the victims interrupted a mugging and the police believe the deceased might have tried to help the victim of that mugging. He could be the key to this case, a man the police would like to come forward. Finally, according to a police source, there has been no positive identification of either of the murdered men, the perpetrators, or the victim of the alleged mugging. They are asking for anyone who was in the vicinity this afternoon to come forward. If you have information, you can anonymously phone this number...'

'So, we are front-page news,' said Sergei, a glass of vodka in his hand. 'Shall we phone them? Can give good description, I think.'

'We could, but I'm not sure that's a good idea, Sergei.'

Chapter 2

The train pulled into the small seaside station on time, not a hint of snow on the line. The few remaining passengers spilled onto the platform except for one. Charles had reached journey's end, a feeling of anti-climax pervading his soul and leaving him unable to leave the warmth of the carriage.

'Are you stopping here all night?' asked a large woman carrying a bucket of cleaning materials. 'I only have a quarter of an hour before this train leaves and you are in my way.'

Charles stepped to the side and after she passed him, still muttering, he took the plunge and stepped into the cold evening air. His business suit was all he had on and it was lightweight, meant for a heated office, not the cold north-east. He shivered from both the cold, his predicament and the knowledge he was without any sort of plan. The platform had emptied of travellers and, apart from the cleaner, the station seemed abandoned. He could see no solution other than to take a taxi and find an hotel.

'Where to?'

'I don't really know,' he said, as he climbed into the rear seat of the last cab on the rank.

'Not been here before?'

'No, a spur-of-the-moment thing. My, er, daughter suggested it and she will be joining me tomorrow,' he lied. 'I haven't booked a room for tonight; can you advise me of a decent hotel?'

'The Esplanade is your best bet; a few hotels are still open up there and you get good views of the town. Shall I take you there?'

'Er... yes, that's fine.'

He was not about to question the driver's choice, happy just to know that his journey was coming to an end. As the taxi pulled off, his mind returned to earlier events. He hardly noticed the passing backdrop and before he realised it, the taxi had stopped.

'This do you, sir, the Sheringham Hotel? It's got a good reputation, I believe.'

'Er, yes,' said a wearisome Charles, pulling the banknote from his pocket before stepping out onto the pavement.

He had no idea where he was, the few street lights giving nothing away and having little choice, he ascended the few steps to a large door. He pushed it open, grateful that it was not locked, and as he entered the foyer he felt warm air engulf him. A welcome relief, and on looking round he saw a desk in the corner with a shiny brass bell inviting him to press it for attention.

'Just one night, sir?' asked a man, suddenly appearing from a concealed doorway. Tall and slender with neat black hair, he seemed friendly and yet cast a suspicious eye over his potential guest.

'I think I will probably stay two nights with the possibility of more. I, er... have some business to attend to and I'm not sure how long it will take,' said Charles, trying to sound convincing.

'Your luggage, sir, do you have any?'

'Er... no. I, erm... This is quite embarrassing really, but I left it on the train. There was a blockage on the line and in the ensuing chaos I simply forgot to take my case. Stupid, really.'

'I see, sir. Perhaps you could contact left luggage, someone may have handed it in.'

'I could, yes, a good idea.'

'If you would like to sign the visitors book, I will show you to your room. We are quiet now, January and February are normally dead months, just a few business people, so I'm afraid breakfast is at eight in the morning, no chance of picking your own time.'

'Oh, I see,' said Charles, the mention of food reminding him that apart from a chocolate bar and a coffee on the train, he had not eaten since leaving for work. The mere thought left him feeling hungry.

'Is the restaurant open?'

'I'm afraid not, sir. We are a small establishment and we just use the dining room for breakfast at this time of year. There is a bar if you would like a drink, failing that, we provide coffee and tea in the room and a small selection of biscuits.'

'That will do fine, thank you. It's been a long day.'

'Then just sign here and I will show you to your room.'

Charles took the ledger, and remembering he was no longer Charles, signed 'Chris Kent' with a flourish.

'Your home address, sir. We need your home address, there, look.'

'Ah yes,' said Charles, confused as he tried to conjure up an address. With Google Maps addresses could be checked and so, after a small hesitation, he wrote down the address of a long-forgotten girlfriend.

'The postcode, sir, please.'

'Of course.'

Now he was stuffed, he had no idea of the postcode

and was left with no alternative but to guess. To his relief the hotelier did not give it a second glance, instead he closed the book and placed it under the counter.

'If you will follow me, sir.'

Great, no problem there by the look of it, thought Charles as he followed the hotelier towards the staircase.

The hotel was pleasant enough, the carpet thick and the decoration in good order. On reaching the landing the hotelier stopped at the first door he came to.

'Here you are, sir, room 101. Don't forget breakfast is at eight sharp. Here is your key,' he said, unlocking the door and handing the key to Charles.

'Thank you,' said the fugitive, stepping into the room and closing the door behind him.

The room was adequate. The bed looked comfortable, the ensuite decent, and on a table near the sash window sat a small kettle with the standard sachets of tea and coffee. Feeling hungry, he opened a packet of biscuits, greedily devouring them while he filled the kettle and once it boiled, made himself a brew.

The day had seemed regular enough to begin with. He had followed his normal routine, sifting through the small pile of mail on his desk, mostly invoices, some advertising trash, and a plain, unremarkable envelope. Checking first the invoices, he filed them and then consigned the junk mail to the waste bin. Finally he'd opened the envelope, taken out a single sheet of headed note paper surprised to see the insignia was that of the Russian Embassy. He was puzzled to say the least, noting that it contained just two lines of Cyrillic text and was signed by the Russian ambassador. That on its own began to ring a warning bell, and although he was intrigued, Charles had limited Russian language skills. He was determined, however, to learn the full content of the letter.

Having worked for the Russian for almost four years, he did not need a working knowledge of the language, just a few words common to the business, though on several occasions he had used a translation app and decided to try it now. Simple enough, just photograph the text and let the app do its thing. It seemed to work and in only a few seconds the app returned a mildly intelligible English text. The content looked English, yet the syntax was not easy to decipher. Working his way through the jumbled text, he did become aware of its meaning, all too aware.

'Oh my God,' he whispered, reading the message again with a more rational approach.

The correspondence was obviously meant for Andrei Potanin, who was not even in London. His connections and bribery had been unable to prevent the inevitable, so how had this letter from the Russian Embassy landed on his desk? If he had read it correctly, Charles was now privy to a damaging secret.

Replacing the sheet of paper in the envelope with a trembling hand, Charles pondered its implication and wished he had never opened it. The embassy was careless, someone had made a grave error in writing such a letter, never mind sending it.

'You alright, Charles?' asked a heavily accented voice from the half-open door.

'Yes, Sergei. I just felt a little faint, that's all, it has passed now,' said Charles, alarmed to see the security man looking in on him.

'You should see a doctor, get your blood pressure checked,' said Sergei Kulikov, head of security and the possessor of an overbearing personality.

'What is it you want?'

'Just doing my job, having a look around to make sure all is in order.'

Charles had known from the beginning that working for the Russians could be a risky undertaking, but the money was a significant inducement. As a large investor in infrastructure projects, shopping centres and hotels, and with business interests throughout Europe, Potanin had his Russian fingers in many pies and Charles, as the head accountant, was privy to some of the most intimate of dealings. It had not taken long for him to become aware that some transactions were not wholly legitimate, and he had known for a while that the Russian was living on borrowed time. The knowledge that the British authorities might soon force his boss out of the country added to his desire to protect his retirement. He siphoned off a small amount of money each time a deal went through, built up a substantial fund and, so far, his dishonesty had gone unnoticed. Yet after reading the letter, he felt strongly that his time working for the Russian was coming to an end.

'So, my friend, Andrei has had to leave us for a while and it is we who must look after his interests. I hope you are not thinking of taking advantage,' continued Sergei, his cold stare unsettling.

'N-no, of course not. You know, I didn't have time for breakfast this morning. I will ask the canteen to send me a coffee and a croissant, that's what I need.'

The security man smiled a non-smile and disappeared and Charles slipped the offending letter into his jacket pocket.

He was worried. If the translation was correct, the letter contents were dynamite and perhaps it was time he put his long-held plan into action. He needed to get as far away as possible, maybe the United States. He had visited New York several times and knew the city reasonably well, he had a few contacts on Wall Street. Could he really go there? No, not immediately. He should hide somewhere first until the problem resolved itself and then, perhaps, he could leave for New York or even return to London.

A thought occurred; the letter could spell his end or, on the other hand, maybe it could save him. A bargaining chip, evidence to protect him, but he must keep it safe. Clasping his hands together, his elbows resting on the edge of his desk, he stared at the opposite wall, a habit that had served him well over the years. The blank wall was a canvas on which to paint ideas, explore moves and, in this case, save his skin. He had a safety deposit box containing his false passport and the codes for the cryptocurrency wallet, and it was the obvious place to leave the letter. As the idea began to unfold, he decided that he would go to the bank on Park Lane during his lunch break.

Sergei Kulikov pared his fingernails as he looked out of the third-floor window, a cup of coffee on the desk beside him. Today was quiet. He had completed his inspection, checked offices, and let the workers know he was keeping an eye on them, and now he was taking a break. His mobile phone rang.

'Sergei, I am calling from the embassy so pay attention. We are on a secure line?' asked the man, Sergei's contact on the Embassy's security detail.

'*Da.*'

'Listen, we have a problem, one we cannot allow to develop. Yesterday one of the secretaries posted a letter from the ambassador to your office. She made a big mistake; the letter was a copy of one sent to Andrei before he left the country and she should never have posted it. It is a communication from the highest level and for some reason she sent it without a recipient name. The letter incriminates the ambassador and we want it back. We are in a difficult situation and bad publicity is not welcome.'

'Who did you send it to, simply the office?'

'More than likely, she says there was no addressee. Please conduct a search and *find* that letter, quickly.'

'I'm on to it, I'll get back to you.'

There was no acknowledgement. The line went dead, leaving Sergei drumming his now immaculately manicured fingernails on the windowsill. Who distributed the mail? That was the place to start, see if anyone remembered the envelope – and then he recalled his intrusion into the accountant's office. He had noticed that Charles seemed uncomfortable. Was he hiding something?

The hotel bed was comfortable enough, though the room temperature was less to Charles's liking. The tea and biscuits had helped warm him, yet still he had climbed into bed complete with socks and vest. He fell into a deep and troubled sleep, his mind grappling with images of the day's events. So vivid were they that he later found himself forced awake. In total darkness he lay sweating, wondering where he was and who those two men were? Their faces were unfamiliar, their complexions strangely pasty, and yet there was something in their manner that bothered him.

He remembered leaving the office and had taken a minute to phone the number given to him by the man he knew as Jake. He had repeated the two-word code and the voice at the other end told him where they would find him.

There was no going back at that point. He had made his decision and, hardly feeling the winter chill, he set off on the half an hour walk to the safety deposit box. His idea was to retrieve his papers, passport, and credit card – all in the name of Chris Kent – and to disappear, though he had not yet decided where he would go.

With his documents safely in his jacket pocket, he had emerged from the glass-fronted reception to head at a brisk pace towards the rendezvous. The street was quiet, just a few cars and two or three pedestrians, and he remembered looking up at the street sign – yes, it was the right one. The voice had told him the street name but not where to wait on the street, so he decided to make his way to the far end and paused halfway to look behind him. That was when the two figures jumped out, emerging from a doorway in front of him. At first, he believed these were the men he was supposed to meet.

'Hello, I'm Charles,' he had said in all innocence, but the response was not the one he'd expected. The men rushed at him, gripping his arms, and he knew he'd got it wrong.

'Where is it?' one of the men snarled. 'The letter, where is letter?'

'What letter?' he had said.

'You are well aware of what letter.'

'I thought that was a joke, I threw it in the bin.'

For an instant the speaker relaxed his grip, pushed Charles's shoulder and turned him.

'You lie, where is letter?'

He remembered feeling faint, his legs turned to jelly, his interrogator's frightening facial expression unreal. Then two strangers appeared and intervened.

'Let him go,' said one.

'We'll call the police,' said the second, revealing a mobile phone.

It was over in seconds. Charles did not witness the full extent of the violence, hearing only a high-pitched scream and seeing a flurry of arms and legs as the murderers did their work, but in that instant an opportunity to escape had presented itself.

Now, alone in the darkened hotel room, he relived those awful moments.

Inspector Mills looked up to see DS Forrest tapping lightly on his office window and waved him in.

'Morning, Graham, what have you got for me? Good news, I hope.'

'Nofing new Eddie. We believe it started as a mugging, a robbery. We have some CCTV showing the initial altercation when the suspects accosted this geezer,' he said, pushing a blurry image across the desk.

'Who is he?'

'We don't know, but there was an eye witness.'

'Good, go on.'

'She lives on the top floor of one of the Victorian buildings and was cleaning a window when she saw the mugging. She says she shouted at them to stop but presumed they couldn't hear her because her pleading had no effect. Would you believe she is a freelance bleedin' photographer and managed to get a couple of shots of the victim of the attack as he ran off? And these two,' he said, pointing to a second image. 'The murderers. They are not great photos because she says she did not have time to set the camera properly.'

'Aren't they automatic these days?'

'Not for everyone. She said she never uses automatic and the last time she used the camera was in low light, hence the lack of detail. But you can make out the one being mugged reasonably well and we're checking all the databases we can to trace him.'

'What about the suspects?'

'Not much luck, I'm afraid. They haven't shown up on any databases as yet, but the team are trawling all the footage gathered so far from within half a mile of the incident to see what we can find.'

'And the two murdered men?'

'Hmm... a real game, this is where things become interesting.'

'Interesting?'

'We have a reasonably positive ID for one of them but we are checking everything we can to make sure. We've contacted the American Embassy for clarification.'

The inspector's brow creased in disbelief. 'Clarification?'

'We ain't got much in the way of brass tacks but we think one is American, and the records we have indicate that he might be an employee of the United States Embassy.'

'Good Lord, that is interesting. Get a positive on that and then I had better tell the boss. I don't expect he will be too happy... Yes, what is it?' he said, distracted by Tabz peering through his office window.

Waving her in, he asked, 'Have you got something?'

'Possibly, sir. We have some more CCTV footage showing the persons of interest and a possible witness. A woman who was parking her car not too far from the incident has called in. She saw it all, a bit shook up like, poor woman.'

'Can she identify anyone?'

'Yes, and better than that, she managed to get something on her mobile phone – the man who she says was taking the beating. Also, we're looking at CCTV from the traffic cameras in the area like. Perhaps if you could come to my desk, Sergeant, I can show you what I have on the computer screen.'

'Thanks, Tabz. I'll be with you in a few minutes.'

She nodded and left. Inspector Mills pursed his lips and looked at his sergeant.

'Well, Graham, from what I've learned, our mystery man was the focus of the assault and the two men killed were not. Now I'm not at all sure what went on. If one or both of the victims were working for the American Embassy then that throws a whole new light on what we are dealing with. Who are the murderers, and the one who was the centre of the assault – who the hell is he?'

Left in charge of the business, Sergei took his new role very seriously but right now he was feeling defensive. At a safe house, under the scrutiny of the Minister Counsellor, a man who suffered fools lightly, he and Markov found themselves having to explain their actions.

'You stupid idiots, what you have done is all over the television news channels. If you're caught and it goes before a British court you will drag the ambassador into the affair. You are not a a registered employee of the embassy, you don't have diplomatic imunity. I thought you would have more sense, Sergei.'

'I'm sorry. It happened all too quickly. We, or Markov, thought they were about to take us on and he reacted. But there is no need to worry, we used the silicone masks, realistic if not examined too closely. I'm sure no one recognised us and nobody but the three of us knows we were involved.'

'I'm still worried about you two. If the police try to

arrest you we will get you out of the country, but until they do come looking for you, we will carry on as normal. We must find that letter. Are you certain it's in his possession?'

'More than certain, comrade. He has it.'

'Did you get any indication of where he might have put it?'

'No, we found him in Duncan Terrace. I have done a search and the nearest safety deposit box company is at Hatton Garden, that's a half hour walk from here.'

'You think that's where he may have put it?'

'I don't know, but it's the kind of thing I would do. No time time to do much else, he could have hidden it or could have posted it on to some other address for pick up later. I don't know where letter is but first, I think we need search his office. He said he simply screwed it up and threw it away. I don't believe but proves he had sight of it I think.'

'Is it likely to be there?'

'I don't know, but we will search office and then have a look in mail room to see if anything went out this morning from him. There should be record, all mail is logged.'

'What about the safety deposit box?'

'If that is what he has done with it then things become a little more difficult, but fifty-pound note might get us somewhere.'

'You need to find him. You say you used the silicone masks; you don't think anybody would recognise you?'

'No, masks are so realistic even your own mother never recognise you. Well, not from more than a metre or two.'

'Find him, and do it quickly. If you need help, I can talk to the ambassador and ask for the security team's assistance.'

'I can tell you now, I suspect we more than likely need their help. We need to find out if he's using a credit card, always good method for tracking someone. I don't have that ability but the embassy might. And his mobile phone – if they have someone on the inside, phone record will be useful.'

'I don't know about that but I will ask, see what we can do. In the meantime you have your company credit card, Sergei. I will increase the limit to one hundred thousand pounds to assist you. Don't let me down, it's cold in Siberia at this time of year. If that Bellingcat outfit ever find out what you've done they will have a field day. Now get out of my sight, the pair of you,' said the attaché.

Sergei and Markov left the house, the irate diplomat, and once out of hearing range Sergei gave full vent to his anger.

'Thanks for trying to wreck my career, Markov. Why the hell did you do what you did? We could easily have avoided killing them and now look at the trouble you've caused.'

'I don't say sorry but I admit it was a mistake, a simple mistake.'

'A mistake! A simple mistake!'

'Yes, I have had some experience of these British; they are devious, crafty, those men could have been accomplices. I was sure one was trying to draw a gun.'

'Really. Perhaps we should have checked them over instead of chasing the accountant. Wait here, I need to check something.'

Sergei walked a few paces past Markov, took out his mobile phone, and after a scroll through his address book he called his contact at the embassy.

'Nikolay, it's me, Sergei. We have a problem; we have just left the attaché and I need your help.'

'So, tell me.'

'You will have heard about two men stabbed today?'

'Yes.'

'Well, it is because of a serious leak originating from the embassy and it is beginning to spiral out of control. I believe a man called Charles Clark is in possession of the letter and he is on the run and I need some help in finding him.'

'Tell me what you want, Sergei.'

Chapter 3

Drawing the bedroom curtain to one side, Charles looked seawards, towards the early morning sun hanging like a ripe orange above the mist. The view was quite something for the city dweller, but it hardly registered with him. Disturbed by his dreams, he had eventually fallen into a deep sleep but now, returned to the cold light of day, the enormity of his predicament weighed heavily once more.

What chaos had he left behind, he wondered? He reached for his mobile telephone, logged onto a source of local London news and scrolled through the headlines. A strike at the bus depot, a story about overflowing hospital wards, and then the headline he had half expected.

TWO MEN DEAD IN ISLINGTON.

There wasn't a lot to learn other that that two men were dead, their identities unknown. The article said that a forensic team had worked all night looking for clues and the chief inspector was to give a press conference at midday, but details were sparse and, surprisingly, there was no mention of him or the attempted mugging.

How strange, he thought. Why would they not mention my involvement?

Perhaps no one had noticed him, or perhaps the journalist was too busy with the story of the murder victims. It did appear strange though, that they would leave him out of the narrative. After all, he was probably chief witness to the crime.

He had made the call to the special number 'Jake' had given him in the hope he might receive help. The deadpan American voice at the other end had reassured him, said he should go to a rendezvous point and that someone would contact him. He had looked for the contact, but there was no one, not until the muggers appeared. At first, he had believed they were his contacts but that idea soon vanished and then the two good Samaritans had arrived. Who were they? Were *they* the ones he was meant to meet? They had to be, and now they were dead because of him.

It was a difficult thought to process. Getting up from the bed, he showered and dressed in his well-worn clothes and finally he did take in the view. The winter sun was already clearing the mist, revealing a flat grey sea and in the distance, a lone fishing boat.

'Oh, how uncomplicated their lives must be,' he said to himself, and with a sigh turned from the window and glanced at his watch, remembering breakfast was at eight. He had eaten very little the day before and now, at least, a hearty breakfast was something to look forward to. Afterwards he would find a shop, buy some new clothes – warm clothes, he thought, as he left his room to descend the staircase.

'Good morning, Mr Kent.'

'Good morning, no one else for breakfast?' he asked on entering the dining room.

'No, sir. Mr James, our only other guest, has already left. He often misses breakfast.'

'He's a regular, is he?'

'Fairly, he spends two or three days a week with us. Travels a lot, I believe. Now, what would you like for breakfast? We have the usual, eggs and bacon, porridge, and some cereal. Can I offer you a coffee? Sit where you like.'

Charles pointed to a table near the window and made his way across the room.

'Well, at least the views are good here,' he said to himself, noticing that the fishing boat had grown larger. For several minutes, he watched its progress.

'Your coffee, sir. Have you decided what you would like?'

'Oh, eggs and bacon, please. Do you have brown bread toast?'

'We do. Marmalade?'

Detective Sergeant Forrest angled the image for a better view and studied the well-dressed, slightly built subject. After a few seconds he pushed it to one side and picked up a second print showing two men with deadpan faces.

'You think these geezers are the killers, Tabz?'

'Pretty sure, sir. From the CCTV and Constable Forrest's witness statement like, I fink it's them.'

'Do we have any positive ID?'

'No, sir, nofing yet, nofing on the databases I have looked at.'

'Hmm... How do you know it is these two?'

'There is no footage of the actual attack, but from surveillance cameras in the area and the witness statements I'm ninety nine per cent certain it's them.'

'But yet you can't identify them?'

'No, sir.'

'Well, we need to – and quickly. I will talk to uniform,

have these pictures circulated and maybe an appeal on the local news programmes might help. Okay, carry on.'

Tabz left the sergeant and walked back to her desk, puzzled that nothing had turned up from her database searches. She had undertaken several of them using well-tried methods comparing the full face, individual features, skin-colour tones and in the end she still had no tangible lead. She would try again, call a friend – a good friend, Jimi Russet, her mentor, a man she had met while attending Imperial College to study for a Master's degree in Security and Resilience. The course had concentrated on various computer systems, methods and algorithms used by the police and the security services, the perfect fit to her degree in computer science. The qualification was a step up and Jimi, it seemed, was of the same opinion.

A well-built man of African descent, most people found it difficult to reconcile his physique with that of a computer expert. At first sight he could be a boxer or a footballer, and yet for such a powerful man he was surprisingly kind and thoughtful. She remembered how they had hit it off and that it was not long before a mutual respect had established itself. Working together in the college library, they had tackled problems together, their constructive arguments stimulating, unlocking new insights that would benefit them both.

'So, what made you want to join the police?' he had asked one day.

'Too much television, my movver says. I loved all the police dramas, especially the ones with a lot of forensics innit.'

'Shouldn't you have studied medicine then?'

'Forensics isn't all about fingerprints and DNA, you know. I enjoy digging out information, a bit like solving

41

a crossword puzzle innit.'

'Crossword, yes, I suppose so.'

'Well, when a crime is committed there will be clues, but as wiv most clues they are not particularly obvious to begin wiv. Sherlock Holmes used a magnifying glass and his intellect to solve crimes. Today it's cameras and computers innit.'

He had smiled at her, his strong white teeth attractive, his eyes bright and intelligent. 'A magnifying glass and his intellect, ha. What about Dr Watson and the policeman, what was his name?' he said, teasing her.

'Lestrade, Inspector Lestrade.'

'Didn't they help Sherlock Holmes solve his crimes?'

'I have never read Sherlock Holmes but I enjoyed watching some of the films, especially the earlier ones wiv Basil Rathbone. Anyway, it was Holmes who solved crimes for the police innit, Lestrade and Dr Watson was never much help like.'

'I think Dr Watson was more than a little help. But you believe computers can take the place of a genius like Sherlock Holmes?'

'I never said he was a genius, though if he was, it was because of his pure deductive reasoning.'

Jimi had laughed out loud. 'Of course, pure deductive reasoning, I see your argument. You think a computer can replace the human mind in reasoning out the solution to a crime.'

'With the right input, yes. What is it – GIGO, garbage in, garbage out? It's the quality of the information fed into the computer what determines the outcome, and that is the part of solving crime that fascinates me. Look at the lecture we have tomorrow morning, it's all about the quality of intelligence and how to use it most effectively like innit.'

'Yes, I agree with you there, too much time wasted chasing false trails. I know from experience how costly that can be.'

'How so? What exactly do you do, Jimi? You have never told me.'

The big man looked into her eyes and held his smile, saying nothing.

'So, what *do* you do, or is it a secret?'

Still Jimi held her gaze and still he said nothing. It dawned on Tabz that this big friendly man was not quite what he seemed.

'You're not going to tell me, are you?'

'Tabz Belafonte, you are asking awkward questions; you might find out one day, but for now I can't talk about my work. Let's just say my interests lie in the same field as yours.'

Tabz felt something she didn't quite understand, and lowered her eyes.

'Come on, we're in the same business otherwise we wouldn't be on this course, would we? Fancy a coffee? We've been at it for the best part of three hours and I'm losing my concentration...innit,' he said smiling.

Tabz began typing and smiled to herself as she recalled those early memories. Then, as the result she was looking for appeared, she picked up her mobile telephone to call Jimi.

I bet he's not in, she thought to herself, he never is. And he wasn't, so she decided to send a text asking him to call her.

'Tabz,' called a colleague, ' I've got a preliminary ID on the man we think was accosted by the two thugs before the murders, I've been checking the Passport Identity Validation Service using one of the images we have of him and I have come up with a name.'

'Good work, Alma,' Tabz said, looking up from her desk. 'That was one of the first fings I did but drew a blank. Who is it?'

'I tried a search of addresses first, people within a mile of the murder, then I tried to narrow it down. The photo we have is not good so I can understand how you missed him. Anyway, after a couple of dead ends, I think the man is a Mr Charles Clark and the address is Shepperton Road. Whether he still lives there is anybody's guess.'

'Thanks, Alma. I'll have a word with DS Forrest, see what he wants to do.'

The girl left and walked back to her desk, leaving Tabz annoyed that she had missed the clues. Luckily the new girl, Alma, had made some progress and together with a few other minor pieces of information, she could now present them to the sergeant.

'Good, I will talk to the inspector right now,' Forrest said a couple of minutes later, dismissing Tabz and rising from his seat.

'We 'ave an address, sir,' he said, on entering Inspector Mills's office. 'I think I should pay a visit. Can you arrange for a warrant if we need to enter the premises?'

'Yes, I think a visit first. We might not need a warrant, just go and see what you can find out about this man and take a uniform with you. That always shows we mean business. No disrespect, Detective Sergeant, but a man in a raincoat doesn't have the same effect as the uniform.'

DS Forrest remained silent; the inspector's pointed comments were familiar to him.

Forrest banged on the door, but there was no answer. He

tried the bell and still no answer.

'Right, Constable, you take the odd numbers and I'll take the even and let's see what we can turn up.'

There were just four doors on the landing and between them the detective sergeant and the constable began ringing their bells. There was no answer from any of them, and so the two policemen made their way back down to the ground floor where a further four doorbells awaited.

'Ah, good morning,' said a relieved DS Forrest as a door opened to reveal a woman, probably in her sixties. 'I am a police officer,' he said, showing his warrant card. 'Would you mind answering a few questions?'

The woman frowned and took on a look of interest. 'Of course, what is it about?'

'We're wanting to talk to a Mr Charles Clark. Do you know of his whereabouts?'

'Charles Clark? I don't know any Charles Clark.'

'We believe he lives on the first floor, those stairs, flat number six.'

The woman pursed her lips thoughtfully and shook her head.

'Here, a photograph,' he said, pulling the image from his coat pocket. 'Do you recognise the geezer?'

'Oh yes, but I've never known his name. He's lived here for three or four years, I think, keeps to himself as do most of the tenants, but I have seen him on occasion.'

'Do you know if he's around? Working, maybe, at home later?'

'I couldn't say. All I know is I think he's an accountant. He must be, judging by his briefcase.'

'His briefcase?' queried the policeman puzzled by the woman's logic.

'Yes, my son is an accountant and he has a briefcase

that looks just the same.'

'Do you know where he works, where he might be now?'

'No, how do you expect me to know where he is?'

'Sorry, ma'am, just a question. Here's my card. If you see 'im, please call me,' said DS Forrest, pointing to a number on the card.

'Yes, but I can't promise I will see him.'

'That's okay, but if you do then give me a call, please.'

The woman took the card and began closing the door just as the uniformed policeman was knocking on another one.

'No luck, Constable?'

'Afraid not, Sarge.'

'Hmm... We'll try this last door and if there is no reply we'll head back to base for further instruction.'

As he spoke, the outside door of the apartment block opened and a man appeared, bare-headed and dressed in a black trench coat.

'Hello, sir, are you a resident here?'

'Er... No, I come to see someone.'

'And who might that be, sir? We are trying to locate one of the residents. Could you tell me who you have come to see?'

Sergei looked at the detective and then the constable and was about to say 'I work for the property company' when the constable lost grip on his helmet and it fell with a dull thud to the floor.

'Sorry, Sergeant.'

DS Forrest frowned and turned back to Markov. 'You were saying?'

'Yes,' said Markov, relieved to have a few seconds of respite to compose his story. 'I work for management company and pay visits to check the state of the building, the walls, the roof, you know – anything that might show signs of deterioration.'

'Who's your employer? It might help if we can talk to your office.'

The questions were coming thick and fast and Markov's intellect was not of the highest calibre. He had to think quickly and as he was not immediately able to pluck a convincing name out of the ether, he hesitated until a name suddenly showed itself in his head.

'Baltic Jet Properties. I work for Baltic Jet Properties and this building is one of ours.'

'Would you know any of the tenants, Mr, er... What is your name, please?'

Markov was beginning to feel cornered and that was dangerous. He had demonstrated not twenty-four hours before how short a fuse he possessed.

'My name is Igor, Igor Husyev.'

'Well, Mr Husyev, here's my card,' said the detective sergeant. 'If you hear of the whereabouts of a tenant called Clark, living in flat six on the next floor, then please give me a call.'

A relieved Markov took the card, nodding acceptance.

'Thank you, you have been very helpful. Come on, Constable, there is nothing much more we can do 'ere. Thank you, sir,' he said, opening the door to the street and making a mental note to check out this Igor Husyev and the property company Baltic Jet. What kind of a name was that?

'Is your helmet-cam working, Constable?' he asked as they left the building.

Breakfast was filling and as good as Charles had ever tasted. Feeling content, he returned to his room and could not resist another hour in bed to lie down and turn his predicament over in his head.

What was he going to do? He should walk into town and buy new clothes, and so after an extra hour in bed and with his breakfast having left him feeling refreshed, he left the hotel and was met by a bright, cloud-free and cold first day. The view over the sea was impressive and, taking deep breaths as he walked, he cleared his mind. Things didn't seem so bad. He believed he was reasonably safe, had shaken off any pursuers and landed in a quite beautiful place.

The Victorian bridge afforded a view of the beach, which was almost deserted save for two or three dog walkers. In the distance, he could see the harbour. He made his way towards the town centre, passing the Grand Hotel, a Victorian marvel in its time but shabby-looking now. The square wasn't busy, just a few pedestrians and a delivery van, and then he saw a figure squatting in a doorway, a dirty sleeping bag pulled up to his waist. Perhaps this pretty little town had a darker side.

The street widened and he saw a cliff lift. Out of curiosity he walked towards the stationary carriage waiting in its shelter. It was going nowhere, an 'out of commission' sign advising its reopening at Easter.

At least one street seemed busy with a few people walking the pavement, coffee shops, though not the bustling metropolis he was used to and he was feeling the cold. He found what seemed to be the one remaining department store and hoped it might fulfil most of his needs, but even if it didn't, the warm interior was very welcome.

He purchased two casual shirts, a pair of trousers and the thickest underwear he could find. He was still wearing his formal leather shoes, had worn them almost constantly for weeks, and felt an urge to cast them off. He had habitually dressed as an accountant should dress – an expensive business suit, tailored, and always the same black leather shoes, polished every day. He rarely wore casual clothing, but today he had an urge to cast off more remnants of his old persona, change his identity.

'How much are these?' he asked the shop assistant, pointing out a pair of trainers.

'Thirty-two pounds.'

'Gosh, that's cheap.'

'I could always charge you a bit more, sir,' said the young shop assistant with a grin. 'Would you like to try them on? What size?'

'Er, nine, I think.'

'I'll bring a pair.'

'I'm more used to leather shoes, they can cost almost two hundred pounds,' he said, slipping them on and wiggling his toes.

'Do you want to try walking in them?'

Charles got to his feet, paraded back and forth, and admired the light blue uppers and dark red mid soles.

'They are a good fit. Okay, I'll take them.'

'Card or cash, sir?'

'Cash if that's alright.'

'Of course, these days cash is best,' he said with a knowing look in his eye.

Charles managed a smile as he paid, aware of the power of cash. Wandering back into the street, he had a wry smile on his lips.

'A few pounds the tax man will not get to hear about, I imagine. Not so different to the thousands I have been spiriting away for the Russians, just a question of scale, I suppose.'

He had all he needed for now, but feeling like a camel

on the silk road, he needed to lessen his load and change his clothes. The business suit he still wore was just not up to the task of protecting him from the northern weather and feeling cold, he retraced his steps back into the department store.

Not sure of where he could change, he found a toilet cubicle, cast off everything he'd been wearing and pulled on his new clothes, not of a style he would ever dream of wearing in London. Still, the change was necessary and after depositing his cast-off clothing in a refuse bin he purchased a well-insulated jacket and at last he felt free.

Charles Clark, the accountant, late of Shepperton Road, London N1, was now Chris Kent, resident of a shabby little northern seaside town.

Chuckling to himself, he mimicked an old television programme. 'Tonight, Matthew, I'm going to be... Chris Kent. Not quite Superman, but the next best thing.'

Chapter 4

Tabz had not stopped all morning, engrossed in her work; she had managed just a ten-minute break to eat a fruit bar and down a cup of lukewarm coffee. Spending the morning searching the Police National Database for the man who said his name was Igor Husyev she could find no trace. A lack of access to the European system was annoying – more than annoying, because with a name like that and the sergeant's report saying that the subject spoke with a heavy European accent, she suspected that the Europol database would have been very useful.

She turned her attention to the constable's bodycam footage, which was good enough for her to use in an image search. It worked; the face pulled a match on the border control system, but the recognition software suggested not Igor Husyev, but a Dutch citizen named Henk Wiersma. Tabz felt she was making progress, but after a fruitless search elsewhere, she felt she was unable to go further. There was simply no trace of a man by that name, no United Kingdom address, no place of work. She sat back in her chair and clasped her hands behind her head.

'I'm sure I have a positive ID, but he's disappeared,' she said to herself.

Sitting forward in her chair, she navigated to the Schengen Information System, hoping some bureaucrat had finally gained access for the British police. She waited for the screen to refresh. For several seconds it did not, and then a notice appeared, denying her access.

'Stupid, it's totally stupid,' she said under her breath, and then her mobile phone rang.

'Jimi, you got my message?'

'Yes, what's the problem?'

'I am trying to locate a suspect but I am getting nowhere. I was going to ask if you knew of some obscure database I may not have come across before – a business database, Facebook, anyfing.'

'Oh, let me think... It's possible to search hidden accounts on Facebook if you know their URL, but you must know what you're doing. Have you got that?'

'Nope, nofing, absolutely nofing. The guy I'm looking for has a Dutch passport so I have just tried the Schengen Information System database to find we're still locked out. I thought they were going to let us back in after all the ballyhoo of our side stealing information like.'

'It's supposed to be imminent, I agree, but nothing concrete yet. Email me with the details and I will see what I can do.'

'What do you mean?'

'We have ways, let's just say that. I will be in touch.'

'Thanks,' said a puzzled Tabz.

She copy-and-pasted Henk Wiersma's details onto an email form, and several miles away Jimi rubbed his chin. Finally making up his mind, he lifted the receiver of his desk telephone. There was a pause of several seconds as the call routed through a secure line and then a voice answered.

'Eric, can I come and see you? I have a small problem I need to discuss.'

Tabz returned from her lunch break to find an email waiting for her. She had been counting on Jimi to circumvent a few rules and regulations and get the information she needed, and was impressed at how quickly he had done so.

That was quick, she thought, opening the email attachment, and finding herself reacquainted with Igor Husyev – or was he Henk Wiersma? One thing was certain, he was working very hard to hide his identity. To compound her confusion Jimi had offered only limited information. He believed that both names were false and that the passports the subject possessed were forgeries – good ones, but forgeries nonetheless.

She had hoped the email would reveal the identity of the man and improve her search criteria, but it wasn't to be. Tabz decided to look again at the footage obtained from the constable's bodycam. It was just about all she had, and perhaps she had missed something.

'It's not always the obvious that can close a case,' Jimi had said to her during one library work session. 'One job I was on last year was a real puzzle. We had info on a drug-smuggling gang and our intelligence pointed to the north of the country, but just where they were operating, we had no idea. It was driving the team I was working with at the time to distraction, until we had a breakthrough, an obscure reference. Some of the text messages we intercepted talked about the "Bitch" and how she had been useful to them, and of course we presumed it was a woman. Bitch is common enough language amongst the criminal class and I thought no more about it until about six months later, when I heard that the local police in a place called Bitchfield had accidentally stumbled upon a stash of drugs hidden in the local church graveyard. Putting the church under surveillance finally broke the case. Such a small clue and I missed it, I should have done a thorough search. It's too easy to lose track.'

Tabz wondered if perhaps she was missing a simple clue here, and decided to run the video at half speed. She concentrated first on the suspect's features, his gestures, glancing periodically at the transcript of the short conversation with DS Forrest. Then she ran it at normal speed through a sophisticated program that looked at pauses in a conversation and changes in the speakers' tones, looking for inconsistencies. The program appeared to confirm the man was lying, yet she was still no further on.

She looked again at the frames taken by the constable's helmet-cam when he had dropped it. Initially she had discounted the short section of video as the helmet had bounced across the floor, but this time she ran the recording all the way through, advancing it a frame at a time to look for anything that might help.

A shoe came into focus – something about it looked a little odd and she wondered what it was. She looked again and then it dawned on her: the soles had unusual-looking segments, wide castellations unlike any she had seen before. Was it a design quirk or was it to give the wearer better traction? She could only speculate, but it was something unusual and that was what she needed.

Opening the file, she scanned through the other recordings, mainly from traffic cameras, and began to run the video files one by one, eventually locating the subject. He showed up crossing a road with a second man, but the video was hardly clear enough to show what they were wearing on their feet.

'Hmm...' she said with a tinge of disappointment, yet

she felt she was on the right track. Maybe she should have a word with the sergeant.

DS Forrest was busy on a call when she approached his desk. Reading her intentions, he pointed to the seat opposite.

'Yes, sir, we have increased uniformed patrols to assure the locals we are keeping an eye on things. Yes, sir. No, sir. I will, sir. Thank you, goodbye,' he said, replacing the telephone receiver and rubbing his forehead.

'Strewth wot a palaver, this double murder has caused some problems, I can tell you. Now what is it, Tabz, you want to see me?'

'Yes, sir, it's only a hunch and there isn't much to show, but I believe the man you saw recently could be one of the murderers.'

'Go on.'

Tabz carefully explained her assumptions, wary of giving too much hope, and yet the more she told the sergeant the more she believed that she could be on the right track.

'But the images of the suspects do not look remotely like the geezer I met.'

'No, sir, I will give you that but they have the same build, and from what I have learned of this Henk Wiersma, he is not what he seems.'

'Henk Wiersma?'

'Oh yes, of course, you know him as Igor Husyev but I have found out he is travelling on a Dutch passport under the name Henk Wiersma like.'

'So, he has something to hide, you think?'

'Yes.'

'We need to tie him to the murder but all you have is a shoe! Have you the maker's name?'

'No, I admit I am skating on thin ice but for now it's all we have. Could we get some footprints like?'

'How? I can't see it after so much time, and the streets are all paved.'

'I will go through the recordings, try to trace his path, see if there is anywhere he might have left a print.'

'Get me as much information on the route you think they took and I will get forensics to 'ave a closer look. Thanks, Tabz,' said the detective sergeant, wondering.

Tabz spent the next hour scouring video footage from traffic cameras covering a slightly wider area. Finding two more sightings, she began documenting times and places. The suspect could have left footprints but as DS Forrest had observed, the streets were paved and there was very little exposed ground where a footprint might reside. Google Street View had proved invaluable on more than one occasion, and from the scant information she had, she could envisage two possible routes the men might have taken.

Meticulously she followed the routes using Street View, searching all the time for open ground the subject may have crossed, eventually focusing on two small areas. It was a tedious and frustrating task, but little by little she eliminated all areas but for a patch known as Islington Green. It looked a promising lead, though whether the suspects had passed that way she couldn't yet tell. The area would need to be searched.

'Have you seen the sergeant, Bill?' she asked one of the detectives.

'I think he's gone out; I don't know where to or when he might be back. You could call him.'

'Fanks, I will,' she said.

'What have you got, Tabz?' DS Forrest asked, when

she finally got hold of him.

Hurriedly she explained what she knew and the sergeant advised her to talk to Inspector Mills. She looked across the room to the inspector's office and could see him moving around in there.

'Excuse me, sir,' she said, tapping on the half-open door. 'I had a conversation with DS Forrest and he said I should talk to you.'

'Come in, take a seat. What can I do for you, is it about the murders?'

'Yes, sir, I believe I might have identified a suspect...' Tabz laid out her suspicions, along with the evidence to support them.

Inspector Mills listened, finally saying, 'I know you have put a lot of effort into this but it is all supposition.'

'If we could find a footprint with the sole pattern, it would at least tie in the man DS Forrest interviewed as a suspect.'

'I don't know... It's late, it will be too dark for forensics to work efficiently and I do believe we are expecting heavy rain during the night. No, leave things as they are for the time being. Thank you for your efforts, but I can't see the merit in despatching forensics on a night like this.'

Leaving the police station at the end of her shift, Tabz's emotions began to get the better of her. Hunching her shoulders, she turned up the collar of her anorak and let her shoulder bag swing wildly against her hip as she walked.

She was bitterly disappointed with the inspector's reaction; she really felt that she was onto something because for the past hour she had revisited the Venn diagram, added a few more details, and could see a pattern emerging. The old-fashioned way of sticking every piece of information, relevant or not, onto a board still worked well enough, but she preferred to use her computer, add to the diagram, and let the app do the work. Artificial intelligence could be useful – she had learned that from the Master's course – and Jimi, it seemed, already had knowledge of the technique.

Walking towards the tube station, she turned over in her mind everything she had learned about Henk Wiersma. First the passport photograph, then the police officer's bodycam footage and the possibility that there might still be a footprint awaiting discovery: it all intrigued her. The inspector was not taking her seriously and the sergeant didn't seem as interested as she thought he should be, but what could she do? Perhaps she should just go home, relax, and try again tomorrow.

Quickening her pace, she pulled her anorak tight against the chill and remembered the inspector's words. 'Rain could wash away any evidence even before we began to look.' She boarded the tube, found a seat, and took out her mobile telephone to look at the Met Office forecast. Sure enough, heavy rain was expected overnight. If they were to make any progress finding footprints then a search would need to take place before then.

Gritting her teeth, she knew that she must do something. She needed help and there was only one person she felt she could turn to.

'Jimi, glad I caught you. Normally all I get is your answering machine,' she said, relieved to hear his deep tone.

'What can I do for you? You only seem to call me when you want something.'

'Have you got a torch?'

'A torch, why?'

'I thought you might like a stroll in the park and if we find what I am looking for then you can take me to dinner.'

'Sounds interesting, anything else?'

'Europol.'

'Mmm... Not the first time.'

'No, but I can't access their database and somehow you can,' she said, smiling to herself.

'I'll pick you up in half an hour.'

Tabz was relieved he was going to help her, and after finding a pair of old boots, she put on her anorak and a woolly hat and stepped outside to wait. When his car pulled up she jumped into the passenger seat.

'I have brought you a torch,' he said as she closed the door. 'These small LCD torches beat anything I've ever used. Here, look,' he said, switching it on and shining it around. 'See, size isn't everything. Now what's this all about?'

'I've been working on the murder inquiry all day and I believe I am on to somefink, but the inspector will not authorise the involvement of forensics and the sergeant is no help eiver like, so I have decided to take matters into my own hands. Tonight, the forecast is for heavy rain and I am fearful any evidence might well disappear liket.'

'So, you thought you would rope me in. What evidence, where?'

'Well, you're always telling me it's the smallest of clues that can crack a case. I believe we might find a footprint somewhere on Islington Green that will link the suspect you identified as using a Dutch passport to the murder of the two individuals innit.'

'And that's what we're looking for here?'

'A footprint, yes.'

'Not a dead body or a gun even, just a footprint. Will one be enough?'

Tabz looked at him, the street light illuminating her scowl.

'Okay, okay, sorry. Where do we start?' he said, pulling up at a public charging bay. 'I might as well kill two birds with one stone,' he said, plugging the lead into the socket of his electric car.

'I don't really know, but I have done a survey of the park using Google Maps. We know where the attack took place like, and there are a couple of sightings of the suspects nearby, so I fink if we start over there by that gate and make our way to the far end of the green, we can hope that something turns up like.'

'What exactly are we looking for? A footprint is a footprint and there will be no chance of finding one on the footpaths.'

'I realised that as soon as I left the inspector's office, but maybe he took a shortcut like. Everyone takes shortcuts if they can innit. If we can establish places where people would cut across the grass or mud, we might find somefing. The footprint, if we find it, should have unusually wide ribs innit.'

In the gloom Jimi nodded his head, impressed by her logic. She switched on her torch and began to scan the nearest patch of grass, and he followed suit. The exercise was tedious, but like Tabz, he had a patient and analytical mind and together they systematically swept beams of white light across the muddy ground.

'Have you a spare battery, Jimi?' asked Tabz, stopping beside a park bench. 'My torchlight is turning yellowish.'

'I'm afraid not, but there is still some life left in mine.

Are you sure they would come this way?'

'Fairly sure, they left by the gate over there, I fink. Let's try just a little longer, though it does feel as if it's the last throw of the dice like,' she said, looking at her feet as she swept the waning beam from side to side.

Doubt crossed her mind. Perhaps she was wrong after all. She was on the verge of giving up when the fading torchlight exposed an imprint less than two metres away. Alongside the park bench was an area of soft mud, and in it a footprint, a deep footprint with wide serrations. She could not contain herself.

'There! Look, Jimi, there innit!'

Jimi swept his own beam across the mud. 'Well, I'll be damned.'

Tabz took out her mobile telephone to carefully photograph the imprint from all angles and then, standing awkwardly, with her own shoe alongside the footprint, she made an image to gain an impression of scale.

'You're sure this is what you are looking for?'

'As sure as I can be. I will need to compare it to his shoes on the video like. I'm wondering if I should purchase a pair of shoes just like the ones he was wearing, print this footprint full size, compare them like.'

Jimi's grin was invisible in the shadows, impressed by her perseverance. 'So, are we having Chinese or Italian?'

'Italian,' said an elated Tabz, slipping her arm through his. 'Just for support, you understand,' she said, smiling up at him.

Kitted out in his new clothes, Charles decided to explore the town a little more before he returned to his hotel.

61

The traffic was nowhere near as overbearing as it was in London, and that made for easy crossings. For all his preconceived notions of the poorer north, he noticed that shoppers were out in force in the town centre, and after a while he found a small café hidden away down a side street. A faint aroma of coffee drifted from the doorway and he couldn't resist. Stepping inside, he noticed just two other people huddled together in conversation and a large woman standing behind the dated Formica countertop reading a tabloid.

'Coffee, please,' he said a little unsurely.

'How many sugars?' she said, folding the newspaper away.

'Oh, no sugar, thanks.'

The woman spooned out the coffee from a large tin and filled the cup with hot water.

'Milk?'

'Yes.'

'There you are,' she said, sliding the cup and saucer across the counter. 'Anything else?'

'A sandwich, please,' he said, looking up at the handwritten board behind the woman. 'Er... cheese and pickle.'

'I will bring your sandwich when it's ready.'

Charles thanked her and carried his over-full cup to a table near a large window. He sat with his back to the wall and gazed out at passing pedestrians. His coffee was too hot and for several minutes he people-watched. When his sandwich arrived his concentration turned more to eating and drinking. The coffee was typically cheap and bitter but the sandwich was surprisingly good. After munching his way through it, he sat back in his seat and noticed, on the opposite side of the street, a small estate agent's office.

If he could find somewhere to rent for a few months, then perhaps he could lie low until his problem went away. He could, of course, go to the police and tell them what he knew, but after the murders in broad daylight he knew he was dealing with incredibly dangerous people. He had no wish to antagonise them further and felt that to remain out of sight in the seaside town was his best option. He had access to the bank account in his new name and a Bitcoin wallet that seemed to increase in value by the day. He had no money worries, no need to work, and once he acclimatized to the northern weather, he felt sure he could survive.

He finished his coffee and left the café, walking across the street to examine the photographs of various properties in the agent's window. To someone from London they seemed remarkably cheap. There was a small terraced house that drew his eye, and he went inside.

'The house in the window, the white one with the slate roof – is it for rent?'

'Which one?' said a bored-looking young man.

'I'll show you,' offered Charles, stepping back outside.

'Oh, yes. Not been on the books very long and it's reasonably priced.'

'Yes, I can see that, but is it for rent? I would prefer renting to buying.'

'I don't know about that. Would you like me to ask the vendor?'

'Yes, if you could.'

'Leave me your details and I will be in touch. Or perhaps you could call back tomorrow some time.'

Suddenly feeling vulnerable, Charles hesitated. Leaving details – his telephone number, the address of the hotel – could be dangerous.

'I'll call back tomorrow,' he said.

'As you wish, Mr...?'

'Kent, my name is Kent,' said Charles, in a less than convincing voice.

'Okay, Mr Kent, I look forward to seeing you tomorrow.'

Rising from his bed just as the dawn was breaking the following day, Charles felt refreshed. He pulled back the curtain and looked out on a grey overcast morning. After the sunshine of the day before it was a mild disappointment, but compared to his mood of just a day earlier, he was feeling on top of the world. For the first time since he had embarked on his adventure, he had a plan. He would return to the estate agent's office in the hope that the owner of the little house had accepted his proposal, then he would explore the town. The view he had experienced the day before had impressed, a wide sweeping beach, a hill with the remains of what looked to be a medieval castle, and nestled below it, a small harbour.

For a second day he consumed breakfast that was twice the size of any he would ever have eaten in London, then stepped out into the fresh salt-laden air.

Surprising even himself at his pace, he strode across the wide footpath, the fresh air instilling within him a feeling of wellbeing he had not experienced and a belief that he was less likely to suffer a slow and premature death as would be his fate amongst the London traffic. He looked up at the sky – grey and less welcoming, but at least the stinging cold had abated. He felt like a child coming to the seaside for the first time and, overcome with excitement at the sight of the sea, decided to head for the beach. It wasn't the Mediterranean, just an uninviting greyness, but he didn't care. Why should he? For the moment he was free, his worries on the back burner, and he had a plan.

Walking along the seafront, he marvelled at the yellowish sand stretching towards the low rollers of the incoming tide. He watched dog walkers and people out for an early morning stroll and, feeling adventurous, he found a break in the railings, leaving the path for the sand. He felt a drag on his feet as he walked, his pace slowed, and after just fifty or so steps he returned to the pathway, deciding that perhaps it wasn't such a good idea after all.

He passed a row of wooden shacks plastered with gaudy lettering proclaiming the wonders of locally caught shellfish. There was a candy floss stall and another selling sea shells, but only two or three hardy shopkeepers were open for business. Beside the harbour he caught his first sight of fishing boats, smaller than he'd expected, and intrigued, he stopped for a closer look at a man working on his nets.

'Not fishing today?' he asked.

The man looked up and scowled. 'No, mate, we can only go out three days a month and today isn't one of them.'

'Oh, why's that?'

'Don't you watch the news? The government have made a complete balls-up. Instead of the rich catches we expected, we're scratting to make a living. Now if you don't mind, you're winding me up.'

A fisherman looking on from the next boat shook his head.

'I'm sorry, I hadn't realised. Perhaps I can buy some fish off you next time you catch something.'

'Aye,' said the fisherman, turning away.

Charles felt the rebuke and thought it best to move on. He tried giving a short wave in the belief that it would make amends, but there was no response. He passed rows of yachts and motorboats moored alongside pontoons not unlike those he had seen in Weymouth, and there was a shack selling tea where several men had gathered. Looking at his watch, he noted the time: ten to eleven. The estate agent must have an answer by now, he thought, and decided to try to get to the office by noon.

Apart from the miserable fishermen he was enjoying his walk, and decided to explore further before making his way to the estate agent's office. An engine's throaty roar turned his head, and he saw a small boat making its way across the harbour. With fascination he followed its progress towards the harbour entrance. He noticed two men fishing, their lines dipping out of sight over the sea wall, and his inquisitiveness got the better of him.

'Do you catch many fish?' he asked as he walked up to them.

'Aye, a few,' said one of the men, looking up.

'What's the main species you catch round here? Cod, I suppose.'

'Yes, cod and pollock, maybe a ling. The boats do better than we do here. You an angler?'

'Not for years, I live in London,' said Charles, momentarily dropping his guard.

'London, eh? Bit different to Scarborough, I imagine. Anyway, what are you doing in Scarborough in January? I would have thought it too cold for you southerners.'

Charles smiled, his guard slipping a little further. 'Well, you have a point there, I must admit. Bracing, I suppose you would call it.'

The two anglers laughed and then one exclaimed, 'I've got something, Joey.' Leaning back, he braced himself.

Charles looked on, captivated as the rod set to a shallow curve, resisting the fish fighting to escape. The second man had a bight and the two of them heaved on their rods in unison, winding madly, and Charles climbed onto the wall to watch as two cold, wet, wriggling fish emerged from the sea.

'You must be a lucky person,' said Joey as he drew the hook from the fish's mouth, a trickle of piscine blood on his fingers. 'You should try your luck.'

'I might just do that. Where can I buy a rod?'

'See the pier over there,' he said, dropping the still-wriggling fish into a bag at his feet.

Charles followed the finger pointing towards a low building.

'There's a fishing tackle shop over there. Why not look in?'

'I might just do that,' said Charles repeating himself.

He hadn't fished since he was a boy and that was only in the local reservoir, but it brought back memories of a time when his father was alive, when he had received love and attention. How that had changed. When he was fourteen his mother had remarried, and between her and his stepfather Charles had been left feeling ignored and isolated, so he had immersed himself in his school work. Alone in his room, sheltered from the unkind comments, he had lost himself in his studies, in the end achieving good enough results. In the same week he celebrated his eighteenth birthday he'd left home to begin his undergraduate studies.

University life suited him. The friends he made were good company, bright people with a lot to talk about, and he flourished, graduating with a good enough degree to find a job with one of the big accountancy firms serving the square mile. His future looked bright but his salary was not as high as he would have liked. Putting up with his lot for a further eighteen months, he persevered until one day he came to the attention of Andrei Potanin. The Russian had said his homeland was becoming just too dangerous, and told Charles that he wished to transfer as much of his business to London as he could. It was a difficult and demanding task, but Charles achieved most of what Andrei had requested, making a good impression on the Russian.

'You come with me, my friend. I have something special for you,' said Andrei one day, when Charles had visited his office for paper signing. 'You like?' he said, leading the accountant into the rear yard of the office block. 'Is a gift for all the work you have done and for making sure no one has come looking for something they should not.'

Charles had swallowed hard. The prospect of owning the gleaming Mercedes pleased him, yet at the same time he was fearful the authorities might scrutinise his work a little too closely. But in the event nothing happened, and as he drove the Mercedes around London those same authorities welcomed the arrival of even more Russian money.

Then came an offer he could not refuse.

'You work for me and I pay you a lot more than your current employer. You know so much about my business that you will be an asset. Of course, there is an alternative,' Andrei had said, putting his hand in his jacket pocket and retrieving a 0.357 Magnum bullet fashioned in twenty-four-carat gold. Placing it on the desk, he looked Charles in the eye. 'What do you say, will you come and work for me

Chapter 5

Transferring the image of the footprint from her mobile telephone, Tabz dragged it across the screen, positioning it alongside one from the constable's bodycam. For several minutes she compared them. A small adjustment in size, a slight rotation, and they matched. She felt sure the man who had left the footprint was the same one the sergeant had interviewed, and the same man who had committed the murders. She did not have absolute proof but it was a lead – a strong one, in her opinion – and she felt she should inform her superior.

As she tapped gently on his office window, Inspector Mills looked up from his work and gestured for her to enter.

'I took on board your suggestion,' he said, not giving her a chance to speak. 'I asked forensics to look in the park for footprints or any other clue that might aid the investigation. They have just got back to me and I'm afraid no luck, the heavy rain during the night obliterated anything meaningful. So, what can I do for you, Tabz?'

Tabz was disappointed the inspector had not acted sooner and was about to tell him of her discovery when something told her not to.

'Don't play your best cards until you know you can win,' Jimi had once said, a piece of advice that suddenly felt relevant.

If he chose to, Inspector Mills could censure her for overriding his decision not to look for footprints and that would harm her career, but more than that, why had he been so reluctant to act in the first place, before rain destroyed the evidence?

'I, er... I'm following another line of inquiry like, looking for the man who seems central to the murders, the one who got away from the attempted mugging.'

'What do you need from me? I'm busy. Can't DS Forrest help you?'

'Sorry, sir, I will talk to him and let him know what I would like to do.'

'Good, I wish you luck,' said the inspector, returning to the document he was reading.

Tabz felt nauseous. Why had she not let him know of her success in finding the footprint? Why had she said she was going to look for the runaway, and what was she going to say to Detective Sergeant Forrest? Something was troubling her and she did not know what it was.

'Relax a bit, girl, get a coffee,' she said to herself. To hell with them.

'Any progress on the murders?' asked a colleague as she retrieved her coffee from the machine.

'Hello, Colin. No, not much, what about your contacts? I hear every informant in London supplies you with intelligence.'

'Hardly, but here's a snippet that might interest you...'

The plastic cup stopped at Tabz's lips and her eyes turned to the detective.

'I have heard recently that there is someone on the manor manufacturing silicone masks.'

'I have heard of those. Some so realistic.'

'That's right. Maybe your suspects were wearing

them. They are expensive and probably not something your run-of-the-mill petty thief would wear.'

Tabz took a drink, her eyes still on the detective yet for several seconds she did not see him.

'Thanks for that,' she said, returning to her desk, placing the half-empty coffee cup on it and picking up the computer mouse.

She would trawl the CCTV footage again, see what might show up. The idea the men might have worn silicone masks was an intriguing one.

Commander Pearson's telephone sprang to life; his visitor had arrived.

'Ben, come in, good to see you again,' he said, welcoming him in.

'Hello, Jeremy, good to see you too,' said the tall American, holding out his hand.

'How is London treating you this time? How long is it?'

'Almost five years since we last met.'

'Must be, I expect a few of those baddies we netted will be released soon.'

'Baddies? You have been watching too many westerns, but let's hope they have learned their lesson. I doubt it, a leopard doesn't easily change its spots and being locked up is part of the job for some. Say nothing, serve your time and pick up where you left off!'

'Learn a few more tricks of the trade, eh?' the commander laughed.

'I suppose so. Anyway, down to business. You know why I'm here.'

'Yes, take a seat. Coffee?'

'I'd love a coffee – a real one, not that powdered muck you limeys drink.'

'I'll have to disappoint you there, the budget only stretches to dried coffee and powdered milk, sorry.'

'That will have to do, thanks.'

'I'm kidding, I'll get some strong proper coffee brought up,' he said, picking up the phone. After a brief conversation he turned back to his visitor.

'So, what have you learned since we last spoke, Commander?' Ben asked.

'Very little, I'm afraid. The police are handling things and will be annoyed if we try to muscle in. It's not really our job to investigate murder.'

'You know as well as I do, this is not just any old murder. Those men were CIA on their way to meet a mole who had just pressed the panic button – an informant who works for a Russian oligarch. He's a minor player but has passed us some useful information in the short time he has been working for us. You Brits seem to like having half the Russian mafia living here in London. We don't like it.'

'Oh, come on, Ben. It's not like it used to be. The Salisbury affair was the turning point and since the Russian invasion of Ukraine, we have been careful as to who we let in. We've thrown a lot of them out, you know – even Premier League clubs belong only to oil sheikhs, American syndicates and the odd Asian now. So, who is this informant?'

'He's called Charles Clark and he is some sort of accountant. He moves the money around for the Russian and writes the cheques for the deals, though of course he is not the one to sign them. He has dabbled in Bitcoin for his employer. I'm sure you are aware many of your guests here in London are not altogether honest men, and Bitcoin is their currency. On top of that, the Agency is aware of a money laundering operation being conducted by our friend the accountant on behalf of his boss, Andrei Potanin. The Russian is sanctioned and we know he left the country recently, one of the last to go, and this accountant and his henchmen are running the business as far as we can tell. We have traced dirty money to Switzerland and the Bahamas, even Peru. The accountant is the facilitator. We let him know a few months ago that we were onto him and that if he wanted to avoid a spell in Sing Sing, then he should cooperate.'

'Is Sing Sing still in use? I thought it was closed down years ago, since Eliot Ness retired?'

'Ha ha, prohibition? I wish that were our only problem today. Believe it or not, Sing Sing is still operational, a maximum-security facility operated by the New York State Department. We let our friend know that we had a room reserved for him if he did not cooperate.'

'And he is?'

'Yes, of course, he's no Superman – and we had to make him more afraid of us than his boss.'

'And someone found him out?'

'Not exactly, though I imagine they will have by now. When he called the number we gave him he was extremely agitated, kept saying he had seen a letter, something from the Russian Embassy and that he dare not tell anyone what was in it until he was safe. So, we sent those two poor guys to pick him up, bring him in from the cold, so to speak. If his information is as explosive as he implied then we could spirit him away to the States and no one would ever find him.'

'But you lost him?'

'We did, and two good men are dead.'

'I'm truly sorry about that. What do you want us to do? We'll help as much as we can.'

'We want this Charles Clark caught. Let the police deal with catching the murderers for now. I suspect they are Russians. You here at MI6 will eventually become involved, you must be, and we want in. The CIA know a lot more than you do right now and we can be helpful. We want this Charles Clark and we want to know what is in that letter that frightened him so much.'

Anita was out of condition, the sweat pouring off her as she took aim one last time, a powerful rail shot that won her the point.

'You've still got it, Anita, that was a really good shot.'

'You think so? From where I am it doesn't look so good. I'm worn out and you were only playing at half speed, I could tell.'

Her opponent laughed, a deep throaty laugh: Jimi's trademark.

'I wasn't going at half speed; you ran me ragged. Come on, let's shower and we'll have a hot chocolate, my treat.'

'Okay, see you in the café in twenty minutes – and stop taking the piss,' laughed Anita.

As a game of squash it ranked as one of her less than spectacular efforts, but she needed to get fit again after her illness. Playing against Jimi was good exercise. He was a clever player, physically strong and agile, and it was a chance to catch up on some of the office gossip.

Together they stowed their rackets and, picking up his bag, Jimi followed Anita towards the shower block. At thirty-two years old, single, Jimi was happy to keep it that way. He had seen the trouble relationships could cause growing up in the tower block. Most teenage friends had sown wild oats and were either stuck in a relationship they did not choose or were on the run to avoid child maintenance commitments. Jimi, though, was luckier than most. His strong-willed mother had kept the family together, his father was never out of work, and there was his physique. Naturally muscular, taller than most of his cohort, he found few bullies were prepared to take him on.

His father was a large-framed and gentle-natured man, liked and respected by all who knew him. Jimi had inherited the same traits; however, he had a streak of determination that was absent in his father. It wasn't as if he was pushed to do well at school, it had come naturally to him and, more than that, he enjoyed learning. While his friends hung around street corners he was happy doing his homework. While they got themselves into trouble with the police, he went on to gain a place at university studying computer science, where he discovered that Oxbridge had not changed so much. Still a recruiting ground for the Secret Service, he had accepted the invitation to talk about opportunities in the civil service, particularly the Home Office, and after graduating he successfully applied for a post within MI6, starting as an analyst.

He spent his first months investigating a few rich men – very rich men enticed by successive governments to deposit their wealth in British banks, invest in British companies. On the face of it a good idea, but not a policy without a darker side. Russian oligarchs with ties to the Kremlin were his main subjects, individuals with pretentions of independence who, in reality, were ruled by the Kremlin.

Once again he found himself investigating them.

Tabz had set an alarm bell ringing with her repeated information requests, and her belief that Russians were responsible for the murder of two Americans. In recent times the British government had confronted the Russians over several incidents – murders, apparent suicides – and across Europe similar cases had surfaced, highlighting the Russian government's contempt for sovereign borders. With the war in Ukraine and their aggression towards NATO, things were becoming ever more dangerous.

Work was never far from Jimi's mind but he knew he needed at least a small amount of relaxation. Stepping out of the shower, he dressed and made his way to the cafeteria.

'You took your time, Jimi; I have bought you your usual. I guess it will be cold by now.'

'Oh, sorry. I was daydreaming a little.'

'You, daydreaming! I don't believe it.'

'Am I not allowed to daydream?'

'Of course, but I know you. If your mind was on something it would be work. Can you talk about it?'

Jimi's eyes momentarily looked away and then he looked back at Anita. 'I can talk a little but not a lot. What do you think about the police being prevented from accessing Europol?'

'It's part of the agreement with the European Union: no fishing, no access to the database, simple. Why do you ask?'

'I have an acquaintance, a friend who works on police intelligence and she has suspicions about the involvement of a Russian, or his personnel at least, in a double murder.'

'The Americans?'

Jimi's dark eyes gave nothing away as he looked at Anita.

'Okay, so what do I think? I think it's totally stupid. There are criminals running around the United

Kingdom and the Europeans are not telling us about them. We only find out after the event when someone is robbed, or even killed, when we could perhaps have prevented a serious crime. Look at that fiasco in Spain,' she said, her voice tinged with anger.

'You mean when the police took out full-page spreads in Spanish newspapers looking for British criminals on the Costas?'

'Yes! Because we were not getting intelligence from Europol, some bright spark decided to put their pictures in the newspaper and ask the public for help. Very Wild West – "have you seen this man going by the name of Jesse James"?' said Anita, laughing at her own joke. 'It did work, though.'

Now it was Jimi's turn to laugh at the absurdity of it. 'Yes, to be fair it did result in a couple of arrests, but most of them just disappeared and we have no idea where they are now. At least when we were working with Europol we had a good chance of nailing some of them without alerting the others. It was working a few years back, but not now.'

'You know that's not strictly true. There is a back door, we all use it.'

'True, but the police don't have that luxury.'

'What's brought this up?' asked Anita, her suspicious mind suddenly alert. In return she received a deadpan look.

'Okay, enough for now. Drink up and let's head for home.'

Charles liked the idea of buying a fishing rod, and after a time looking through the shop window, he made up his mind and pushed the door open.

The weather was showing a kinder face, what he had

seen of the town he liked, and the cheerfulness of the second two fishermen had helped him make up his mind. Happier childhood memories returned, times when his real father had taken him fishing and taught him some rudimentary techniques. He decided he would try it. He could not return to London, not for a while. His pursuers would be searching for him elsewhere and he reasoned that he could not just sit around doing nothing. Why not sit around fishing for fish?

'How much is that one?' he asked the stout, red-faced man sitting behind the counter.

'Which one?'

'That one,' he said, pointing to a slender green rod sitting in the window.

'Fifty-three pounds and ninety-five pence.'

'I'll take it,' said Charles, perhaps a little too eagerly.

'Done much sea angling, have you?'

'No, thought I would try it, it looks interesting.'

'Interesting? Ha. Have you got a multiplier reel, and what about clothing? It gets cold this time of year. We don't want pneumonia, do we? And you will need a tackle box for your hooks and sinkers. Have you got those?'

Charles puffed out his cheeks, bewildered by these new complications.

'I must confess I am a complete beginner, just fished when I was quite young at the local reservoir with my father and not since then.'

The shopkeeper cocked his head slightly to one side and gave Chris a sympathetic look as he totalled up the potential sales. 'How much do you want to spend?'

'What?'

'How much do you want to spend?' he repeated. 'We can go over all the tackle you need and look at the different stuff I have in the shop. A good reel can set you back three hundred pounds, or you can buy a cheaper one for less than a hundred. One like that is a simpler mechanism but it's good enough. You can buy a Scarborough reel on eBay for a tenner but it will probably cause you more problems than it's worth.'

'No, I'll take one of those. You said a tackle box?'

'I did,' said the shopkeeper, showing Charles the few he had in stock before proceeding to present the novice fisherman with everything else he might need, finishing with a selection of clothing.

For no other reason than because he was on the run, Charles ignored the more fashionable waterproof suits and settled for the same camouflaged clothing the local fishermen were wearing.

'I will be more at home in the jungle,' he mumbled, hardly believing that he would be invisible on the sea wall.

Perhaps it was a uniform of sorts. He had noticed a lot of anglers wore the same clothing.

'It is a sort of camouflage,' he said to himself. 'At least I will not stand out.'

The news that the small house was available to rent had pleased Charles, and today was the day he would sign the six-month lease and after ten days at the hotel he would be moving into a place of his own.

'The landlord says he was going to put most of the furniture and fittings into a saleroom, throw some away. But I'm sure you can make use of them,' said the mordant estate agent as he countersigned the lease.

Charles hardly heard his comment, his mind more on the fact he was getting his own place. A small house, yes, but tucked away from view – a place where he might be safe. They had asked for a reference, said they needed to check his credit but his offer of six months' rent in advance no questions asked had sealed the deal. He signed on the dotted line and paid with his new credit card in the name of Chris Kent.

'Bit unusual not to have a proper credit check,' said the young man. 'I suppose it's the cost of living squeeze, you paying so much up front I mean.'

'Yes, must be,' said Charles relieved that he had got away with it.

'Well, here are the keys. I expect I will see you in six months with the next rent payment – or not?'

Why had Inspector Mills been so reluctant to search for footprints, only authorising a search when he knew there was a very good chance the rain would make them invisible? It was a question Tabz could not let go – and what if she told him she had found the footprint on her own initiative, what would he do then? If he wanted to, he could wreck her career.

Now there were more video recordings available from traffic cameras, so she left thoughts of Inspector Mills and concentrated on this new footage using the artificial intelligence program's face-recognition facility. As a technique it was new to her, and she had to refer to the command list on more than one occasion, but after viewing an instructional video she felt ready to get going.

She had two images of the suspect known as Henk Wiersma and, loading those images into the search box, proceeded to run the new video streams. At first she drew a blank and on examining the camera's location, she realised that one of the routes the killers might have taken was probably wrong. She had a second path, one that would have taken the suspects past another camera around the time of the murders, and within minutes the screen flashed up a result.

'That's him,' she said under her breath, leaning forward to examine the frame in more detail, 'and there is the second man.'

So far so good, she thought, re-running the video to determine where they were heading. She looked at her list to determine which camera, if any, might have picked them up next. She was in luck: a traffic camera on the A104 provided some video recorded just half an hour before the attack, and as it was sited not far from where they had found the footprint, it could provide crucial evidence.

She was more sure than ever that Henk Wiersma and the second man were involved, yet the witness statements did not match the evidence. The most convincing witness, a woman who had just parked her car, had described two men wearing hats. Having trawled the video tapes, Tabz could not find them and the facial-recognition software could not make a match.

She was tired, her head buzzing from concentration and disappointment at a lack of results. She needed a break, so stretching her legs, she visited the coffee machine, an oasis in a sea of chaos.

How could they disappear like that? she kept asking herself. She had times and places and could, with some accuracy, predict their whereabouts – but they had disappeared into thin air. She decided to make prints of the suspects, study them on hard copy, see if that helped.

Sitting back at her desk, she sent a file to the office printer and sipped the remains of her coffee before walking to collect her images.

'Ah, Tabz, I have been meaning to talk to you,' said Inspector Mills, approaching. 'How is the case progressing? Unfortunate that we could not find your footprints; the weather, unpredictable as usual.'

'Yes, sir, unfortunate. There is nothing much I can tell you, sir.'

'What is this you are doing, are those your suspects?' he asked, his eyes fixed on the images for a few seconds. 'Oh, and the man who ran away, have you anything on him?'

'No, sir, he seems to have completely disappeared.'

In truth she had not really tried to locate him, engrossed as she was in trying to find her murder suspects. Perhaps she *should* spend some time trying to find him – he was key to the inquiry, after all, and he would have some answers. But where to start?

The facial prints were not at all bad, better than they might have been with such magnification, but she could see clearly the faces of the two men crossing the road towards Islington Green – so why were they not showing up after the last sighting? Other cameras should have picked them up, surely. They were reasonably distinctive, both bare-headed, one wearing a blue anorak, the other a short camel-coloured overcoat.

She looked at the images again, studying their features: good-looking men, powerfully built. The witness statement said one had a rounded nose. These two didn't, and as she looked closer, Tabz noted they had sharp features. Was she chasing ghosts? They had disappeared almost as ghosts and she felt totally deflated.

'Hi, Tabz, how's it going?' said a voice. She looked up to see Colin, the undercover detective.

'Not good, I've lost my suspects on the A104.'

'Oh, where?'

'Near Islington Green.'

'That's a maze of criminality on any evening. I've caught a few drug dealers there in my time. How come you've lost them? There are loads of cameras around that area.'

'Look, here they are crossing the road and that's the last I've seen of them.'

'Silicone masks.'

'What?'

'Silicone masks. I told you, someone on the manor is, or was, producing silicone masks. They can be so realistic. Have you thought that your suspects might be wearing them?'

Tabz's body stiffened and she jumped up from her chair to wrap her arms around her colleague and give him a kiss on his cheek.

'Whoa, steady on.'

'Colin, you have made my day. Of course they could be wearing masks! And a witness stated they were wearing hats like.'

'Well, they would, that would help their disguise.'

Feeling a little embarrassed by her show of emotion, she sat back in her chair and watched the undercover detective walk away grinning. Maybe she had made his day too.

On the screen Andrei Potanin's face projected anger. Returning to Russia, he had become aware of the letter sent in error by the embassy. Just a day earlier he would have received it personally, but having to leave in such a hurry meant that it was up to Sergei to look after his interests.

The Kremlin had made him aware of the letter's

contents, and for him to make an enemy of the state was not a good idea. Should the operation fail, his masters would hold him responsible. He needed that letter back. Somehow Charles had got hold of it, he was sure, and the accountant could have guessed its meaning.

'Sergei, you must find this piece of dog dirt and screw him into the ground. He cannot be allowed to live,' said Andrei, his face reminding Sergei of a scene from *Red Dwarf*, one of his favourite English television programmes.

Sergei's eyebrows rose only slightly, all signs of amusement banished. He had no idea what the letter contained or what Charles Clark knew, but if Andrei wanted him eliminated then he must be.

'We don't know where he is, we chased him but he simply disappeared,' Sergei replied. 'I sent Markov to check his apartment and the police were already there.'

'I am not surprised they are looking for him. I will speak with someone who might shed some light on his whereabouts, someone close to the police investigation. When I have that information you must move quickly. That's all for now.'

The screen went blank. Sergei left the small office, locking the door behind him, while in the Russian capital Andrei Potanin thumbed through the address book of an encryption app and called a number.

'Hello,' said a voice.

'You know who this is?'

'Yes.'

'I am looking for someone, a man I must find.'

'Who?'

'Charles Clark, an employee of mine. I understand that you are looking for him as well.'

'It would seem so, yes.'

Chapter 6

The man now known as Chris Kent settled into his new life surprisingly quickly. In just one week he had found a new dwelling, made the occasional friend, and was about to discover the joys of sea fishing. Although perhaps a little naïve to believe his life could continue in such a manner, he had begun to relax, the adrenalin rushes subsiding as the memory of his escape faded.

He was beginning to enjoy life. The tiny house tucked away down a side street was ideal, comfortable, and easily managed. He had treated himself to a few extra comforts: a thick duvet, and a new set of pans to replace the disgusting pile of implements he had inherited, and he was beginning to settle in.

The world kept on turning, and on this new day when he pulled the curtain to one side to look up at the patch of sky that was visible between the buildings opposite, he was disappointed. A second grey day in succession, yet the greyness was not going to dampen his enthusiasm. He would take his new fishing rod to try it out. It may be a grey day, he thought, but it was the first day he felt truly free to do what he wanted. Gathering his fishing tackle, he left on his adventure.

Although the weight of his new equipment slowed his pace, he felt unnoticed in his camouflage clothing and soon found a place on the harbour wall not far from Joey and Malcolm, his new found friends. With a wave and a grin, they greeted him as he baited the hook and clumsily cast his line, no more than five or six metres out over the water. Sitting on the wall he watched the float as it bobbed to the surface, its red and yellow a contrast to the dark waters. He closed his eyes for a few seconds, reflected on how his life was changing, the traffic, the crush of people and the hustle and bustle of the city almost a distant memory.

However, the tranquillity did not last; an exclamation a few metres away announced a bite. He turned to see Joey springing into action, grabbing his rod from its stand and winding furiously, the slender pole curving in response to a fish desperately trying to escape. The contest had begun and all heads turned to witness the struggle. Chris watched as Joey's rod curved markedly in response to the force of the flailing fish, the rod dipped and bent until finally the writhing silver body broke the surface to swing helplessly in an alien world.

'Well, hello,' said Malcolm to Chris, as his friend unhooked his catch. 'Look what I've found. I see you've got yourself kitted out. Nice-looking rod. How much did that set you back?'

'Two hundred and thirty-eight pounds and twenty-five pence all told.'

'About two hundred and fifty pounds then,' said Malcolm, laughing. Well, it looks good and I see you have an Ironloop reel, they're not cheap either.'

'I got a discount on that: one hundred and seventy-nine pounds ninety-nine pence.'

Malcolm grinned again, amused at Chris's precise costing – but then he didn't know he was dealing with an accountant. 'You seem to be struggling a bit with your casting. Do you want me to show you the best way?'

'That's very kind of you, er... Malcolm, isn't it?'

87

Malcolm, amused, mimicked the new angler. 'Chris, isn't it?'

'Yes, Chris Kent. Not quite Superman, I'm afraid.'

The big man roared with laughter and, picking up the rod, reeled in the line. He played out some line, cast the hook and sinker three times the distance Chris had managed, and reeling back in, handed the rod to Chris.

'Here, hold it like this, and string out some loose line to start with. Ready?'

Chris nodded and practiced flicking the rod as Malcolm had shown him.

'Not bad, see? Nice and easy. Think you can manage?'

'I'll have a go,' said Chris, swinging the rod over his shoulder, and with a flick of his wrist made a passable cast.

'That's right, you'll soon get the hang of it.'

The following day Chris once more set off for the harbour. Thanks to his new friend's expert instruction, he felt confident that he would catch his first fish. Although he had failed to catch anything the day before, he had begun to feel he was making progress and another day's fishing, he was sure, would bring results.

On the advice of Malcolm to try different bait, he called in at the tackle shop.

'You again,' said the red-faced man. 'Have you caught much yet?'

'Just a few tiddlers, but they seem to be getting bigger,' Chris bluffed.

The man laughed. 'Well, that's the best fisherman's tale I've heard this week. Perhaps it's wishful thinking.'

'Maybe. Have you some better bait? I think I should try something different today.'

Looking thoughtful, the red-faced man replied,

'Maybe you would be better off this time of year with lugworms. Here, how about these,' he said, opening the door to the freezer. 'If you want live bait you will need to dig them up yourself. Not much fun this time of year, though.'

Chris saw no reason to argue as he felt for some money. Taking the cold packet, he managed a wave of his hand as he left the shop, believing strongly that he would have better luck today and looking up at the sky, noticed an increase in the strength of the breeze. Though he was no weather expert, he did know that a weather front had passed through during the night and although the sun was breaking through, today was very different. The sea looked angrier than he had yet seen it, crashing violently into the sea wall, and throwing up a spray. He was aware from conversation with Malcolm and Joey that the tide affected the fish, and on Malcolm's advice he set his rod down a good twenty metres from his usual place.

'We're safe enough here but if you go over there,' he had said, pointing, 'it can be dangerous in a big sea, particularly at high tide.' Then it had occurred to him to ask Chris, 'Do you understand the tides?'

'Well, sort of.'

'You've a lot to learn, mate.'

The advice was good and Chris, took it, picking the safest place he could find to make his first cast. It wasn't good and he had to try again. This time he was more successful, the float bobbing up beyond the breaking waves and well clear of the rocks. He settled down and for an hour watched the float until his mind began to drift.

The memory of his flight from London was never far from his thoughts and feeling sorry for himself began to drift into a depressive state until jolted back to reality. His bright red and yellow float suddenly disappeared, dipping beneath the waves, and his line straightened. A bite. A bite! he mouthed, and feeling the tug of a powerful fish, began to reel it in. The rod bent to an alarming angle but playing the fish just as Malcolm had taught him he began to get the better of it. It wasn't the same as fishing with his father from the reservoir of his youth – no, this was a raw, crashing fight against a sea monster and a moody sea. He felt spray blow in his face, and in his imagination he had Moby-Dick on the end of his line and the waters were those of the South Atlantic, not the North Sea.

It was no Moby-Dick, not even a marlin: just a codfish weighing rather more than a bag of sugar, but the thrill he felt knew no bounds.

'Wow, that will make a good dinner,' was all he could say, but after several hours' more casting into a receding sea, just a few tiddlers were all he could manage.

In high spirits, he returned home to gut and fillet his fish, he made a batter mixed with half a bottle of lager and fried the fish to perfection, feasting as if he were Henry the Eighth.

'Wonderful,' he said out loud, as he wiped the last of the bread across his empty plate. 'And now for a nice cup of tea.'

He took his plate into the tiny kitchen, set the kettle to boil on the gas stove and, whistling an out-of-tune obscure song, prepared the tea. He was warm, his appetite satisfied and with his mug of tea steaming on the side table, he turned on the 1950s-era radio. He had discovered it while rummaging in the scruffy second-hand shop not far from his house. Yes, it was old-fashioned, but the idea of living the simple life appealed. He still had his mobile telephone if he needed it, and as it was just six o'clock he tuned into the BBC. There was no mention of the murders, no mention of an accountant, and that left him feeling content.

The United States Embassy in Nine Elms Lane had plenty of problems to deal with and the British press was one Frank Martinelli could do without. Someone had passed information to the press and the story that the murdered men were American undercover agents had made the front pages, but there was no mention of the fugitive.

'It's getting a bit hot, Raul,' he said, looking across the desk at the station chief. Have we learned about the guy since I called you yesterday?'

'No, sir, nothing. I am in contact with the Metropolitan Police and was hoping they would have a lead by now, but so far, they have drawn a blank. The guy has just disappeared into thin air.'

'I hear he worked for an oligarch. Any progress on that front?'

'Yes, and that's what made him useful to us.'

'What do you think, Raul – Russians?'

'Definitely a Russian hit, it's got their fingerprints all over it. The guy worked for them and he was passing us information. I can't understand why the Brits think it *isn't* the Russians. I sometimes wonder about their police. I think we should keep things quiet, do the investigating ourselves. Maybe ask MI6 for some help if we need it; they are far more competent than the cops.'

'Well, keep me informed. In the meantime, I will talk to a few people. Try to keep the lid on the story,' said the deputy ambassador.

'Yes, sir, I will.'

Raul Martínez had been station chief in London for just six months, and during that time his dealings were mostly routine: gathering intelligence, running agents, and keeping his antenna switched on. But the way things were going; six months might be all he would manage.

In the days since the deaths of his two agents, events had not turned out as he would have liked. He needed to move the operation up a gear, he needed to kick some ass. Another visit to the Metropolitan Police might be a good idea. After his first meeting with Inspector Mills he had expected more, but now he felt that the Brits were somewhat behind the curve and that was worrying.

Yes, another meeting. Picking up his desk phone, he punched in the number.

He didn't have to wait long.

'Mr Martínez, nice to hear from you,' said the inspector.

'Thanks. Look, I need to talk to you. My boss is getting agitated about the case, not happy with progress. I think it will be a good idea if I drop in for a chat, get an update on what you have.'

'Of course, let me have a look at my diary. Ah... I'm tied up for the next few days, but how about Monday next week?'

Raul felt the hairs on the back of his neck stand up. The guy was fobbing him off.

'Let's put it this way. I'm free this afternoon at two o'clock, so unless you want someone on a far higher pay grade than you involved, I suggest you clear your appointments for this afternoon. I want an update, everything.'

Inspector Eddie Mills swallowed. The voice at the other end of the phone meant business and was not easily put off.

'Of course, Mr Martínez. Two o'clock in my office.'

'Thanks, and you can call me Raul.'

Replacing the receiver, drumming his fingers on his desk, Inspector Mills considered his options. He was running the case, not the Americans. *He* would decide on what course of action to take. The last thing he needed was for the superintendent to become involved, to question his ability, dig too deep. He would have to cooperate and he needed something to give the American.

'Tabz, anything turned up yet?' he asked, approaching her desk.

She looked up from her screen. 'Yes, some traffic-camera feeds I am working through. I fink our murderers were wearing masks.'

'Masks?'

'Yeah like, I have learned that there is someone on the manor supplying silicone masks. I did a search on the internet and I must admit they are realistic. They are becoming a regular feature in some places like.'

She hesitated. She had still not informed him about the footprint. Should she tell him of her suspicions? Jimi had asked her not to say too much until he got back to her, but she was conscientious and didn't feel comfortable with holding back evidence.

'Er... I still believe that the man DS Forrest interviewed is involved in the case, sir.'

'You did say, and I asked forensics to have a look for this footprint you mentioned. I told you – nothing there. Too much rain, they said.'

'Yes, sir, I know, but I found him on one of the video feeds from a traffic camera. He is with another man and certainly heading in the right direction. Perhaps the sergeant should interview him again – and the other man in the video, if we can find him. Witnesses did say there were two men like.'

The inspector looked thoughtful. 'Well, I suppose we do have a suspect: two, probably. I will get DS Forrest to follow it up. Keep looking for the man who left the scene, will you? He could be crucial in solving this case. I have a visitor this afternoon who will be interested in your assessment, I'm sure.'

As he left her, Tabz returned to her notes, the witness statements and as well as the traffic camera files, she had the short video provided by the woman with the car. The shots of the fugitive taken by the photographer were useful to a degree, but none showed a distinct view of his face. Her only reasonably clear image of him was his passport photo, which did contain nodal points for facial recognition and that might prove crucial in identifying him. Perhaps the traffic cameras on the main road near Islington Green had caught something? She had some video taken from a local public house, usually a good source of intel. Anti-social behaviour did have its positive points.

'Tabz,' said Detective Sergeant Forrest, interrupting her, 'Inspector Mills said you might have something for us, a lead.'

'The man you interviewed when the constable dropped his helmet.'

'Oh yes, the foreigner.'

'Well, if you have a look at this,' she said, bringing up a few seconds of video showing two men crossing a main road, 'I think that is him and they are not far from the scene of the murder like.'

'This geezer, where is he now?'

'That's what I'm trying to find out. I don't have a

positive on him and he seems to have a few aliases, that's all I can say.'

'What about the man who left the scene, the one whose flat we had a look at?'

'I'm just starting a search for him.'

'Well, good luck with that. Anything you can turn up would be useful.'

'Yes, sir.'

As he walked away, she turned back to the computer screen and opened the file containing images of the victims and the suspected murderers, and added one of Charles Clark. She had quite a workload on her hands and had to enlist the help of Alma, the new girl assigned to the office, her task to plot nodal points for each image. Whether it was inaccuracies or simply poor-quality video, she wasn't sure, but there were so many false positives with facial recognition she felt she needed a new approach. The search was taking longer than she would have liked, she needed more images, better data sets, better face maps, but that wouldn't happen any time soon. Overworked she felt a migraine coming on and decided to take a break, visit the coffee machine.

She noticed Detective Sergeant Forrest was not at his desk. Looking across the office, she could see the inspector and another man in what looked to be a heated discussion. The inspector seemed under pressure and, in her opinion, she felt that he was not handling the case at all well.

Returning to her desk, she ran the video from a traffic camera, looking at a section of the main thorofare. Suddenly a box appeared, a positive sighting, she hoped. She stepped the tape back thirty seconds. A man appeared from a side street and again the facial recognition picked him out. She saw a black cab pull up and disgorge a passenger, obscuring the view of her suspect. Seconds later it pulled away and of the suspect there was no sign.

'Hmm... What happened there?' she mumbled, and ran the sequence again.

He must have got into the cab – that was the only conclusion she could come to. But where was it going? She had a view of the number plate but it was practically illegible. She felt frustrated and, looking at the time on her screen, saw it was 6.15. Tabz realised that she should get a move on, Jimi was taking her for an Indian meal as promised. She should leave for home straight away; the black cab could wait until the morning.

It was raining when she left the police station; the underground lay a quarter of a mile away and she was going to get wet. Pulling up her hood, she set off. Remembering she was out of shampoo, she decided to call in at the all-night pharmacist on her way. She looked at the time on her mobile phone: she would need to hurry if she was to catch the underground, and decided to take the shortcut through a poorly lit side street. It was a risk but she was running out of time. Quickening her pace, she was unaware of someone watching her from the shadows.

The dark figure raised his collar and let Tabz open some distance between them before he began to follow, careful to keep far enough away so as not to alert her. For several minutes, both shadowy figures made their way along the dark wet street.

The rain increased in intensity and when eventually Tabz emerged onto Chapel Market, she was relieved when a man emerged from the shop and held the door open for her. Gratefully she dodged inside the store.

It wasn't the first time she had shopped there; she

was familiar with the layout and went straight to the shelves by the window to look for her favourite shampoo. The lighting strip above the shelf was out of commission, the illumination practically non-existent, and she had to squint to see the labels properly. She turned her head to utilise the street lighting and, seeing the bottle, reached to grasp it and as she did, she noticed a man rushing by outside.

Who is he? I know that face... she thought.

Then recognition dawned and her adrenalin began to pump so hard she felt she might faint. Pulling back, she tried to hide in the shadows. The face she had glimpsed a second earlier was the one she had spent some time looking at only that afternoon. She knew who he was and she could not let him see her. He had taken the same path as her, heading in the direction of the underground station.

He was following her.

She felt sick, and with a shaking hand fumbled in her bag for her mobile telephone.

The street lights seemed to burn brighter than normal, reds and yellows reflecting off pavement puddles as the falling rain splashed everywhere. In a doorway, sheltering from the worst of the downpour, Tabz shivered – but at least she felt safer in the shadows. She had a view of the street, occasionally peering round the door frame to look for the car. To her relief she saw it pull up outside the burger bar just two doors away, and splashing her way towards it, she waved frantically.

'Thank God. Oh, I'm so glad to see you.'

'And me you. What's this all about?' said Jimi as she landed in the passenger seat.

'Just drive, I'll tell you, it's him,' she said, her words

97

jumbled and incoherent.

'Okay, hang on. Where do you want to go?'

'Home, I'm soaked.'

Tabz showered and Jimi carried two cups of steaming coffee into the lounge to wait for her.

'Phew, I feel better for that,' she said, appearing in a full-length dressing gown, her hair wrapped in a white turban-shaped towel.

'So, what's this all about?' said Jimi, offering a mug. 'You said "it's him" but you haven't enlightened me any further.'

Tabz looked into the big man's dark and friendly eyes and burst into tears.

'Sit down,' he said, still holding the mug. 'Compose yourself and then tell me what's happened.'

She took the loose end of the towel, dried her eyes, and sat down beside him. For a second time he offered her the mug.

'It's okay, take your time.'

'I've had a shock.'

'That's evident. What kind of shock?'

'I fink I was followed by the murderer like, the one whose footprint we found.'

'Where?'

'I fink he followed me from the police station when I left work. I fink he was waiting for me,' she said, beginning to stare into her coffee mug. 'I'm frightened, Jimi. If he killed those two Americans, he could kill me innit.'

Jimi blew out his cheeks. 'Let's start from the beginning. Why would he follow you, what is he after? I can't see that harming you would serve any useful purpose.'

'There is somefing I need to tell you, you're the only person I can trust.' Jimi frowned as she continued. 'The footprint. I believe it is important to this case like, and now that this Henk Wiersma, or whoever he is, followed me, I am certain it is his footprint and he is the murderer.'

'What does the inspector say?'

'That's the problem, I haven't told anybody about what we found. The inspector doesn't seem particularly interested and I don't want to risk my job like, but after tonight I need to talk to somebody.'

'Get dressed and you will.'

Sergei Kulikov was annoyed, angry to the point of thumping the wall. Unlike Markov he was thoughtful and scheming; murder was not beyond him but he would have handled things differently. Markov could be a violent man, as he had proved, but this time he had gone too far and he was feeling under pressure.

The upheaval of the past few years had changed everything. Andrei had known for some time that he had outstayed his welcome, and as one of the last Russians forced to leave the country, he had left Sergei in charge of the business – but Sergei was no businessman.

Initially, Sergie and Markov had entered the country on false passports, Markov under the name of Henk Wiersma and Sergei travelling on a Swiss passport. So far, the British authorities had not questioned either documents' validity and believing that he was safe enough, he had been left to run the business with the help of several managers and the accountant, while his boss had not been so lucky. Now the accountant was a problem, disappeared, and everywhere Sergei looked turned out to be a dead end – until now. An informant had provided a lead, he had discovered that a woman working on the double murder was narrowing the search for Charles Clark.

She was the best chance he had of finding the accountant and he had tasked Markov to find out where she lived. The plan was simple enough: follow her home and after a nod from the informant, pay her a visit and extract the information needed to find the runaway accountant. They would make it appear like a simple burglary gone wrong and gain a head start on the police, but Markov had bungled it already. A simple task and he had messed up. They could try again, but losing her so easily led Sergei to believe that she might have become suspicious. Following her in future might be difficult, so the informant was going to have to earn his money.

Then there was Markov's visit to the accountant's apartment, leaving him surprised at Markov's belief the police had not even been near the place. That was rather odd, that after a week or more he would have expected the police to have discovered Charles Clark's identity. But he knew the real reason.

Staring out of a window and trying to make sense of the situation, he ran through recent events – the telephone call from the embassy alerting him, and then Andrei calling from Moscow. What was so important about a letter, why did the accountant run after reading it? He might have remained quiet, left the letter where it could be found, and no one would be any the wiser.

They had seen him walking alone, and entering the park they had hurriedly pulled on the silicone masks they had reversed their jackets for added disguise, but by the time they caught up with Clark he had quickened his pace, and was crossing the busy road. Too busy, and so they had followed him into a side street.

Easy enough, it seemed. Overpower him, find the letter, and instil the fear of God into him to keep his mouth shut. Sergei had no intention of killing him, not in the street, but then those two strangers had appeared and everything changed. Markov had exploded into violence and within seconds the two strangers were lying dead in the street. Sergei now knew from the newspapers that they were Americans. He remembered standing over them as the accountant made a run for it and in a desperate attempt to catch him they had searched nearby streets but of Charles Clark there was no sign.

Again, Sergei thumped the wall, cursing the accountant and realising that his best hope of finding him was through the police informant. Andrei knew the informant's identity but kept it to himself. Anything Sergie wanted to know had to go through Andrei Potanin and he was reluctant to say they had lost him but he needed something, a clue to where the accountant might be.

After several days following sightings of the two murderers, Tabz turned her attention back to the escapee. She started with the taxi cab, sharpening and toning the image enough to read just a small part of the number plate. But it was enough, because after searching the Vehicle Licensing Agency database, she came up with a few likely numbers for the cab. Cross-checking those with the capital's cab companies, she finally hit paydirt and discovered the company running the cab.

Wary of the inspector and the detective sergeant, she enlisted the help of Colin, the undercover detective.

'Why me, what's wrong with DS Forrest?'

'Trust me, Colin. I need a favour and you're the man to help like.'

'A favour, eh... Okay, leave it with me.'

Colin liked to work alone, poking his nose into any useful place, find out things the rest of the detectives could not, and he had often wondered about Blue Line taxis. Now was his chance to take a closer look, and if it helped the pretty little analyst then so much the better. That same afternoon Tabz received a phone call informing her of the taxi driver's name and telephone number.

How was she going to handle the call? Chances were that he wouldn't cooperate just with her. Why should he, she had no authority to interview a suspect? She would have to ask Detective Sergeant Forrest to talk to the man but did not relish that idea. She needed a lever, and after a search of the police database she felt she had one.

'Mr, Patel I wonder if you might answer a few questions?'

'I'm busy, what's this all about?'

'A woman has made a complaint about you and I would like to talk about something that has come to light.'

The line remained quiet long enough for Tabz to believe he was falling for her ruse.

'What about her? I never touched her.'

'That will be for the court to decide, sir, should it get that far. I need to know if she rode in your cab after you dropped the fare you picked up at the end of Raleigh Street, five days ago around two thirty in the afternoon.'

'How do you expect me to know that?'

'Perhaps there was something notable about the earlier fare. He could have been distressed.'

Mr Patel remained quiet. 'All I can remember was I

did pick up a man from there and he did seem a little breathless.'

'Where did you drop him off?'

'King's Cross station, I think – yes, there. What has that got to do with the complaint against me?'

'Nothing, sir, it seems our information is incorrect. Sorry to trouble you.'

'What is—'

Tabz cut him off and hoped no one would ever find out what she had done. Feeling flush with success, she began typing a request for relevant video files from the King's Cross security team.

The wait for a reply seemed interminable, but the email arrived during her lunch break the following day and attached were several video files. The search for Charles Clark had so far proved to be a tedious and unrewarding process, but she hoped that using the facial-recognition algorithm would mean progress, and for the rest of the afternoon she worked her way through the material.

'How's it going?' asked Alma as she passed Tabz's desk.

'Not very well. I have been checking the camera covering the drop-off area and I looked for the cab. Plenty of them coming and going but I haven't picked up the number plate. Black cabs all look the same and so far, there is no sign of our friend like.'

'Maybe if I have a look at his image again, tweak the data points?'

'It's worth a try. Have a go,' she said, typing a command and wondering if the image she was using was the problem.

She would wait for Alma's updated biometrics, but in the meantime she'd follow the lead she had received from Colin about the artisan producing the silicone masks. Perhaps a visit from the police might convince him to confess the identity of the person for whom he had made the masks.

Her mobile phone began to buzz.

'Jimi, this is a surprise. What? Fifteen minutes? Yes.'

She listened for a few seconds longer before she picked up her bag, slipped her jacket off the back of her chair and made for the door.

Jimi had insisted she tell no one. 'Just get out of there and I will pick you up,' he had said, and with only two people working at their computers and no sign of the detective sergeant, she took her chance to leave. Breathing a sigh of relief, she walked quickly down the stairs and out into bright winter sunshine. Her instructions were to make her way to Grant Street and wait near the laundrette, where a car would pick her up. Strange, but then she was learning that Jimi moved in mysterious ways.

Within a few minutes she had reached the rendezvous and, moving close to a dark and reflective window, she unobtrusively observed the street and minutes later she noticed Jimi's car.

'In here,' he said as he pulled up, his arm waving her towards him.

'What's this all about, Jimi?' she asked, climbing into the passenger seat.

'We are going to meet some people who are interested in what you have been doing. You have already signed the Official Secrets Act and you will be asked to sign a coda, and then you will learn a little of what you have become involved in. Trust me, Tabz, this is serious stuff and it's important.'

She turned to look at him but his eyes were firmly on

the road. Then she looked out of the window and wondered where they were going. Familiar landmarks appeared: Blackfriars Bridge, the National Theatre, and when they crossed the river from the Albert Embankment it began to dawn on her where their destination might be.

Chapter 7

Chris wrapped his cold hands around the mug of tea, a small oasis of warmth. The air was chilly and the reality of living beside the North Sea was dawning on him: overcast skies, the cold wind off the sea, cold hands. Even the two hardened anglers standing next to him seemed subdued as they took their tea from the kiosk counter.

'How's the fishing going, Chris, have you caught much? I saw you land a couple of small cod the other day.'

'Yes, going quite well, thank you. Nothing spectacular, though I did land a biggish one the other day and tried my hand at filleting. Not the best attempt, I grant, but the fish was delicious with a squeeze of lemon and a sprinkling of salt to bring out the flavour. Really nice. If I catch anything of any size today, I will be taking it home for supper.'

'Where's home?' asked Joey. 'Do you live in town?'

Chris paused, gripped the hot mug. The less people knew about him the better.

'Er... yes, up there,' he said, waving his arm broadly. In that moment a feeling of uncertainty overwhelmed him.

'Are you alright?' Joey asked, noticing a change.

'Yes, I'm just feeling the cold. Maybe I'm going down with something.'

'It's that time of year,' said Malcolm. 'Sitting for hours on the sea wall doesn't help. Piles can be the worst.'

'Do you two do any work? You seem to fish every day.'

'We're builders. We take on anything, no job too large or too small, but building outdoors in January is no fun. We take the month off and if the weather lets us, we fish. Why not? We're busy all summer and never get a summer holiday. We enjoy fishing so that's what we do.'

'What do your wives say?'

The two anglers looked at each other and smiled. 'We don't have wives to bother us.'

'Oh, me too, my wife left years ago. Were you married?'

Again, the men looked at each other and smiled.

'No, never bothered,' said Malcolm, looking up at the sky. The cloud cover was beginning to thin and the sun had broken through in parts. 'It's still a wee bit cold but the sun is trying to break through,' he said. 'I reckon it will be a nice enough day when this cloud clears. It's already started.'

Chris looked up as streaks of yellow penetrated the greyness. He hoped the man was right.

'Well, it's been pleasant talking to you, gentlemen,' he said. 'Thanks for the tea, my turn tomorrow. If you will excuse me, I think I will try further along the sea wall.'

The two fishermen simply grinned, amused by his politeness, but Chris was feeling vulnerable and needed to be alone. He had pushed his problems to the back of his mind, the tranquillity and joy of fishing helping him to forget, but now he realised it was giving him a false sense of security. What if the murderers were still looking for him? What if they were able to find him here in this obscure seaside town?

Tomorrow he would look for some other place from which to fish. An angling magazine he had purchased spoke of beach fishing and how the codfish swam close to shore at this time of year. Perhaps there was a quiet cove along the coast where he could try his luck. The days were lengthening, and if he could find somewhere secluded and not too distant, perhaps, he would be safer there.

Entering the United States Embassy was not the biggest surprise of the day for Tabz. Jimi took that honour with the way he took charge, his self-assurance.

'Here's your security tag,' he said with a smile.

The security man stepped out from behind the front desk. 'Will you please follow me?' he said. 'I must accompany you to the meeting room. You understand.'

'Of course,' said Jimi, ushering Tabz after the man. Feeling a little bewildered, she followed until they turned a corner and the guide halted.

'Thank you,' said Jimi, knocking on the door before opening it and walking into a spacious, bright room, gesturing for Tabz to follow. The walls were hung with portraits of men and women she did not recognise, except for the far wall where the current President of the United States looked down on them. A man stepped out from behind a wide, expensive-looking dark wood desk and held out his hand in greeting.

'Good to see you again, Jimi, Miss Belafonte,' he said, shaking both visitors' hands. 'She knows she must sign the confidentiality agreement?'

'Yes, no problem there,' said Jimi, turning to Tabz whose jaw had just dropped as she recognised the man – the office visitor who had berated Inspector Mills.

'Good. You will have realised by now that what we are

about to discuss is of importance to both our governments, Miss Belafonte. You must not divulge anything you hear today with anyone outside of this room. You understand?'

Tabz's heart began to race. Until this moment she was simply an analyst for the Metropolitan Police Service, but now she found herself in the embassy of the United States, at the heart of power and with a sheet of paper to sign. She looked at the legend: 'Classified Information Nondisclosure Agreement'. Taking a deep breath, she looked at Jimi for support.

'It's okay, Tabz, but you must sign it before we can begin the briefing.'

Briefing? Bloody hell... she thought, taking the offered fountain pen, and carefully she signed her name.

'Good, that's the formalities over with,' said Raul, screwing the top back on his pen and replacing the non-disclosure agreement back in its envelope. 'I would offer you coffee but I don't have much time. You understand,' he said, looking at Jimi.

Then he turned to Tabz. 'I'm sure you will have some idea of what this is all about. Since losing two of our agents on the streets of this city, your police have been trying to trace the murderers and, just as importantly, the man the agents were trying to protect. He is known to us as "Crypto". He is the chief accountant for a Russian oligarch called Andrei Potanin, who has interests in this country and across Europe. Potanin has the ear of the President of the Russian Federation, and like all those in a similar position, he is working for Mother Russia as much as for himself. It goes without saying that he would be foolish not to. Unfortunately, Mr Potanin is no longer with us and unlikely to return to the UK soon.'

Tabz found her voice. 'Where do I come into all dis like?'

'You have been working on the case, and Jimi here tells me that you are the one person making any real progress.'

Jimi nodded. 'You are turning up information that's useful to the case, and I know about the problems you're experiencing with senior officers. I have talked at length with Raul here about your suspicions regarding Igor Husyev – an alias, we presume. We do not know yet who he really is but we suspect he could be Russian foreign intelligence, or SVR, real name Markov Kalman. He works with Sergei Kulikov, who we think is running Potanin's business in his absence. Your evidence points to Kalman as being the killer, and no doubt Kulikov is involved too. Both have history and are of interest to us. We could bring them in, but there is a bigger mystery to solve and we believe you can help with that. Your talent for digging up information from obscure sources has proved invaluable on previous cases. You have already demonstrated your worth on this one, and now we need you to find Charles Clark, "Crypto", who we believe is in possession of some important information. We think he was about to pass it on to Raul's agents when the two thugs arrived to spoil the handover.'

'What Jimi says is true, Tabz. Crypto was, and still is, working for us. He is privy to information we would both like to get our hands on.'

'We don't know what it is he wanted us to know,' Jimi continued, 'but it must be important otherwise the Russians would not have gone to the lengths they have to retrieve it. We know he has dealt in cryptocurrency, on behalf of his employer. That could be for something as innocent as a new Ferrari, but more likely it is to buy arms for terrorist groups or to move embargoed oil around the world. We know the Russians are bankrolling several groups who are supplying them with technical help, advanced microchips, hiding oil movements – that sort of thing.'

Raul nodded. 'Crypto is not the most robust of individuals. He was relying on our protection when he called the emergency number, saying only that he had in his possession a letter from the Russian Embassy and was not prepared to divulge the contents over the telephone. A sensible course, I suppose. It will be the job of the British Secret Service to bring him in, and we need you to help find him without your superiors knowing too much about it.'

'What about the Met?' Tabz asked, her head spinning. 'It's their case, surely? And I work for the Met like.'

'Not any more, young lady. Your police are under-performing and we need to get a move on. Through Jimi here you will be working indirectly for the government of the United States. So, what's the latest?'

Tabz cleared her throat. 'I can't tell you much except that I fink I found where he went after the attempted mugging, though I don't yet have a positive identification. I was about to look on a CCTV feed from King's Cross railway station when Jimi rang. I fink Clark got into a black cab somewhere near the murder scene. I contacted the taxi company and found out that the driver dropped his fare off at King's Cross.'

'I see,' said Raul, looking at his wristwatch. 'What about his mobile phone? That can be traced I believe.'

'Yes, of course, and I would have looked if I knew his number but I don't.'

Raul pursed his lips. 'I have a meeting with the deputy ambassador in ten minutes so we need to wrap this up. I would appreciate knowing of anything you find as soon as possible. Liaise with Jimi and he will contact me. Anything you get I want to know immediately, you understand?'

Tabz nodded.

'Thank you for your time, but I really must wind this meeting up. I'll be in touch, Jimi.'

As Jimi and Tabz left the building, he said, 'There you have it. The double murder is one thing, but the Americans believe there is a much bigger problem to solve. We will let the Met pursue the murderers in their own inimitable way while we find our friend the accountant, but remember that anything you turn up about his whereabouts is to remain confidential until I decide otherwise.'

'Why did I need come to the embassy, Jimi? What's with the non-disclosure agreement? Surely the Official Secrets Act is enough innit?'

'Normally it is, but you have just technically visited American soil. You are working for them as well as us and they want you legally bound. You're in the loop and you already know too much.'

'What do you mean?'

'The Americans are conducting their own investigation, naturally, but you are ahead of them and they want you onside. This way they can give you classified information should you need it. You have to admit this investigation is beyond the Met. The CIA have some knowledge of what our Russian oligarch friend has been up to, thanks to Mr Clark, Crypto, and to say they are unhappy with the Met's performance would be an understatement. That goes for the government too; HMG doesn't fare much better. The loose regulatory regime was a godsend for Andrei Potanin and his masters. When Clark called for help, he let the Americans know that he believed something big is about to happen, and once he disappeared the CIA asked for our help. They cannot operate in the United Kingdom quite as freely as we can. Charles Clark is a useful tool and they want you to find him.'

'You're not all you seem, are you, Jimi?' she said, looking at him.

'We're on the same side. That will have to do for now.'

Tabz had been absent for no more than two hours, and on returning to her desk she found Detective Sergeant Forrest looking at her blank computer screen.

'Where have you been? I've been waiting here for ten minutes, no one seemed to know where you were.'

'Sorry, sir, I had to drop off some papers at the annexe,' she said, letting her bag drop to the floor. 'What can I do for you?'

The sergeant gave her a disbelieving look, and was about to quiz her when he heard his name called.

'Sir,' he said, turning away. 'Be right with you Inspector. I had better go,' he said to Tabz, giving her a suspicious look.

As he turned away she blew out her cheeks and crossed her eyes in a gesture of release. She had survived a close call; the sergeant was rightly suspicious but she had ridden his misgivings. Hooking her jacket over the back of her seat, she sat down to take up where she had left off.

'You're back,' said Alma, coming to her side.

'Yes, I had to nip out for a while – paperwork, you know how it is.'

'I do. Anyway, I have done some more work on his face. I'll email you a copy and you can have another go.

Let me know how it works out. I'll see you tomorrow, I'm away now – dentist.'

'Thanks, Alma, I'll get straight on to it.'

The girl walked away and Tabz returned to her screen, found the email from Alma, and opened it. In truth, the image of Charles Clark looked no different but she knew the extra nodal points embedded within the image could help her find the fugitive. She saved the file and looked at the time on her screen – almost four 'o'clock, almost time to finish her shift and go home, but the urge to find Charles Clark was proving too much. For a further two hours she used the modified image to search her King's Cross video files, her persistence eventually rewarded when a search box locked onto a face in the crowd.

'Bingo,' she exclaimed. 'That's him, I was right.'

The fugitive had appeared just as a black cab drove off and now, as he mingled with passengers and rail employees, she tracked him into the station precinct. She had files from other cameras situated in the station provided by the British Transport Police, and for a further hour she ran videos, finally locating Clark boarding a train. After checking the time and the platform, she discovered it was the three o'clock train to Edinburgh.

So, he was heading north, and she guessed he would be going all the way to the end of the line. Looking up the contact details for Edinburgh Waverley station, she sent an email requesting video files from their security cameras, timed for the arrival of the London train. Then she noted that it was nine o'clock, and suddenly she felt weary.

'Enough for today,' she said to herself.

After putting on her coat, she slung her bag over her

shoulder and wondered about taking the tube so late in the evening. Believing someone might still be following her, she decided that for once she would call a cab. She was exhausted, her search efforts coupled with her visit to the United States Embassy had left her feeling weary and unable to calm her mind.

Arriving at her desk the following morning she discovered an email from Edinburgh Waverley waiting in her inbox. That excited her – a result, and so quick – but then she read the text. Video footage of the arrival of the three o'clock from London was not available due to snow on the line. The service did not in fact arrive until much later in the day, after passengers were bussed to Northallerton. Did she still require the video files?

The delay was news to her. She needed to know who had disembarked from the London train and, if possible, find a clue as to where her subject might have gone. She couldn't wait for an exchange of emails, and after looking up the transport police number for Waverly station she called the office.

Raul Martínez's meeting with the Deputy Chief of Mission was not going well.

'Ma'am, we are doing our best and I agree with you. That is why I have taken the unusual step of asking the British Secret Service for some additional help. The police have a strong suspicion who the murderers are, and it should just be a matter of time before they arrest them. However, we have a potentially more urgent situation. Crypto, as you know, is someone we are using for intelligence-gathering on the Russian, Andrei Potanin. We recruited him in Dubai some time ago and he has been feeding us information on the Russian's activities. We think his organisation is involved in the movement of sanctioned oil and he is the reason we lost our agents. His call for help set wheels in motion and unfortunately those wheels have come off.'

'So, this man is the accountant for the Russian's organisation and he is on the run?'

'Yes, ma'am, that's the one. He has been feeding us information about some dark-web deals, the oil, shipping insurance. Crypto is something of an expert on cryptocurrencies. Without his help I don't think we would have cracked the Medrun case, the arms deal the Turks were involved in. The whole enterprise was funded with Bitcoin, and we wouldn't have known anything about it if it wasn't for Crypto.'

'So where do you think he might be?'

'I'm sorry, ma'am but we have lost him. The Russians caught our agents by surprise and that's when Crypto took off.'

The DCM spoke at some length about her knowledge of the case, asking for his overview, pausing to listen to his replies.

'Ma'am, catching the murderers is important, of course, and after talking with the British Secret Service we are pretty sure who they are... but there is a problem.'

'What problem?'

'Crypto was extremely agitated when he called the number we gave him. He said there was an operation in progress but did not give any details, said he needed some reassurance we wouldn't dump him once we knew his secret.'

The DCM spoke again, querying the reason why.

'It seems Crypto has a document, said he has evidence of some sort of operation but for his own security he's lodged it in a safe place. Our agents were to meet him and bring him in, but that didn't happen and it's causing us a problem.'

'What are you doing about it, what progress have you made? I need something, Raul, this case looks to be spinning out of control.'

'I am liaising with the Brits, ma'am; they have a contact in the Metropolitan Police who is tracking Crypto. She's exceptionally good at her job and we have high hopes she will turn up a lead. The police and MI6 are keeping an eye on the two suspects we believe murdered our agents. We haven't brought them in yet because of what Crypto said. Either there is some operation in the pipeline or it is already happening, and the Brits say they need more evidence before making arrests.'

It had been a difficult conversation but he had what he wanted: a free hand to work with the British Secret Service. They were professional and competent and their involvement meant he could leave his own agents on the sidelines which, considering he was two men down, was not a bad idea.

Just an hour later, after calling his counterpart, he entered an office at Vauxhall Cross.

'Commander Pearson, you know Raul.'

'Yes, we have met,' said the intelligence officer. 'Good to see you again, Raul, though we never seem to meet in settled times.'

'No, Commander. The nature of the beast, I guess.'

'Indeed. Jimi here has briefed me. Seems we know the identity of your agents' murderers. I'm sorry about that, none of us like to lose colleagues and certainly not in such circumstances.'

'Yes, they were caught off guard, a shame.'

'So, you believe there is something brewing on the Russian front and you would like us to take the lead.'

'So long as it's within your own borders, yes. If the operation leaves these shores, then maybe we will have a different perspective.'

'Of course. Normally it would be within the remit of MI5 to carry out an operation within our borders, however, as there is Russian involvement the PM has asked us to take it on. Where do you suggest we start?'

'It must be with our contact Crypto, he's the key. We need to find him, and fast. Jimi here has already been working with an analyst at the Met. She has almost single-handedly figured out who the murderers are and she is on the trail of Crypto as we speak. Isn't that right, Jimi?'

'Yes, she knows her stuff. I have asked her to inform me, if and when she locates him.'

'If?'

'She will, Commander. Give her time and she will find him, I'm sure.'

'Time! We don't have that luxury.'

Tabz had a video record of the London train's arrival at York but the facial-recognition algorithm was not turning anything up. Perhaps the quality wasn't good enough, she thought, and began to view the video at half speed, her eyes searching the arriving passengers. But of Charles Clark there was no sign.

Half an hour later, frustrated by a lack of success, she went to Alma's desk to see what help she could offer.

'Can we try a different set of nodes? Do you fink that would help like?'

'I doubt I can make the images any better. You know the London train terminated at York? What if he didn't catch the coach to Northallerton? What if he stayed in York and took a train from there?'

'It had crossed my mind but he is on the run and would want to get as far away from London as possible innit.'

'The modified image you have should work. It brought him up almost straight away when you first tried it.'

'True. Maybe I am looking in the wrong place,' said a thoughtful Tabz. 'I received a file from Newcastle but there are no surveillance cameras in either Northallerton or Berwick-upon-Tweed. I'll try Newcastle, see if he got off there like,' she said. 'I need a coffee first, though; my head is spinning.'

Alma smiled at her colleague, aware of the effort she was putting in. 'I will take another look at the images we have of him; I'll post them to you when I'm done.'

'Thanks,' said Tabz, leaving for the coffee machine.

Trying the algorithm on the Newcastle video file, she found similar results to Edinburgh – plenty of subjects but none resembling Mr Clark.

A movement caught the corner of her eye and she looked round to see Detective Sergeant Forrest.

'Found anything, Tabz?'

'No, nofing yet. I'm working on the feed from Newcastle station. I believe that and Edinburgh are the best hope of finding somefing.'

'Well, I suppose you must keep looking. You really have no idea where he might be?'

'No, sir,' she said.

'It's vitally important we find this geezer; he is a witness to the murders. We need to question him. Keep me informed, will you?'

'Of course,' she said, turning back to her computer.

For almost two hours she trawled the video feeds from the two most northerly stations. She was about to give up when she was alerted by the arrival of an email.

It was from Alma – the image of Charles Clark with adjusted nodal points. Tabz added it to the algorithm's data and searched the Edinburgh video again, and yet still there was no result. She sat back in her seat. The York video had turned up something, so maybe she should try the new image where she had already made a positive identification, make sure it worked before examining other footage.

It had an immediate effect; within seconds the facial-recognition algorithm found the suspect cold and miserable-looking walking behind a group of passengers. She had already looked at that same video and not seen him, but the new image was working – it was him; she was sure. She re-ran the video a second time at reduced speed, followed the crowd along the concourse and there he was, the location box bouncing along with him until he suddenly disappeared.

She stopped the video. Where had he gone, what was he up to? She was feeling a little tired and felt a headache developing. She needed to speak with Jimi.

'Jimi?' she said when he answered.

'Yes, it's me.'

'Listen, about Clark... I think we've lost him.'

Silence for a few seconds. Tabz could sense Jimi's mind whirring.

'Have you a hunch, any idea where he might be? Somewhere I can go, feet on the ground?'

'I am one hundred per cent sure he got as far as York. I am also certain he did not take the coach for the connection at Northallerton, which means we can discount Newcastle and Edinburgh. There is no sign of him leaving the York station, so I think he must have caught a train somewhere else.'

'That's a blow.'

'What do you want me to do? My boss will expect something and I must tell him what I have found out sooner or later, time's getting on and we don't seem to be getting very far.'

Chapter 8

According to the fishing periodical the bay was supposed to be good for cod during the winter months. It said that big fish come close to the shore, especially after a storm, and with the weather improving Chris decided to give it a try. Arriving as the tide was going out, he was delighted to find the bay deserted and, confident in his anonymity, he lay his tackle box and rod on the shingle before pulling on his waders.

The breeze off the sea was chilling but the city dweller in him was acclimatizing. After casting his line into the gently undulating sea, he settled down to watch the float bobbing up and down. He felt happy and relaxed and looking around noted that the cove. was a mixture of dark yellow sand, shingle, and mud – not an ideal place for sunbathing, secluded, and that suited him. But he was not completely alone. A man appeared, walking his dog. He came close and nodded a brief greeting, and further along the shoreline a woman was collecting pebbles.

Winter was at last changing into spring. *Change*, a simple word, yet for him the significance was profound. To live, exist, in a place he would never have dreamed of visiting just a short time ago seemed surreal, and yet he had settled easily into a routine. The fresh North Sea air, even the topography, had noticeably improved his fitness, and fishing had added a tranquillity to his life he had not known before.

Who would have believed it? he thought, a wry smile creasing his lips. Living the life he was could not be more different from that of a London accountant. Immersed in the hustle and bustle of the capital, fencing each day with a new set of problems, that had been his lot. But now, wrapped in the solitude of the cove, he felt content.

The float bobbed suddenly, his thoughts abruptly ended and his concentration focused solely on one small area of seawater. The float didn't move again, a false alarm – there was no fish eager to take his bait, an awkward ripple had fooled him. Slipping back into his thoughts, he daydreamed until another twitch caught his eye. This time a bite, a real bite, and as the float bobbed beneath the surface, Chris grasped the rod with both hands, lifting it high. Curving under the strain, the slender rod seemed that it would bend in two. Carefully, he worked the line, relieving the pressure of the fish fighting to escape until suddenly its thrashing silver body broke the surface.

'Looks a good catch,' said a voice as he reeled it in.

'Yes, hopefully,' he said, not taking his eye off the fish, reaching out to grasp its cold wet body.

'Aw, it looks so helpless. Are you going to kill it?'

Chris turned his head to see a woman wrapped in a thick coat, her face just visible under a woollen hat.

'Do you think I should?' he said as he began to unhook the hapless creature.

'No, definitely not. It is one of God's creatures and deserves life. Look at all the damage we are doing to the planet, all the species under threat of extinction because of our selfish ways. Don't kill it, or I will never speak to you again.'

Stunned, for a few seconds Chris wondered who she might be. Then he could not help but burst out laughing at her comment. For the first time since he had left London, he genuinely felt like laughing.

'Here, watch,' he said, as he finally extricated the hook. With a swing of his arm he let go of the writhing body, watching as it arced towards deeper water. After a faint splash, it was gone.

'Bravo,' said the woman, silently clapping her gloved hands in appreciation.

'The least I could do for such a charming lady,' he said, suddenly feeling embarrassed.

She grinned. 'Do you fish here a lot? I walk down here two or three times a week but I haven't seen you here before.'

'I have only fished here today.'

'Well, it's nice to meet you. I hope you catch more fish and throw them all back,' she said, her bright eyes cheery under her woollen hat. 'Then I might speak to you again.'

'What's your name?' he couldn't help asking.

'Jade, Jade Trevelyan. And you?'

'Chris Kent, not quite Superman,' he said, laughing.

'What do you mean?'

'Superman is Clark Kent; I am just Chris Kent, so... not quite Superman.'

'Ha ha, that's the strangest thing to say. Can you fly?'

Now it was Chris's turn to look perplexed. 'Fly? What is it, what's the meme? Oh, I know – is it a bird, is it a plane? No, it's—'

'A flying fish,' she said, her smile returning, and they both began to laugh, Jade because she was amused and Chris to relieve a deep-seated tension.

'That was funny. I must be going now. Nice to meet

you, Superman. Well... not quite.'

She laughed again and Chris watched her go, his enthusiasm for fishing suddenly taking a back seat.

Raul Martínez had a habit of drumming his fingers on any surface to hand when his thought process was in overdrive. Today his briefcase was the recipient of the almost noiseless rhythm.

He found it hard to comprehend that the Metropolitan police had made so little progress, and that was annoying. He had arranged for the bodies of the murdered agents to be flown back to their families in the States, and although he was sure who the murderers were, his hands were tied.

'He will see you now, sir,' said the girl on the desk, replacing the telephone handset. 'If you would like to put on this pass and follow me?'

Raul looked up, his concentration broken. He nodded as the girl got up and led him down a long corridor, stopping outside a closed door and tapping lightly on a polished panel.

'Your appointment, sir,' she said when the door opened, making way for the American to enter before she left.

'Raul, good to see you,' said Jimi. 'Come in, take a seat. You want to talk about Crypto?'

'Yes, my boss is getting impatient. She says she needs some good news. We have just repatriated our agents' bodies and she is concerned some newshound will pick up on the case, let the whole world know what happened. It is not general knowledge that the Russians killed our agents, and if it were, there could be trouble. With all the tricks they have played over the past few years we don't think the American public will take too kindly to it. You guys are supposed to be keeping an eye on our Russian friends, Tom and Jerry. We hoped they might lead us to Crypto but that hasn't happened, has it?'

'No, we don't know where they are.'

'Well, that's not encouraging, is it? How's your star analyst doing?'

'Not so good either, I'm afraid. She tracked Crypto to York but then she lost him. I sent one of our men to have a look in his flat, see what we could turn up, but he found very little of use. There is no indication he has any connections with the north of the country. This is a purely random flight, we think. The only way we are going to find him is through surveillance videos or a response to a missing-persons request, but that is the police's responsibility, not ours. All we can do is talk to the Foreign Secretary, who will talk to the Home Secretary to instruct the police to pass on intelligence to us and then, only after the Home Secretary speaks to the Foreign Secretary can we act. Sounds long-winded but it isn't.'

'Hasn't that been done already?' asked the American.

'Not to my knowledge.'

'Is it worth a try?'

'With a caveat. No one outside the police or MI6 should know we're looking for Crypto in case we alert him. The real danger is that the Russians get to him first and we never find out the secret he's keeping.'

'We need a plan, Jimi, and we need it now.'

'I was afraid you might say that.'

Tabz was making progress, she knew Charles Clark had reached York – but where did he go after that? The information she had suggested several scenarios. First, he could have taken the coach to Northallerton. The group she was watching certainly seemed to be heading in that direction, but then again, once he had left the station precinct he could have gone anywhere. She believed there was a strong possibility he had wandered into the city, and if he had then she would be facing a whole new set of problems.

Sitting back in her seat, she looked at the images of the figure walking along the platform and wondered what he would do. At least she had him at the station on a particular platform, and from that she could work out which cameras were most likely to pick him up next. She would need to meticulously check the video feeds around that time, so starting with the passengers leaving the London train, she followed their progress to the exit and was about to examine footage from a camera overlooking the platforms when a familiar voice interrupted her.

'Have you found anything, Tabz?' asked Inspector Mills. 'It's been almost a month since you started looking for our friend.'

'Almost. A monf on Tuesday, sir.'

'Have you anything we can use?'

'I'm afraid not, sir.'

'Right, well, let me know as soon as you turn up anything.'

Tabz was about to answer him when her mobile announced an incoming call.

'Mind if I take this, sir?'

'No, that's fine,' he said, giving no indication of leaving, and as she took the call her brow creased into a frown.

'I wish you had told me earlier about this,' she said down the phone. 'I'm having lunch, can I call you back?'

Jimi took the hint and broke off the call.

'A boyfriend, wants me to go to a concert with him like. Sorry, sir, it's not important.'

'Hmm... Well, remember what I said and let me know as soon as you turn anything up. The Super is breathing down my neck and I don't like it.'

'Yes, sir, I will,' she said, relieved to finally see him go.

'A boyfriend?' said Alma, having overheard the conversation. 'I didn't know you had a boyfriend; you never mentioned it.'

'Oh... No, not really. He's a carpet fitter,' said a flustered Tabz. 'He's, er... just decided that he can't fit my new carpet until next week and, er... just asked me out.'

'Are you going?'

'Oh no. He's nice enough, but no.'

'They are all the same, work when it suits them and charge you the earth. Humph, I've had the same problem. Did I tell you about our new bathroom suite...?'

Tabz hardly listened as her colleague unloaded her problem. She was more concerned by the short conversation with Jimi. What did he want?

'I need the loo,' she said, looking at her mobile phone, and before Alma could say anything she left the office.'

Alma pouted. What was the hurry? 'I bet he is her boyfriend,' she said to herself, disappointed that she couldn't boast about her new bathroom, but Tabz had more to worry about than to engage in small talk about bathrooms.

Instead of going to the Ladies, she walked out of the police station, found a secluded corner, and called Jimi.

'I'm sorry, you were busy,' said Jimi. 'No matter.

Listen, something's not long come to light. I had a meeting with the Americans and decided to send a team into Crypto's flat to scrutinise it properly. I can't understand why the police didn't do a thorough search... Anyway, an album tucked away in a drawer in the kitchen had several decent pictures of him; something better for you to work with, I guess.'

'You guess!'

'Look, I know you have been working hard to find him. Perhaps these new images will help. I'll scan them and email you.'

The email arrived not long after Tabz returned to her desk. There were six images in all, mostly taken from oblique angles with the subject's face never full on, and Tabz knew that could be a boon in her search for the elusive Mr Clark.

'Alma, come and have a look at these.'

The girl walked over to Tabz's desk. Looking over her shoulder, she examined the new images.

'Where did you get those?'

'Never mind where I got them, can you do something with them?'

'Yes, of course, send them across.'

'Hello, how is it going?' DS Forrest had entered the office. 'Anything new?'

'Tabz has got hold of some new images of Charles Clark. I'm going to see what I can do with them and then I suppose we will do some more searching.'

Tabz compressed her lips, annoyed at Alma for letting the world know about the images. They hadn't done anything with them yet, they might be no better than the passport photo – and on top of that, Jimi had asked her to be discreet.

'That's interesting. Send me copies, will you? And let me know immediately if anything turns up.'

Flustered at his request, Tabz said, 'Can't do it straight away, we need to work on the clarity a bit before we can use them.'

'I want them as soon as you can let me have them. Do I make myself clear?'

Tabz looked at him inquisitively for a second or two before returning to her computer screen.

'Yes, Sergeant. I will get them to you when we have finished tidying them up.'

'Good,' he said, turning away.

Why the hurry? she thought. Why was he so interested when he hardly seemed on the case?

The surf broke over Chris's waders, and he took a step back. He was getting the hang of beach casting but had strayed a little too far into the sea and the water was beginning to overwhelming his waders.

'Damnation,' he said, annoyed at his lack of awareness and settling back onto safer ground raised his rod to cast his bait.

He had learned the basics and, casting with some skill, watched as the hook and sinker arced out over the water to land with a splash ten metres or so out into the bay. The brightly coloured float popped magically to the surface. He let the line pay out a little further, surveying the red and green float as it lolled lethargically on the surface. Content that he had got it right, he set the rod on its frame and sat on a large flat rock to watch the float and to daydream.

A cloudless sky and a lack of breeze made for a pleasant morning, and as he rejoiced at his good fortune, he took from his pocket a pair of newly acquired earbuds. He had spent the previous evening acquainting himself with the new-fangled technology, learned how to connect them wirelessly to his mobile phone, and after a little fiddling he heard the first strains of Handel's 'Water Music' – an apt suite, he felt. Closing his eyes, he let the music flood his mind as he waited for a bite.

He couldn't help feeling that his life was looking up. He had his new home, his health was improving, and he had found a wonderful preoccupation in fishing for fish. How long was it since that day? He did not really want to work it out and instead settled upon the fact that today was Sunday. It could be any Sunday, and that was the point. He didn't want reminding of his recent past; instead he was content with the present, and when he finally opened his eyes again, he realised that the cove was unusually busy. Several dog walkers, a couple, and a woman bending down to the shingle.

The forecast was for a calm morning but with heavy rain around midday. Looking up into the sky, he could see the first of the dark clouds looming. His float hadn't budged for the whole musical movement, and deciding he really should pack up and go before the rain started, he began to reel in his line.

'Bugger it, one last cast,' he said to himself, removing the earbuds and stuffing them in his jacket pocket.

'Are you still trying to catch something?' said a familiar voice beyond his line of sight.

'Oh, hello,' he said, turning.

'Hello.'

'Out for your walk, I see.'

'Yes. Not for long, though, it looks like rain.'

'That's the forecast. I am wrapping up in a few minutes, head home before the storm hits.'

'Probably a wise thing to do. You don't want catching

out down here if it pours down, there's nowhere to shelter except that old wartime pill box,' she said, looking to the far end of the beach. 'It stinks of urine, disgusting place. Chris, isn't it?'

'Yes, and I remember you – Jade. I saw you rummaging about earlier in the shingle. Do you live around here?'

'Up there,' she said, pointing. 'A small cottage overlooking the sea.'

Chris looked up to a row of three or perhaps four small, single-storey buildings; typical cliff-edge dwellings with a view, but not much in the way of a future.

'Oh yes, nice view,' he said, surprised to see her on all fours scratting in the sand. 'What are you doing? You were doing that earlier – what have you found, treasure?'

'This,' she said, standing up and brushing the sand from a dark red pebble. 'Treasure to me, just what I was looking for. The colour will go well with my latest creation.'

'Creation?'

'Yes, I'm an artist. I used to live in London but the pressure of people and traffic did for me, so I came here. I'm attached to this place, I used to spend summer holidays here as a child.'

'You came here from London for your holidays?'

'No, we lived in Leeds in those days. When I was ten years old my dad got a job in London and we went to live there. I have never forgotten the happiness I felt here, though, and on the spur of the moment I decided to up sticks and move here. The cottage convinced me. How about you? You don't sound like a local.'

Chris felt a surge of delight to know he wasn't the

only one to make a leap of faith. 'No, I'm not local. I too hail from the metropolis,' he said, casting caution to the wind.

'Where, exactly? I came from Richmond.'

'Islington, last stop.'

'What brings you here? You obviously don't work, I have noticed you when I'm looking for materials.'

'Are you well known?' he asked, avoiding her question.

'Fairly, I suppose. I have had a couple of retrospectives at small galleries and they seemed to go down well.'

'Do you sell much? What kind of art, painting?'

'I'm a sculptress, I use what I find here to make my art. I do paint but I prefer something tangible in my hands, even if it's just a lump of kid's plasticine. I used to do a bit of animation for a studio when I left art college, that was all plasticine.'

'Wallace and Gromit?'

'Oh yes, stuff like that. What do you do?'

Chris had daydreamed occasionally as he waited for a fish to bite, wondering if he should have a story prepared just in case someone asked him too many questions.

'Banking. I was in banking. Took early retirement.'

'Very early by the look of you. Drat, it's starting to rain. The last thing I want is to get drenched. Do you fancy a coffee? You could come to the house and I can show you some of my work?'

'That is the best thing I have heard all day. Just let me pack up my fishing gear.'

'You had better hurry. I don't like the look of those clouds.'

The rain was falling well before they reached the cottage. It was a small, half-brick half-wood structure that sat precariously on a receding cliff top. The tiled roof of dark slate contrasted well with the green-painted woodwork, and a narrow chimney breast ran up one side. Chris could understand the attraction of the place.

'This way, round the back. I always use the rear entrance so I can kick off my muddy shoes.'

Chris followed, looking on with some concern at the short front garden and the half-collapsed fencing teetering on the edge of the cliff.

'Oh, don't worry about that. It will be years before we fall off the edge. The council are spending millions propping us up. Come on,' she said, reaching the door and fiddling with her key until finally it turned and she ushered him inside. 'Welcome to my abode, put your stuff over there,' she said, kicking off her shoes and slipping on a pair of paint-stained moccasins.

'Take your coat off, Chris. There's an old pair of slippers over there should just about fit you.. Come into the workshop, I will show you some of my work. Do you want to dry your hair? I can give you a towel.'

Chris shook his head. 'I'm fine,' he said, placing his tackle box and the rod against a wall. 'Is it a workshop? I thought artists had studios.'

'Call it what you like, it's a shed really. I work hard in here,' she said, pushing the door open. 'In my opinion studios are for talking in. Have you seen those programmes on the television when they go into a studio? They just sit or stand and talk a lot of waffle.'

Chris couldn't help laughing, eliciting a wide grin from Jade, and for some reason she added, 'By the way, I don't have a television.'

'Good for you. I have one but I hardly use it.'

'Look around while I put the kettle on.'

Chris watched her cross the small yard, and with the aid of the natural light streaming through the transparent roof panels, he explored. The place was untidy to his eyes yet it had an attraction – an ordered chaos, perhaps. Colours, shapes, half-finished sculptures that declared a talented artist. The beach seemed important to her, featured extensively in her work: sea shells, pebbles, and old bits of wood, but the one exhibit that really drew his attention was a painting.

He walked towards it, intrigued. Was it one of those paintings they did with a palette knife? The surface was uneven, light danced around its surface and it looked almost three-dimensional. He took a pace back and folded his arms to admire the work.

'You like? It's an expression of the trash polluting the sea,' she said, returning with a tray of refreshments. 'How do you like your tea?'

'Oh thanks, just some milk will do nicely.'

'There are a couple of Garibaldis for you. Do you like them?'

'I do. You are a clever lady, they are my favourites.'

She smiled and he felt comfortable.

'Come on, I'll show you round. I see you like my rendition of the cove down there.'

'I do. How do you make it stand out so?'

'Ah... that would be telling,' she laughed. 'If I tell you, I'll have to kill you.'

She was funny as well as talented. He couldn't help but appreciate her wit – aside, that was, from her last comment.

'What do you think, is it a studio or a workshop?'

'Both,' said Chris diplomatically as his eyes roamed. 'What are you working on at the moment?'

135

'This, a sculpture representing the demise of the fishing industry. It shows, I think, that it's their own fault for over-fishing.'

Chris stood back and for several minutes tried to understand what she meant, the connection beyond him. 'Lovely, I see what you mean,' he said diplomatically.

'There are quite a few half-finished, I'll get round to finishing them one day. Look, this one here is where I will use the pebble from this morning. Can you see how the red contrasts with the blue glass fragments I found earlier? It will represent the blood of countless fish caught and thrown away because they were too small. Such a waste of a natural resource. We haven't many left in the sea, I find it all rather depressing. This is my way of helping the fish fight back.'

'Commendable, I must say,' said Chris, looking a little bewildered.

'Cheers,' she said, lifting her cup to his.

'Cheers.'

'Don't look so sad, fisherman. I'm teasing, that is a commission for a lady who lives in Leeds, a well-off lady who likes my work. Quite frankly she almost single-handedly pays for my lifestyle, frugal as it is.'

'So, you are not campaigning to save the planet after all, and I can carry on fishing.'

'Ha ha, my little joke. The number of people who take me seriously amazes me, and the number who argue against me when I am just teasing. I care about the planet, of course I do, and I care about the fish. I find that quite a few people get it through my art; it's my way of addressing reality, and coupled with a good argument it makes an awful lot more people take seriously what is going on. At least I'm having a bit of an impact. I would prefer to do a Hockney and reach a lot more people, but I'm afraid I'm not so well known.'

'Or a Banksy?'

'He's great, I love his stuff. Do you want something to eat, I can rustle up a bit of pasta?'

'That sounds a good idea. I'm not putting you to any trouble, am I?' said Chris, eating his second Garibaldi. He was quite hungry.

'No, it's nice to have some company occasionally. You must be a bit solitary. Are you?'

'I suppose so, but I am comfortable with my own company. I never had a lot of friends back in London. Don't suppose I'll be missed.'

'That's a bit sad, Chris. Come on, you're not lonely, are you?'

'No, not really. But there is a reason.'

'And the reason is?'

'I can't tell you.' He paused and grinned. 'If I do, I'll have to kill you.'

'The plot thickens,' she said, laughing. 'Where do you live? Can't be far away if you walk here every day.'

'Oh, a couple of miles, I think. Up on the south side, a little house not unlike this one.'

'Have a look round a bit more and I will find that pasta, a tin of tuna, maybe. You're not allergic to tuna, are you?'

'What makes you say that?'

'Just a joke, you're a fisherman. It wouldn't look good if a fisherman was allergic to fish. I'll call you when it's ready.'

Chris watched her go, impressed both by her looks and her intellect. He hadn't jousted with someone like her for a long time, not since university – those drunken evenings when they would dissect the way of the world.

As he quietly reminisced, Jade walked away, murmuring to herself: 'He's hiding something.'

Tabz was annoyed with Detective Sergeant Forrest. How had he failed to find the photo album in Charles Clark's flat? The passport image was good enough for the immigration scanners, but had proved less than useful with everything else. This new material gave her more scope to search the videos, to be able to re-examine the footage in a more detailed way, but she should have been able to do that weeks ago if only DS Forrest had done his job properly.

She ran a tape from York station, watching as the passengers left the London train. The crowd was moving away from the carriages and through the concourse. At the rear a digital frame appeared, enclosing a face, a man hunched up against the cold.

It was him.

'At last,' she sighed, and for a few more seconds she followed him as the box danced in unison with his movements. She was confident of the match, but then he disappeared.

'Blast, where did he go?' she said to herself, rewinding the video. She slowed it to just a fraction of full speed, noting every detail of Charles Clark and his surroundings.

'It's him, but where is he going?' she muttered. 'Alma?' she called to her colleague. 'Can you have a look at this? I need your help.'

The girl looked up from her work and nodded before getting to her feet. Just a short distance away, DS Forrest looked up.

'I have found our subject, Alma. I'm certain it's him, he is on the platform in York station. Look here,' Tabz said, running the tape. 'See? He walks past that hoarding but I don't see him again.' She pointed to her computer screen. 'Where did he go? Did he catch another train, one out of sight of the camera? And if so, which one?'

'Shall I check the timetables for that day?' Alma said. 'It seems to me that if he's on the run he will not hang about. With the Edinburgh train stopped at York and no sign of him elsewhere along the route I think he might have changed any plan he had; he could well have caught another train.'

Tabz looked thoughtful; Alma's reading had merit. 'But where?' she groaned, exasperated that she may have to start her search all over again at numerous other stations.

'I think looking at departures around this time are our best bet,' said Alma.

'Agreed. I will see if there is anything else on the video that might identify where he went. A map of the station could be useful, a plan of the platforms like. Get me a layout and a list of trains leaving within, say, twenty minutes of the video's time stamp?'

'Leave it with me,' said Alma, returning to her desk. DS Forrest's eyes tracked her all the way.

Tabz returned to her screen and ran the tape for a few minutes before consulting her notes. She added to them her sighting and the time, and then she sat back in her chair, wondering what a fugitive would do in that situation. She was still thinking about it when Alma returned with a sheet of paper.

'I have just three trains leaving close to the time stamp – Leeds, Doncaster, and Scarborough. The Scarborough train left almost to the minute, the other trains seven and twelve minutes after that. Here's a print of the station layout.'

'Thanks,' said Tabz, studying the print and comparing the details on her screen with the elements shown on the plan.

She could see a bridge across the track but her subject did not cross it. Instead, he passed behind a nearby advertising hoarding and from that she had to deduce which platform he was most likely to go to. She glanced at the train schedule.

'Scarborough fits,' she said to Alma. 'The timing is about right and he is close to the right platform like.'

'If he did catch the Scarborough train where would he get off, Malton or Scarborough?

'I think as he's on the run, he will try to get as far away as he can. It must be Scarborough.'

Tabz consulted the station plan and nodded her head slowly.

Sergei waited patiently in what was originally Andrei Potanin's office. He was acutely aware of his boss's displeasure, and although Andrei was now in Moscow, and this was nothing more than a video call, the pressure was getting to him. Since starting the war, Russian businessmen were less welcome in London and in a scramble to move assets, some had lost vast amounts of their wealth. Andrei Potanin was not one of them, as his business registrations had moved offshore, and that provided some protection. Sergei was left to oversee the rest.

The screen flickered into life, an audible warning, the connection confirmed.

'Sergei. We still have a problem, I understand?'

'I'm afraid we do but we're working on it.'

'Yes, I'm sure you are. The accountant is causing

problems, real problems. I don't know to what extent, but my instruction comes from the Kremlin and they are not happy. Anyone with detailed knowledge could decipher the meaning of the letter and we think our erstwhile accountant has made some sort of connection. Luckily for you, we may have found him.'

'Oh, where?'

'Just a few minutes ago I received a call from one of my informants; they have learned that our friend is in a place called Scarborough. I believe the information is genuine because my informant demanded a large sum of money in exchange.'

'Scarborough? Where is that?'

'I don't know exactly – the north of the country, on the coast somewhere. I have spoken with the embassy; they think it will be easy enough to find our man, as it's a small place. You are to go there immediately, find a needle in a haystack, as they say.'

'*Da.*'

'Take Markov – and make a better job of it this time. You don't need to bring the accountant in, just find that letter and then you can dispose of him. You still have the company credit card for any funds you might need?'

'*Da.*'

'Good. Make contact with the embassy and let them know you are going there. Oh, and be aware that the British will have the place under surveillance.'

The camera was innocuous, looking no different to any modern DSLR camera on the market, but it was slightly heavier and the software more advanced.

'You will not be using this under low light conditions, I think,' said the technician, his face serious as he proceeded to demonstrate the best way for Sergei to use the instrument. 'It is a modified off-the-shelf camera with the ability to recognise a face that has been input to the memory from a second source. You will only be able to use it effectively at less than fifty metres; any more and the sensor will not pick up the subject. We find the most useful way is to take a series of stills and analyse them using a laptop. We are aware you must locate your target in real time and that is where this little baby comes into its own. It can identify a subject but to obtain a better image you will need to upload to a computer.'

'Are you telling me that with this camera we can find a needle in a haystack?'

'Most likely, but you will have to do some legwork. You will need at least one clear image of your target. We have two approaches, the first just using the camera. It has a facial-recognition facility that is not unusual in modern cameras, but unlike most, this one has a special sensor that can discern targets at a distance. You could alternatively download images and view them on a laptop, but the preferred technique is to constantly upload to a cloud-based AI software that can scan the images quickly and accurately. You will probably need that facility because you will most likely be using a wide-angle lens to capture as much of a scene and as many subjects as possible, which means vastly more processing, hence the need for a computer.'

'We will have an image of our target somewhere, it's a condition of employment.'

'Good. Any questions?'

'Not really, I understand the capabilities of modern cameras and I can see you have simply taken it a stage further.'

'Yes, that's right. I think the best thing we can do now is for you to find a busy street and go take a few pictures.

I will instruct one of my subordinates to accompany you. Try to find him in a crowd and then you can analyse the images, familiarise yourself with the instrument.'

The silent shutter, operated by an equally cutting-edge camera, took several images of Sergei Kulikov and a second man in quick succession. They were leaving the Russian Embassy in a black BMW and, as with the Russian camera set-up, the software wasted little time uploading the images to the cloud. In a room at Vauxhall Cross, Jimi viewed them one by one.

'Well, at least we know the suspect has access to the Russian Embassy and that suggests the Russian government's involvement, but to what degree?' he said.

Anita looked over his shoulder and pointed at Sergei. 'I know this one. I have seen him before, when we had problems imposing sanctions on some of the Kremlin's puppets. His boss is Andrei Potanin, right?'

'Right.'

'So would you like to tell me why I am here, Jimi?'

'You will remember the two Yanks who were murdered back in January?'

Anita nodded.

'He is one of the killers, of that we are sure – and he was not alone. Here is the other suspect,' he said, bringing up an image of Markov Kalman on the screen.

'I have come across this character before, too,' she said. 'Unsavoury is a description that doesn't do justice to these two.'

'Yes, and you have probably already guessed that for now they are of more use to us on the street than behind bars. Sergei Kulikov is supposedly ex-FSB, he acts as security for a Russian businessman, Andrei Potanin. But we don't believe *he* is ex-FSB.'

'Oh yes, another of the Kremlin's stooges. Where is this leading, Jimi?'

'The Americans have specifically asked us to let these two roam freely, to give them a false sense of security. Secondly you are going to find a person of interest in sunny Scarborough, an asset of value to the CIA. They want him found before these two get to him,' said the big man.

'That's a bit risky, isn't it? Why not just arrest them if there is evidence?'

'The Americans believe they are far more useful as they are, especially as we have these surveillance images of Tom leaving the Russian Embassy.'

'"Tom"? Don't tell me.'

'Yes, the Yanks have christened them Tom and Jerry for this operation. They are looking to pin anything they can on the Russians. If they can implicate the embassy directly in the murders of the two CIA men, then it will be a publicity coup and another nail in the Russians' coffin.'

'Tom: that's Kulikov's codename, right? So Kalman is Jerry?'

Jimi smiled and Anita looked at the ceiling, shaking her head.

'Who thinks up this stuff?'

Sergei found a parking space on double yellow lines as near to Portobello Street market as he could possibly get. The market was just a mile from the embassy and his instructor had told him that it would be a good testing ground, a chance to familiarise himself with the camera in one of the busiest areas of the city.

'If you can make the facial-recognition app work here, you can make it work anywhere,' said Sergei's instructor.

'I will head off into the market and you can see if you can find me.'

Sergei was a little nervous, which was unusual, but he felt that he was drawing attention and that was a situation he hated. Still, he had a job to do, and for half an hour he wandered past the stalls, pushed through the crowd taking pictures as he went, and each time he interrogated the instrument for a result. Apart from just one image amongst many, illuminating a face with a green square, there was little else to show for his effort and at the pre-arranged time he made his way back to the BMW. To his surprise the embassy employee was not alone. With him was a figure in a dark blue and yellow uniform, a traffic warden, and he was issuing a ticket.

'What's going on?' Sergei said angrily.

'This your car, sir?'

'Yes, is mine.'

'Can't park here. One: you're on double yellow lines, and two: you parked on a pavement. Both are offences under the Traffic Management Act 2004.'

'I park where I want.'

'I'm sorry, sir, but you can't. There are rules, the law, and this is a no-parking zone. I'm afraid I must issue you with a fixed penalty notice. You will need to pay at the town hall or you can do it online.'

Sergei was about to burst and the embassy man could see it. Interceding before the situation escalated, he said, 'Yes, we are aware now that we can't park here, but we are leaving so you don't need to issue a ticket.'

'Sorry, I have to,' said the parking warden, placing the ticket under the windscreen wiper.

'Thank you, officer, the fine will be paid.'

Still fuming as he climbed into the driver's seat,

Sergei looked at his passenger.

'We are under strict instructions to keep a low profile,' the embassy man said. 'I got the feeling you were about to push back. If paying is a problem, I can ask the embassy to take care of things.'

'No, that will not be necessary,' said Sergei, calming down. He knew he was wrong but the situation had jangled his already edgy nerves.

'Did you get a result?'

'Just one, I think.'

'Good. Let's go back to the embassy and debrief.'

After learning as much as she could of the case, Anita returned to her desk. Jimi had given her free rein to locate and bring in Crypto; he said an analyst working in the Islington police headquarters had done a good job so far, suspecting he was in the small northern seaside town. She would travel north, but first she wanted to speak with the police handling the murder enquiry and arranged to visit Islington police station. They were not making much progress and she wanted to know why.

'Ah... you must be Mrs Simms,' said a man just leaving an office.

'Yes, and you are Inspector Mills?'

'Yes, I was expecting you. Shall we get ourselves a coffee and you can tell me what this is all about?'

Anita blinked in disbelief. 'No thank you, I don't have a lot of time.'

'Right,' said the inspector, mildly perplexed. 'In here,' he said, standing aside for Anita to enter his office. 'Please take a seat, how can I help?'

'I am working for the Foreign Office and I have authorisation to ask questions. This meeting is off the record for the time being, by the way.'

Inspector Mills did not reply, instead he weighed up his visitor.

'You are investigating the murder of two men which took place five or six weeks ago. Americans. What progress have you made?'

'Not much, I'm afraid, evidence is scant. We have one suspect, a Dutch citizen by the name of Henk Wiersma. My sergeant has been looking for him.'

'What about the fugitive, the man who appeared to be at the centre of the incident? I understand he may be somewhere in the north. Have you issued a missing-persons inquiry with forces in that part of the country?'

'No, not yet.'

'Right, I want you to get an image of him circulating. Tell them he is a suspected burglar or something. He is harmless enough, we believe, but we don't want him spooked by an overenthusiastic bobby. Who is the analyst who has been tracking him? I would like a few words. Have you a private room I can use?'

'You can use this office; I must see the superintendent in a few minutes anyway. I will get Tabz.'

Anita smiled weakly; the lack of urgency was annoying and, looking round the unimpressive office, she wondered if the inspector was holding back the investigation for some reason.

'Hello, I am Tabz, you wanted to see me?'

'Hello, Tabz, come on in. My name is Simms, I'm from the Foreign Office. Take a seat – your boss's, I suppose.'

Tabz grinned and Anita took an immediate liking to her. 'This meeting is confidential, as I am sure you are aware, and I must stress that it comes under the Official Secrets Act.'

Tabz nodded; the statement was not entirely

unexpected. 'I understand. Jimi has briefed me a little and I presume you work with him?'

'Yes. I want to know everything you know about the man we are looking for, Charles Clark, code name Crypto. The department here is investigating the murders, I know, but I am interested only in the man on the run. Where is he and how have you found him?'

'I don't know exactly where he is, but I believe I have traced him to a small seaside town in Yorkshire. I have searched video footage from a wide variety of cameras — traffic and railway stations, mainly — and I am ninety per cent sure he is in Scarborough. Finding him in York was the breakthrough. Most passengers disembarked to carry on their journey by coach, and for some York was their destination, but he took a different path. I located him as he passed a kiosk towards the platform for the Scarborough train, but then he disappeared. I did not see him board the train but the platform is not for through trains, just the Scarborough line. My colleague Alma checked the timetable, and one left only minutes later. My guess is he was on that train.'

'You don't have video of the Scarborough station?'

'No. I mentioned that perhaps I could obtain some video files in the vicinity of the station from the local council, but the inspector told me not to waste my time.'

'Did he...'

'Yes, I have quite a workload relating to ongoing cases and he felt I should use my time on them like.'

Anita looked at the analyst, an attractive woman with honest eyes. From what she knew of her, she was good at her job. She had performed useful work so far and seemed to have her teeth into Crypto, and in Anita's opinion she should stay with the case. MI6 did not want the Met too involved; they were hardly making progress anyway, other than finding Crypto in York, and that was down to this woman.

'We need your input but we do not want a third party involved.'

'The Met?' said Tabz.

'Yes, the Met. We will involve them or any other police force when the time is right, but for now you are working for us.'

Tabz's eyes grew a little wide, guessing that Simms was probably MI5 or something. The prospect of working with the Secret Service was intriguing and she was pleased that someone was at last taking her seriously.

'I will speak with my superior, get you seconded for the duration. It may well be that you work from here, but preferably I would want you to move to one of our offices where there is less chance of prying eyes.'

Events moved quickly. Tabz learned that MI6 and not MI5 was to be her new home for the immediate future, and she was amazed at how quickly she landed at her new desk not far from Vauxhall Bridge. The building was non-descript, hidden away, her only view that of the old gas works. It was secure, of that she had no doubt, and as she touched her new security badge she stared out of the window at a rusting skeletal gas holder.

'No distraction there,' she said to herself, as a knock announced a visitor.

'Here's a coffee,' said Anita when Tabz opened the door. 'I think you have earned it after all the upheaval. Are you happy with the set-up? We thought it necessary to move your computer and your files here, keep continuity, keep confidentiality. We need you to hit the ground running. You understand?'

'Yes, of course.'

'The security briefing you had earlier was important. There are other people in this building doing crucial work of national importance, and we don't want anyone poking around who shouldn't be. The outside world has no idea of what goes on in here and we want to keep it that way.'

Tabz nodded. 'I have been finking that we should obtain video from any camera the local council controls,' she said. 'Although there are no cameras inside the station, there may be one with a view of the surroundings innit. If I could find him on there, I can place him positively in the town like.'

'I have already had someone look at the camera situation in Scarborough,' Anita replied. 'They have just spent some money upgrading their system to more modern high-definition cameras. This new system should produce images of a much higher order.'

'That's good, and there is something you could do for me. I will work faster if I can have a direct feed from their system, monitor the cameras in real time like. I think that's possible but someone needs to tell them to give me access.'

'I will follow that up.'

'Let's hope they have a facial-recognition facility. Sometimes privacy considerations get in the way innit.'

'What does that mean?' Anita asked.

'Well, there is software out there that I can use in conjunction with the video feeds, an overlay, so to speak. There is one called Clearview that allows real-time interrogation of video, but it's use is contentious. I could not use it working for the Met.'

'You're not working for the Met now. I will talk to someone. There are laws about National Security issues that allow us to do things other agencies cannot. One of our boffins is coming to talk with you, should be here any time. He will discuss your needs to make your job easier, and if there are technical issues that need addressing, he will take care of them.'

The difference in management styles between the two organisations was noticeable. If Tabz needed something from the Met it might take weeks, whereas here it happened almost immediately. She had a problem with her computer's connectivity but within an hour of asking for help she was back up and running, her attention turned back to the fugitive accountant.

MI6 had worked fast; she had already received the video file taken by the local traffic-monitoring camera in the town centre. Her screen showed the scene outside the railway station on the day in question, just minutes after the arrival of the York train. It had been raining, street lights and car headlights reflected from cold wet surfaces giving an unnatural glow, sharpening detail and making her job easier.

After the York passengers dispersed and the taxis had left, she could see that just a few pedestrians remained. A man crossed the street, a dog walker paused to investigate a shop window, and from the station entrance a lone figure appeared – a small unremarkable figure. She could not be certain if it was Crypto. He came closer to the camera, came into full focus, and then she was sure it was him. Lonely, shivering, and bewildered. He paused to look around – for a taxi, she guessed – and sure enough he made his way to the one remaining cab. The car was a long way off, the number plate indistinct, and after he climbed inside, she watched it leave. Picking up her mobile phone, she called Anita.

'Mrs Simms, I have somefing. He did arrive in Scarborough as I suspected, and then he caught a taxi, though there is not much I can do to determine its destination like.'

'Good work, keep me informed.' said Anita.

Sergei had not addressed the question as to whether Charles Clark may or may not be in Scarborough, he was taking it in good faith that he was. After consulting the car's satellite navigation, he opted for the A1 trunk road, a slower but slightly shorter route. That suited him; less traffic driving on the wrong side of the road to worry about. Hunched over the steering wheel, he peered into the gathering gloom as Markov Kalman sat beside him, eyes closed, peaceful, the state in which Sergei preferred him.

He turned over in his mind what he knew, began to think how he would look for the accountant. The information given to Andrei by his informant indicated that Clark would be in Scarborough, but not where, and that presented Sergei with a daunting task. The camera the boffin had provided was essential and he was determined to make full use of it, though he would do that alone. He could not afford Markov's temperament to become a liability; a good man in a fight but not a diplomat to say the least. When they reached their destination, he would leave his companion to amuse himself, only calling on his skills when he needed them, when he had the accountant in his sights.

'We're nearly there, Markov,' he said, alerting the man from his doze.

Markov opened his eyes and looked out of the window. 'Are we here?'

'Almost. The sat nav indicates that we were just a few

streets away from the hotel. Keep your eyes open for a place called the Royal.'

'Royal, sounds grand. No expense spared this trip, eh?'

'I don't think expense is foremost in anybody's mind. Is that it?'

'I think so,' said Markov, peering out of the windscreen. 'Yes, it is.'

Sergei followed the curve of the street and slowed the BMW, pulling up outside the hotel entrance.

At the same time, out on the M62 motorway the heavy transports were stopping for the night, leaving just a few vehicles for Anita to negotiate. The speedometer showed eighty, then ninety, and although she would have liked to push the car further, she restrained her urge to do a Lewis Hamilton. Glancing at the car's satellite navigation system, she noted just forty minutes before she reached her destination, Scarborough's Royal Hotel.

The theatre company lined the stage to the audience's enthusiastic applause, and sitting amongst them Jade and Chris joined in with enthusiasm. What a revelation and such a wonderful little theatre, Chris thought, as he watched the actors taking their bow.

'What do you think, did you enjoy the performance?' asked Jade as the lights came up.

'I once saw the film *Blithe Spirit*, but this is the first time on stage. Interesting.'

'I've seen it several times, once at the Gielgud with Angela Lansbury a few years ago. That was a really good performance.'

'Better than this?'

'No, not really, she was obviously a star but these

actors are good professionals. Some who come here are quite well known and I thought they performed very well.'

'Ah yes, they did, and the theatre in the round, I must say it makes for an interesting viewpoint.'

'Shall we have a drink?'

'Yes, I would like that,' said Chris, standing to follow the retreating audience members as they shuffled, chatting, towards the exit.

'There is a wine bar just round the corner. We could have a nightcap, talk a little. So far you haven't told me a lot about yourself,' Jade teased, determined to find out what it was he was hiding. 'Help me on with my coat and I'll treat you.'

As they emerged from the theatre, she slipped her arm in his.

'Come on, mystery man. There, across the street,' she said, a gentle nudge directing him towards a large picture window through which shadowy figures moved. 'G and T for me.'

Chris took the hint, approaching the small bar as they entered.

'Gin and tonic, please, and a Merlot if you have some,' he said to the busy barmaid.

'Cash or card?' she said, placing his drinks before him.

'Oh, card,' he said, fumbling in his pocket for his credit card. Taking the drinks, he walked towards Jade who had managed to grab a small table.

'Oh, lovely,' she said, pouring the small bottle of tonic into her glass. 'You a red-wine drinker, Chris? I had you as a whisky man.'

Chris looked at her, not sure of how to respond. He had never been very good with women and he could never be wholly sure whether Jade was serious or not.

'Er, yes, usually. I'm not much of a drinker, a couple of glasses of red wine usually suffices.'

'What's it like? Probably plonk.'

Chris took a sip, rolling the wine around in his mouth. 'It will do.'

'What does that mean?'

'At the price I have just paid I am not complaining. In London, with the prices they charge, perhaps I wouldn't be too happy.'

'That's one of the attractions of living here, the price of stuff. My house only cost one hundred and seventy thousand. What would it be in London – a million and no views?'

'You have a point; I'm renting but a month's rent here would barely cover a week in London.'

'Do you fancy buying a place?' she said, probing.

'No, not now. I don't know what the future might hold.'

'Are you thinking of moving back – to London, I mean?' she asked, the question catching him off balance.

After his recent experience his life had altered beyond recognition, but it had still left him with an inability to think more than a few days ahead, the worry of discovery constantly at the back of his mind.

Jade peered over the top of her glass. 'You're not thinking of moving back any time soon, are you?' she said, pressing her question. Her intelligent eyes were penetrating, intense, and he knew then that she was not easily lied to.

'No, I don't think I am.'

'Good, that's settled then.'

He smiled weakly and took a mouthful of wine. 'It's not too bad, you know. By the way, I was going to ask

155

about that painting, the one you are doing with a whatsit, a palette knife.'

'Yes, the one in the studio.'

'When will you finish it, do you think?'

'I could finish it in a couple of days, I suppose, but it's on the back burner for the time being.'

'Will it be for sale?'

'Already sold, I'm afraid. The lady from Leeds wants it. She pays me a visit every couple of months or so. She came last week and said she would take it.'

'Oh, shame. It would look well in my living room. The place is a bit drab and could do with some colour, some excitement.'

'Excitement? I wish all my work could conjure up excitement. Why don't I do you one? You could let me know a theme, perhaps. I know, why not sit for me and I will do a portrait of you?'

Chris grinned and finished his wine. 'I'd love that. No one has even taken a photograph of me for years, never mind painted a portrait. Thanks, why not?'

Chapter 9

Anita slept well after her dash from London, waking before seven to the sound of seagulls. Taking a shower, she thought about the work she had to do. Her controller had advised the local police of her visit, deciding on a story that she was looking for a missing person believed to be in the town.

I wonder how well up they are on surveillance? she thought. A small parochial force probably had limited capability, but she would need their cooperation if she was to make any headway.

Dressing in slacks and a jumper, she looked at her jacket and wondered if she should carry the Beretta, an out-of-production Nano that suited her well. No, she thought, she did not want to fall foul of the local police so soon in her investigation. Better to leave it in the small safe in the boot of her car. Her task was to locate Crypto, let Commander Pearson know, and then he would call in the heavy gang.

She was hungry, having eaten very little the day before, and reasoned that a proper breakfast would stand her in good stead. One last look in the mirror and picking up her jacket from the bed, she left the room for the ground floor.

It was early and she was almost the first guest to arrive; there was just a middle-aged couple and a lone businessman in the spacious deserted dining room. She filled her plate at the self-service counter, collected a glass of orange juice and found a table near a window, a reasonably obscure position from where she could observe – a habit honed over years in the service. After washing the last of her food down with the orange juice, she watched as the room began to fill.

An elderly couple was sitting not far from her, and several men in a group – workers, she guessed. Then two men, well-built and well-dressed, casually entered the dining room. At first, she did not recognise them. She watched as they approached the self-service counter and began loading their plates. Then, somewhere in her head, an alarm bell began to ring.

Of course. Tom and Jerry, the two dangerous Russians.

The men were hungry, large-framed and in need of a lot of calories. Tucking into their breakfast, they did not notice the dark-haired woman leave.

'What are you going to do today, have you a plan?' Markov asked.

'A sort of plan. Cruise the streets, take photographs. If anybody asks, we are working for a travel firm putting together a brochure about hot spots in the north of England.'

'Hot spots?' growled Markov.

'Maybe not. Look, we have no idea where our friend might be so we need to tramp the streets, see if the facial recognition works.'

'What about a photo of the accountant? We could make a couple of prints, show them to a few locals and maybe find him that way?'

'It's an idea but we need to be discreet. We could make out we are undercover police, that might work.'

The overcast sky was threatening rain, Anita thought, as she walked towards the police station. Yet that was nothing compared to the discovery that the two men staying in her hotel were the same men the police were looking for in London.

It was a real puzzle, a dangerous one. Tom and Jerry had come to her attention during her briefing for the mission, two characters whom the CIA believed were their agents' murderers but also SVR agents. Now she was aware of them, she believed they were probably looking for Crypto as well – but how had they known to come here? she wondered as she entered the local police station.

'Good morning,' she said to the burly sergeant standing behind the counter. 'I have urgent business here.'

The policeman frowned, looking unhappy. 'Keep your hair on, let me just finish this,' he said, writing something on a pad. 'Now, what is it you're in such a hurry about?'

'I would like to see the officer in charge.'

'Have you an appointment? He's a busy man.'

Anita produced her warrant card, causing the desk sergeant's ruddy complexion to fade.

'Sorry, ma'am, you should have said. Just wait here.' He returned a minute later with a second police officer.

'You wanted to see me, I believe.'

'Yes, my name is Simms. You should have received some sort of notification that I was coming.'

'Ms Simms, yes, I was expecting you. I am Superintendent Lester. Come through. Sergeant?'

The sergeant left his position behind the desk, reappearing to hold a side door open for her. 'If you will come in here,' he said.

Thanking him, Anita passed through to see the inspector opening the door to his office. 'Take a seat,' he said.

'You know why I am here?'

'Yes, a missing person, I believe.'

'Yes, it is imperative we find him and I need your help. I don't know how much you know of the case, but the man I am looking for is of particular interest to us. I cannot say exactly what that interest is, simply to say that we need to find him with some urgency.'

'And what assistance can we provide?'

'I will need access to your surveillance system and I would like your uniforms briefed on the man's appearance, to see if they can locate him. We don't want him arrested, we just want to find him and then I will decide on the next step. Is your system capable of facial recognition?'

'We do not monitor the CCTV. We cannot offer twenty-four-hour cover so now the local council hosts the system in a building behind the town hall. We can go there and you can have a look round.'

Chris felt the irritation in his nostril grow until he could not resist twitching.

'Stay still, Chris. I can't get it right if you keep twitching your nose, it makes you screw up your eyes.'

'Sorry, got a tickle and I couldn't get rid of it.'

'Okay, we need a break. Relax and I'll put the kettle on,' Jade said, putting down her brush. She had already sketched an outline of his face, his aspect a little towards her, and now she was ready to add some paint.

'Eyes are always the hardest,' she said. 'If I get those right, it gives me the confidence to make a good job of

160

the rest. Hair and texture are not easy sometimes, but really it's the eyes. You must get them right for a good portrait.'

'Remind me not to blink.'

'I'll certainly do that. You can relax now. Here, I have some scones.'

Chris could not resist the offer and standing up, he stretched his arms and puffed out his cheeks.

'I didn't realise how hard it is to sit still for a portrait.'

'That's the essence of a good model. Some life models remain in a pose for a very long time. They are much sought after by the art colleges.'

'I can believe it. I wouldn't like to do it for long, especially without my clothes.'

Jade just looked at him. 'No sugar?'

'No sugar.'

'We will just do another two-hour session today and then you can leave me to paint in part of the composition. Come back the day after tomorrow and we'll progress it a bit more. Are you fishing this afternoon?'

'No, I must visit Town Hall to sort out the rates on the house I'm renting. The bill came in saying it's a three-bedroomed house and it isn't, it's just two.'

'Good luck with that one.'

'Why?'

'Local councils are not the easiest to deal with, especially if there are changes involved.'

'Will you work on the portrait all day?'

'No, I always need a break after half a day. If I feel like it, I might spend some more time this evening. My plan is an intense session in the morning so I can do fuck-all in the afternoon.'

'That's not very ladylike language.'

'Sometimes I'm not ladylike. Tell you what, bugger working this evening, you can take me to the Valley for a drink.'

'What's the Valley?'

'A pub. Guess where it is.'

'In a valley?'

'Well done, Chris, go to the top of the class.'

'So where is it, and what's so special?'

'The Valley runs towards the seafront. Thursday night is music night, a folk band or maybe some blues. Do you like blues?'

'I do, and do they sell real ale?'

'I thought you were a wine drinker?'

'Not where music is involved. I like it a bit raw and real ale is raw.'

'Gosh, you do surprise. Bring your tea and we'll have another go at making you pretty.'

Although it was a short walk from the police station to the council offices, the inspector insisted on providing a car which gave Anita some cause for alarm. The Royal Hotel was not so far away, and what if the two thugs saw her get out of a police car? She had little choice, though, and stepping from the car she followed the inspector into the council building. He led her up a wide staircase and along a corridor, stopping in front of an oak-panelled door.

'In here,' he said, opening the door and walking into a large office.

'Superintendent Lester,' said a man, recognising him and rising from his desk. 'How are you? I see Newcastle aren't doing so well now.'

'No,' said the inspector with a grimace. 'May I introduce Ms Simms? She is here from London and we are to give her all the assistance she needs.'

'Good morning. I am Barry Sparkes, pleased to meet you,' he said, holding out his hand.

'Likewise,' she replied, shaking it.

'Now, what is all this about? I did receive an email yesterday saying someone was coming to look at our CCTV system and that you would be present, Graham, but I presumed it was just some sort of inspection.'

'That might be your assumption, Barry, but it's not the reason we are here.'

First name terms, all a bit friendly, thought Anita. What kind of an operation was it? Deciding she needed to take some control, she said, 'I am here on a more serious matter and I need the use of both your CCTV system and an operator. I am looking for a missing person.'

'You didn't need to come all the way from London for that, a picture would do.'

'It's a little more involved, Mr Sparkes. Is there somewhere more private we can talk?'

Sparkes nodded his head, looked at the policeman and ushered his guests into a side room.

'It is important the missing person is located as soon as possible; he is part of an ongoing operation,' Anita said. 'I can't tell you a great deal more at this stage. My instructions are to find him and I will need your help to do that.'

'It's from above, Barry,' said the inspector, his expression serious. 'We are to afford Ms Simms here all the assistance she needs, and that includes the use of my officers.'

'I have to warn you, Mr Sparkes, that this is a confidential investigation and so the fewer people who are involved the better,' added Anita.

The man remained silent, thoughtful. He was simply a local government officer. 'First thing,' he said. 'Have a look at our operations room, I think.'

'Yes, good idea,' said Anita, glad that formalities were over and she could at last get down to business.

'If you will follow me.'

Anita and the inspector fell in step behind the council employee, entering the CCTV control room where an array of monitors filled one wall.

'The operators work twelve-hour shifts, manning the unit twenty-four hours a day. If they need assistance, we can bring in extra staff at short notice.'

Anita looked around, impressed that such a sophisticated operation existed in an out-of-the-way town. She looked at the monitors and noted several scenes.

'Are they in the town centre?' she asked.

'Yes, and these here,' said Sparkes, pointing, 'are more towards the outskirts of town. Those ones cover the seafront area.'

'Do you monitor the main roads?'

'Yes. Can you bring up the A64 and the Filey Road cameras, please,' he said to the female operator. Immediately one of the screens switched to overhead road scenes, showing traffic flows to and from the town.

'You seem to have good cover; I understand you have facial recognition?'

'Yes, since the government relaxed the rules,' said Sparkes.

'I have two decent images of the missing person; I can download them from my mobile phone if you like,' said Anita, producing her phone.

'Can you take care of that, Victoria?'

The operator turned in her seat and beckoned Anita

towards her. 'Take a seat and I will help you transfer them onto our system.'

'So, how many cameras are working your area, Mr Sparkes?'

'We have a total of forty-one cameras covering Scarborough, Filey and Whitby. Most are in Scarborough, with six covering the town centre and the others at various locations. We have surveillance across most of the borough. Do you expect to be looking for your subject in Whitby or Filey?'

'I don't know. I am guessing that he will not be roaming far, but who knows,' she said, feeling more confident in locating Crypto than she had so far. If he was indeed in the town, she would find him.

Sergei was not sure where to start. His plan was to take random pictures around the town in the hope that the software in the camera and on his laptop would find the accountant somewhere in the mix. The informant had said Clark arrived via the railway station and that seemed the obvious place to start, so after breakfast he and Markov had made their way there. Soon after arriving, however, Sergei began to realise how daunting the undertaking would be.

'What do you want me to do, Sergei? There doesn't seem a lot I can do if you're taking photos. How about getting those prints and showing a few people, ask around?' Markov suggested once more.

Sergei thought for a minute. It was a good idea under the circumstances, and probably an easy matter to find a shop specialising in photographic printing.

'I think we will have to. Maybe I can use a copy, quiz the taxi drivers, see if anybody remembers picking him up from the station.'

Markov managed a thin smile; he was pleased Sergei was taking notice. After the attack, Sergei had seemed wary of him even though he had tried to explain that he believed the men were reaching for concealed weapons. He was simply protecting his boss.

'What was the alternative?' he had argued. 'We were isolated in the street wearing those masks. If they had prevailed, we would have been exposed and Clark would have got away just the same. They were going for their guns; we had no alternative.'

The 'we' rankled with Sergei. Perhaps it was the only course of action, but the ramifications if they were ever caught could be catastrophic, and it would be he who would shoulder the blame.

'Okay, see if you can find a shop to make us a couple of prints while I take some pictures around here. Then we'll ask around. It's a long shot, but you never know.'

Chris twisted his torso to relieve some tension. After posing for his portrait for a fourth time he thought it might be easier, but still the tightness across his shoulders returned and, rubbing each in turn, he stood up.

'It's bloody hard work sitting for a portrait. How they managed back in the day dressed in all that finery, I will never know.'

'We – you – are not dressing like that. I wouldn't call a tee shirt and jeans finery, would you?'

Chris laughed and looked down at the jeans, the latest component of his transformation.

'No, I'm just plain old Chris Kent, no airs and graces about me.'

'That's what I like about you,' said Jade, wiping the paint off her brush. 'Do you want a look?'

'Is it really finished?'

'More or less. I might touch up here and there later, but to all intents and purposes it's done.'

The news that his ordeal had at last ended helped relieve the tension of sitting. He walked towards her, excited yet apprehensive about seeing the canvas. He had marvelled at Jade's skill as the work developed, intrigued at how she had transformed a very good sketch, but this was the first time he would see his portrait complete.

'You really are very good,' he said, gazing at the work.

'You are too kind, sir. It's been a pleasure. I haven't done a portrait with a sitter for ages, and it was good to have some company. Sea shells and flotsam are rather mute, you know. What's wrong, something you don't like?' she said, noticing his expression.

'I seem almost sorrowful, the look in my eye...'

'Not sorrowful, it's a faraway look – the look of someone with his mind on something. Your mind is always on something, Chris. What is it?'

'Always on something? What do you mean?'

'Come on, Chris, you are a man of mystery, you know. You have appeared from nowhere and you don't seem to have any recent history. Yes, you have told me all about your childhood, university and about your ex – but there is a chunk missing, isn't there?'

Chris was dumbfounded, speechless. Jade noticed the look of alarm on his face.

'You okay? I've hit a nerve, haven't I... Do you want to talk?'

Chris simply exhaled through half-closed lips and the colour drained from his face, leaving Jade to change the subject.

'I'll put the kettle on. Come on, let's go into the house

and we can talk over a cuppa.'

So, the time had arrived. He could no longer bottle up his anxieties. He knew it would happen one day; inevitable, he supposed.

'Do you want a scone?' Jade asked. 'They're a day old, but they won't kill you.'

'You might be surprised,' he said as a shiver ran down his spine.

'It's serious, isn't it?' said Jade, reading his mood. 'That's the thing with portraiture – having your subject near for long periods, talking, learning about the inner self, putting it all on canvas. That's what it's all about. I wouldn't do it if all I had for a sitter was a cardboard cut-out.'

'You're a very perceptive woman, Jade.'

'So they tell me.'

Chris lifted his cup and took a sip of tea, cleared his throat. 'Phew, this is hard,' he said, looking her in the eye.

'Take your time, we have all day.'

'I, erm...' He still couldn't tell her the whole truth. 'I stole a large sum of money from my employer, mostly Bitcoin and some cash.'

'Are the police after you?'

'I expect so.'

'Well, at least no one has died. So what's the problem?'

Chris swallowed, the image of that day all too vivid. Someone *had* died. He was unable to tell the full story, instead falling back on a daydream he had concocted as he fished, staring into the abyss as the hours passed. He had let his mind wander and during those moments of calm he had come up with a story.

'How much did you take?' Jade asked.

'I honestly don't know. Bitcoin is volatile and I haven't really checked for a while. A million, maybe two.'

'Gosh, someone will not be very happy when they find out.'

'I don't think they will, not without a lot of digging. I'm pretty sure I have got away with it.'

'Bloody hell, you are a dark horse, Chris. No wonder you have a faraway look. And no one knows you are living here?'

'I don't think so, I think they would have found me by now.'

'What will you do with all this wealth?'

'I just want to live a quiet life... Fish. Go fishing for fish.'

'Fishing? You have the bug for it, I can see.'

'The weather is getting better all the time. I do enjoy it, beach-casting down there and...'

'And what?'

'And meeting you.'

'Me?' She smiled.

'Yes, I like your company, your humour. You have made me the happiest I have felt in years.'

'Well, thank you, Chris. I like you too. And not a word about cryptocurrency any more, eh?'

He shook his head. 'No more talk of Bitcoin. But I will check to see what the price is today...'

Their conversation petered out, the day-old scones disappeared, and he worried he had said too much. Jade, meanwhile, worried that he hadn't said enough.

'What are you doing with the rest of your day, Chris? I have some work to do around the house. You can stay for tea if you like.'

'No thanks, I have some work to do at my own house.

I bought some paint and if I leave it any longer it will be solid in the tin.'

'I know the feeling. Nothing worse than to squeeze a tube of paint and find it too hard to be of any use. It's expensive.'

'I'll be off, I think. Thanks again for the tea,' he said, reaching for the door handle and just a short time later he was walking down to the cove and, in a way, he was happy to have shared part of his problem.

Now he didn't feel quite so alone, but he was still wary of disclosing fully what had happened to him, why he was really on the run – the murdered men, the Russian thugs. He couldn't burden Jade with his problems. She was a talented artist and he was glad to have met her. A simple, honest person wanting nothing more than to pursue her art.

By the end of their chat, Jade had seemed unconcerned and Chris had left in reasonably good spirits. For her part, she felt she should look again at the portrait, see if she had captured the anxiety in his eyes that she had just witnessed.

The canvas was an old one, repurposed, no more than eighteen inches or so tall, and under the light from the translucent roof she looked hard at his image. His eyes did indeed show a hint of anxiety, a reflection of his inner self perhaps, and she felt an artist's pride about it being the look she had wanted to capture.

The old clock on the chest of drawers where she stored her paints showed it was not yet two o'clock. She would forget her chores, take her bicycle, and visit her friend Sherilee.

The images produced by the photographic shop were

good and Markov had the prints in his hand within the hour.

'Not bad, Markov, well done. We can leave these with a few shopkeepers, see if any of them recognise our friend, perhaps keep a lookout for him. I will carry on taking pictures while you distribute them,' said Sergei, adjusting the camera setting. 'There is a train due in less than ten minutes, I will give a couple of prints to the taxi drivers before the train gets in.'

Markov peeled off two of the prints and gave them to Sergei before setting off for the seafront and his own assignment. Sergei walked towards the railway station where he approached the first taxi in line on the rank.

'Excuse me, sir,' he said to the driver, showing him the print. 'I look for friend of mine who came to this town about a month ago. This man here, slightly built, wearing business suit. You wouldn't have any idea, would you?'

The man looked at the print, pursed his lips in thought and slowly shook his head. 'No, mate, doesn't ring a bell. What day would it be? We work a loose rota, so if you know the date then maybe you can find out who was working then.'

'That useful, thanks,' said Sergei.

He looked towards the next car but the latest train had already arrived, and soon passengers would begin to appear. He needed to be quick before the taxis departed.

Slipping on a light anorak, Jade locked the back door and went to the disused coal shed. She kept an old bicycle there for her runs into town, as the walk was too much on a regular basis and she hated catching the bus.

The shed door squeaked as she pulled it open and there in the gloom sat a bicycle that had seen better

171

days. Its original green paint had peeled in places and the wickerwork basket was showing its age, but this bike was her lifeline and she loved it. Dragging it out, she swept the back of her hand over the saddle to disperse any lodgers that might have made their home there and pushed the bicycle onto the narrow path. Pointing the bicycle in the direction of town, she pushed it forward, mounting with a practiced skill. Soon she was careering along the bicycle path alongside the bypass and then through the back streets, avoiding the bulk of the traffic. Twenty minutes later she freewheeled down the incline towards the foreshore.

There was no mistaking Sherilee's art gallery at the bottom of a steep and narrow cobbled road. It sat amongst the remains of a long-demolished theatre, the remaining part of its wall covered in an array of graffiti depicting cats, footballers, a tall dark angel, and a whole house front. There was no mistaking the local artist's crossroads.

'G'day, Jade, good to see you,' said the slight, grey-haired Australian proprietor.

'Hi, Sherilee. Can I leave my bike against this wall?'

'Course you can, dear. By the way, I sold one of your pots this morning. I can give you the cash now if you like.'

'Oh great. Is there much interest in my work?'

'A bit, although we've been quiet for the last few days. Trouble with good weather, everyone wants to be outside. Nothing like a bit of rain to bring in the punters. Have you come about the exhibition? Your sculptures always go down well, have you something new to show?'

'Yes, two small pieces I would like to show, and I have just finished a painting you could use.'

'A painting, great. I haven't seen you paint for a while,

dear.'

'It's of a chap I know, a portrait. I did it as a present for him.'

'Sounds serious, gal.'

'No, he's just a nice guy, good company. He likes to fish from the beach below the bungalow, so I see a lot of him when I'm scavenging for materials. We hit it off, he's from London.'

'London, eh? Big city boy.'

'Well, we know a few of the same places. I've been to the theatre with him and dinner a couple of times.'

'You will have to bring him to show me. Another exhibit,' she laughed. 'What about the painting then? Shall I get John to swing by later? Tell you what, we could put your work here near the window, your art is always a draw.'

Markov had only seen the foreshore from the hotel bedroom and was enjoying his walk past the ice-cream stalls and amusement arcades. Although well before the tourist season a spell of good weather had encouraged locals and day trippers alike to savour their good fortune. It was a busy sort of day, crowds meandering and crisscrossing the road through slow-moving traffic. They wouldn't know anything of the accountant, no, he needed to find locals to quiz – but where to start? The café near the harbour with seats outside, he would start there; perhaps one of the staff had seen him.

'Excuse me, you haven't seen this man recently, have you?' he asked, showing the girl at the serving hatch one of the prints.

She looked at the image and shook her head. 'No, I don't think so.'

'Your friend, has she seen him?'

'Sarah, come and have a look at this,' she said to a second serving girl.

'What?'

'He's looking for someone. Any idea?'

'What's he done? He's not a murderer or anyfing, is he?' she said in all innocence.

'No, he is missing from home and we are trying to find him.'

'Undercover cop, are you?'

'Er... Yes, but don't tell anyone. Have you seen him?'

'Might have. A man looking a bit like that passed here a few times earlier in the month. Carrying a fishing rod if I recall.'

'A fishing rod?'

'Yes, I fink so.'

'Thanks, you have been a help,' said Markov, moving on.

'Tough-looking bugger, isn't 'e, Sarah.'

'Well, you do pick them, Maureen,' said the girl leaning out of the kiosk window to watch Markov wander away.

If he had a fishing rod, he must be going fishing... So where would he go to fish? mused the Russian, looking for another likely candidate to quiz. Anybody fishing might recognise Charles Clark; it stood to reason that fishermen would notice other fishermen.

He walked onto the harbour wall, seeing several men, their rods reaching over the sea, but first he came across two fishermen packing their gear into an old Ford van.

'Have you seen this man round here? He would probably be fishing like you,' asked Markov, holding out the picture.

The men examined the photograph but showed no sign of recognition. He left them to consult anyone else he could find, but behind him the two anglers spoke quietly.

'That's our London friend, isn't it, Malcolm?'

'I think it is. Who's he, anyway? Big bugger, sounded foreign – police, maybe?'

'Dunno. I wonder where Chris is these days, he hasn't been fishing off the pier for, I suppose, two weeks. Maybe more.'

'Aye, must be. I haven't seen him. He's a nice enough bloke and I'm not going to drop him in it.'

'No, me neither.'

Anita stood behind the CCTV operator, casting her eye over each monitor in turn and listening as the woman informed her of the camera locations and their scope of view.

'That one and that one, they look out over the main street in Filey. That one is surveying the Coble Landing, we sometimes get youngsters causing trouble down there. Not enough to do, I suppose.'

'And that, I suppose, is Whitby?' Anita asked. 'I know a little bit about the area.'

'Yes, these six cameras are in Whitby. We have a multi-screen which I can switch to full-screen for any camera. Here, I'll show you,' she said, bringing up each image of the seaside town one by one.

Anita looked closely at figures moving around the streets and was impressed by the detail. 'And the rest, they are in Scarborough?'

'Yes, Scarborough is a bigger town so most cameras are in the borough.'

'Where would you expect our subject to go if he arrived by train in the late evening? My information is that he arrived one evening in January and it was one of your traffic cameras that picked him up, but we do not know where he went after leaving the station.'

'If he was new to the town then other than wandering the streets, he might have taken a taxi, there are plenty in the station forecourt.'

'Ask the driver for advice?'

'That would be my guess, At that time of day it would be dark and January is quite cold at times.'

'What are you suggesting?'

'He caught a cab, probably, and if it was me, asked where to find a decent hotel for the night.'

'The analyst working on the case seems to think the same but the video file she has is inconclusive. Have you files covering the time and date he arrived?'

'If you can supply me with the time, yes I can look into the archive but I will need authorisation.'

'Who from?'

'The police.'

'Now I have a better understanding of your system and what it can do, I think I need to talk to Superintendent Lester. What time did you say your relief comes on?'

'Six this evening.'

'I'll be back to talk to her. Thanks for now,' she said.

It seemed to Anita that the best approach might be a two-pronged attack: use the surveillance cameras, but also quiz the taxi drivers working out of the station forecourt. For that she would need the help of the local police, and on visiting the police station, she found Superintendent Lester receptive to the idea.

'I can spare a detective constable to speak with the taxi drivers. I think you're right; they could give you a start for your search if one can remember the fare. A lot of them have cameras in their taxis in case of trouble, but after such a long time the chance of finding a recording of your subject looks slim.'

'It's worth a try, but just to know where a taxi dropped him off would help. Can I leave it with you for now, Superintendent?'

The policeman agreed to keep her informed of developments, and after leaving him Anita thought about what she had learned so far. The walks to the police station had given her a rough idea of the town's layout. The proximity of the hotel to the town hall made it easy for her to visit the control room, but taking in all the information had left her a little weary. She felt like a break. Perhaps it was time for a word with her controller, so finding a quiet place, she called Commander Pearson.

'Anita, good to hear from you. How's it going?'

'Well enough, they have a decent surveillance system in place here, much better than I imagined.'

'How are you getting on with the local police, are they much help?'

'Yes, helpful, but we're not very far along the road yet. I have asked the officer in charge – Superintendent Lester – to find out if any of the taxi drivers working the railway station remember picking up Crypto. I don't know how successful it will be, but if I can locate the drop-off point, I will have a good start in finding him. They have a facial-recognition facility and that's where I think I will do best. By the way, Tom and Jerry are here in Scarborough.'

'What! How did they know to go to Scarborough?'

'That's what is bugging me. My belief is that someone is passing on information. I have no idea who, but if there is a mole, we need to find him or her.'

'Jimi has let the analyst return to the Met; she did good work finding Crypto's location but right now there is not much more she can do.'

'There is.'

'What?'

'If there is a mole in the Met, chances are the informer is based in Islington police station and she might have an insight. It might be her, how else could Tom and Jerry have learned of Crypto's whereabouts?'

Sergei's powerful laptop ran on the latest Intel chip and it had a number-crunching capacity with which a mainframe of even just a few years earlier would find it difficult to compete. Sitting on the edge of his bed, he inserted the camera card. With over two thousand high-definition images taken, he had plenty for the identity search software to examine.

'Well, here goes, Markov. Let's see if I have caught anything.'

Markov inclined his head momentarily before turning back to the television. He had told Sergei the girl at the ice-cream stall thought a man fitting Clark's description had passed by at some time, and that she remembered him carrying a fishing rod, and he said he had spoken to a few men fishing from the harbourside, shown Clark's picture, but no one recognised him. Now that Sergei was pinning his hopes on a result from the camera, Markov was happy to carry on watching television.

'It's found something,' said Sergei, a rare trace of enthusiasm in his voice. 'It's found something. Well, I never. It's him, I am sure.'

Suddenly the television wasn't so interesting and Markov joined Sergei to look at the computer screen.

'There, look, the red square. That's him, I'm sure.

What do you think?'

Markov looked hard at the image on the screen and as Sergei zoomed in, he could see Charles Clark – the accountant– amongst a small group of people.

'Is him.'

'I took the photograph here, on this street, in front of the hotel,' said Sergei. 'Look, you can see the statue of Queen Victoria. He has just come out of the building opposite.'

'Well, that seems to prove he is in the town, but where exactly? That doesn't look like a place of residence.'

Chapter 10

Jade's friend Sherilee had always dreamed of having her own art gallery, and after meeting her partner and moving to Yorkshire she had finally realised that dream. It was a modest affair, tucked away next to the seafront, where she took pride in giving local artists a platform for their work. She organised exhibitions and workshops, a vehicle for the local community's talent, and today she was putting the finishing touches to her latest showing. She called it 'Springing into Summer', the prequel to a busy summer season, she hoped.

For a small town, many of the exhibits were of a high standard. A pair of modern-day amphorae stood sentinel at the entrance to the gallery, welcoming its visitors; a white panelled platform against one wall was adorned with pottery and glass in all shapes and sizes; avant-garde nudes in wire and clay donated by a local artist stood on a table opposite; and lesser sculptures of people and animals created by young art students wanting to show off their work were scattered thorough the gallery. The centrepiece, however, was Jade's portrait.

Sherilee still had not met the mystery man, though judging by Jade's talent, she expected that he would look very much like his portrait. Now she wondered how best to present it. The lighting in the window was strong, and those eyes would not lend themselves to direct sunlight, yet she felt that as a centrepiece it would entice customers into the exhibition.

'It's good, isn't it?' said her partner. 'Stunned me when I picked it up last night.'

'I'm not surprised, John, it is good. I'm hoping it will bring in the punters. She should enter that competition for portrait artist of the year. She would walk away with the first prize.'

'She could. Let's hope it drums up business for the gallery, we could do with some.'

'It's wintertime, John, we can't expect to make a fortune out of the locals at this time of year – but a few quid would be nice. We're opening at ten this morning, as planned. I have a decent guest list; a few glasses of wine and some canapés will get them in the mood. Maybe a few early tourists will come in for a look and we can get some sales.'

Sergei was pleased with the results. The camera had done its work and he now knew for sure that Charles Clark was somewhere in the town, but the question remained as to where he was based. He had run the collection of images through the software again, in the hope of finding Clark at some other location, but was disappointed by the result. One sighting was not particularly helpful. He needed more, and that probably meant searching further afield but at least it would be worth the effort.

'I will head to the railway station, show this new image to the taxi people,' he said. 'No one seemed to recollect picking him up last time I asked but they are always coming and going, this new image might jog someone's memory. Markov, you go back to the harbour, there must be someone who remembers him. Find someone who might know of him.'

The big Russian nodded, happy enough to stroll around as he pleased, showing the copy to anyone he felt might be able to help recognise Clark. He set off for the seafront while Sergei headed for the railway station and the line of waiting taxis.

As Sergei passed through crowds of shoppers he took more photographs. Who knew, maybe Clark was amongst them right now, and the more pictures he took he believed the more chance he had of finding him. Reaching the end of the shopping precinct, he crossed over to the station and approached the taxis looking for a driver he had not already quizzed.

'Excuse me, sir, I am trying to trace this man. Have you seen him?' he asked, offering the print for examination. 'Was he a fare of yours a few weeks ago?'

The driver shook his head and Sergei moved on to the next in line. Again, he drew a blank. A third he recognised from his previous enquiry and moving on he came to the last in line already beginning to doubt his approach. But this time the man nodded.

'Yes, I think I picked him up. He was freezing cold; the silly man was wearing just a thin jacket. No good in winter.'

Sergei's eyes lit up: some success. 'Where did you take him?'

'Oh... somewhere up on the South Cliff, I think. Yes, he didn't seem to have much idea of where he was going, just wanted a hotel for the night. I dropped him off at the Chevron, I think it was.'

'You take me there now?'

'I'm not supposed to jump the queue. Try the taxi in front, he should get the first fare.'

'Chevron Hotel?' said Sergei to the driver, after

retracing his steps to the front of the line.

The taxi pulled up outside the Chevron and Sergei stepped onto the pavement. He passed a banknote to the driver, waiving any change due, and looked at the hotel. No cars sat on the forecourt, all the ground-floor windows had their curtains drawn, and the place appeared deserted.

Was this really the hotel Clark had come to? Was he still here?

Puzzled that something didn't seem quite right, Sergei walked up the short flight of steps to the hotel's front door and turned the handle. There was no movement. He pushed but it seemed locked and so he tried the bell. There was no answer, and looking around for signs of life, he walked towards a ground-floor window where he noticed the curtains did not quite meet. Cupping his hands to keep out reflections, he peered in, dismayed to see the furniture covered in white sheets.

What's going on? he thought, returning to the front door where, with a mixture of anger and frustration, he used his clenched fist to thump heavily on a panel. There was no response and so he pressed his ear to the door and listened. Nothing. He was about to give up when he heard a voice from inside.

'What do you want?'

'I am looking for someone, a guest of yours. Open the door, will you?'

There was no immediate reply until the sound of a key in the lock, and the door swung open to reveal a white-haired old man peering out at him.

'Are you looking for Brian?'

'Brian? Who's Brian?'

'My son, the owner. You have just missed him, they went to Tenerife this morning. The decorators are starting tomorrow and I am keeping an eye on things.'

Sergei's lips parted a little, a narrow stream of frustration exhaled into the sunlight. 'You closed, nobody here?'

'That's right, pal, we're closed 'till Easter.'

The Russian gritted his teeth and turned round in frustration. The taxi had gone, stranding him. He had little choice but to call a radio cab, but then his mobile telephone began to vibrate.

'Markov, what?'

'I've found him – well, nearly.'

'What do you mean "nearly"?'

'Where are you?'

'At a hotel on the Esplanade, the South Cliff. Why?'

'Meet me by the harbour.'

'What's happening?'

'You'll see, and you will forgive me for killing those two Americans.'

'This better be good.'

The line went dead and Sergei felt irritated by Markov's cryptic comment. What did he mean, he would forgive him? He didn't have time to waste and a taxi was not forthcoming. It was quicker to walk, so at a brisk pace he made his way towards the harbour.

Victoria squinted at the left-most screen as it switched automatically to a camera covering the southern end of the seafront. A red box had just appeared to enclose a subject. Adjusting her glasses, she used her mouse to freeze the frame and zoom in.

'That looks like our man,' she said to herself, reaching for the mobile phone on her desk.

'Ms Simms? Hello, it's me, Victoria from the town hall. I think you should get over here right away, I might have a sighting of the man you are looking for.'

Anita was just finishing her coffee in a small café, a tactic to avoid coming face-to-face with Tom and Jerry in the hotel. If they recognised her and suspected her of working for the security services then she could be dead meat – literally.

'Thanks, I'm on my way,' she said, dropping several coins near her cup before hurrying into the street and speed-dialling her controller.

'Commander, I am on my way to the control room. The operator sounds positive that she has a sighting. I will call you back as soon as I have seen the evidence and assessed the situation on the ground. You might want to warn Jimi.'

Commander Pearson listened carefully, and once Anita rang off he called his colleague on the secure line.

'Simms thinks she has a positive. There is a complication, though. She believes the two suspects in the murder of the CIA agents are in Scarborough right now too. I was going to contact you later this morning to discuss the operation, but her call suggests that things are taking a more serious turn and she may need backup. What do you want to do about the local police, do you want them involved?'

'No, I will request a helicopter and get up there as soon as I can, should be there within a couple of hours. On second thought, maybe we *should* involve the local police, it could be useful to have an undercover car waiting for me. Can you organise that?'

'That was quick,' said Victoria, as Anita appeared at her side.

'I don't mess about. Show me.'

Victoria stepped the recording back ten minutes and Anita looked intently at the screen. Charles Clark had been found walking along the seafront road with an unknown woman.

'There, they are just coming into view.'

Anita's eyes scanned the screen, the road, and suddenly the red square appeared to encompass a face.

'That's him. Well, the computer thinks it is, but maybe you would like to make a positive ID.'

Anita took out her mobile phone and brought up the images she had of Charles Clark, looking first at the screen and then the mobile telephone. She looked again. 'I think it is. Who's the woman?'

'I don't know.'

'Have you still got them?'

'No, unfortunately they have gone off the main foreshore road up a side street where there isn't any coverage.'

'So where could they be?'

'They have gone up a street called Blands Cliff. It leads to the indoor market, or even the town centre. I don't think they would go up there if they were going to the harbour, pointless really.'

'Where is this Blands Cliff?'

'Not far, let me show you,' said Victoria, turning to a laptop computer on the desk. 'Here, look at this street scene. We are here and they went up there. It's only a short distance away. I think your best bet is to go to the main street back there and turn right. You might spot them if they are walking slowly.'

'Thanks, keep looking,' said Anita, heading for the door and emerging into the street to run towards the main thoroughfare.

The street was busy with locals and tourists alike. A steady stream of light traffic flowed past, and looking down the street, she was disappointed that of her quarry there was no sign.

'Blands Cliff, oh yes, I see,' she said, walking towards the sign on the wall. Turning the corner, she began to descend a steeply cobbled street.

Markov first saw Sergei hurrying along the path on the opposite side of the wide foreshore road, and raised his arm. Waving twice, he caught Sergei's eye and beckoned him over.

'What have you found?' said Sergei, his chest heaving from exertion.

'Charles Clark. Come, I show you.'

Markov began to retrace his steps past bells, whistles, and the commotion of noisy arcades until they reached a steep side street with bright murals painted on every surface imaginable.

'What, here?'

'Come,' said Markov in triumph. 'There, look. What do you see?'

'Mother of God. But where is he really?'

'The artist will know.'

'Of course,' said an incredulous Sergei, unaware of Agent Simms staring at him from just metres away.

Shocked by the sight of the two men she least wanted to meet, Anita stopped dead in her tracks. They were staring intently into a shop window. Realising that they had failed to notice her, she dodged into the nearest alleyway. Blending in with the shadows, she held her breath, deciding what to do as she peered round the corner. Her expectation was that she would come face-to-face with Crypto and his friend, but instead she had almost run into Tom and Jerry. There was no sign of Crypto or his friend, and why were the Russians so intent upon the shop window?

Not daring to expose herself on the street, Anita carefully observed the two Russians and was surprised to see them enter the shop, unaware that only seconds earlier Crypto and his female friend had stepped inside the gallery.

'What do you think, Jade?' Sherilee said. 'Looks great, doesn't it? Is this your new friend?'

'Yes, meet Chris. Chris, this is Sherilee, the lady I was telling you about. If it wasn't for her, I think Scarborough would be full of Philistines. She runs this wonderful little gallery, the best gallery in town with the help of her partner John, and she makes sure as many people as possible know about it.'

'Pleased to meet you, Chris. You alright, Blue? You look as if a possum got your sandwich,' she said, noticing the look on his face.

Chris wasn't alright, far from it, because looking through the window were the two faces he feared most.

'Is there a back way out of here?'

'What?'

'A back way. I can't explain, but two very bad men are looking at the painting and they want to kill me.'

'Strewth, cobber, sounds like real trouble,' said Sherilee, but she was nothing if not quick-thinking and shrewd. 'Through there, along the alley and past the dustbins. It brings you out further up the street.'

Chris didn't say anything, he simply turned towards the door at the rear of the gallery and disappeared.

'Blimey, Jade, that was a bit sudden, wasn't it? You

alright gal? You look as if you're taking a turn now.'

Jade was dumbstruck, her brain working overtime as she watched the door close behind Chris. She had suspected there was more to his sudden appearance in Scarborough than he was telling her. Okay, so he said he'd stolen a couple of million pounds, but the look on his face had betrayed a real fear, a fear for his life, and that didn't quite tie in with simple fraud.

'Are you the owner?' asked an accented voice, attracting the attention of both Sherilee and Jade.

'Yes, can I help you?'

'The picture in the window, the portrait, is it for sale?'

'Er... no, it's part of the exhibition. Once we finish the artist will take it away.'

'Oh, the artist – and who is he, would he be interested in a commission?'

'Er... he... might be, I don't know. You would have to ask him.'

'Do you have a telephone number or his address?'

'I'm sorry, I can't give you that without his permission, but I will ask. Perhaps if you come back tomorrow?'

'We leave tomorrow. Please can you find out today? I will come back this afternoon, in an hour. It's important to me. I like to invest in real talent and this man has got something.'

'You are so kind. I will pass the message on and let you know.'

Sergei resisted the temptation to grab the woman by the throat and wring the information out of her, but instead he gave her a watery smile and left the shop followed closely by Markov, who was feeling equally belligerent.

'It's him for sure, and that woman is hiding

189

something. We'll come back and find out who the artist is and where he lives. Clark cannot be far away.'

Chris Kent wasn't very far away, just fifty metres, in fact, stumbling through the dank passage in a blind panic. Anita was still peering round the corner of the alleyway and wondering what had interested Tom and Jerry so.

There is something going on in that shop, she reasoned. Something they are very interested in, and that something has to be Charles Clark...

She heard a noise and her ears pricked up. Footsteps, heavy breathing, and she turned round to see a figure stumbling towards her.

'Ahh...' was all the man said as he tried to push past her.

'You alright?' she asked suspiciously, as he came into the light, and with a feeling of shock she recognised him. 'Charles Clark.'

'Ahh...' was all the distressed Chris Kent could manage to utter. In a panic he attempted to push past, but Anita was having none of it.

'Stop, I'm a friend. Just calm down.'

'I don't believe you.'

'Well, you better had,' she said, barring his way and taking a quick glance down the street. 'Shit. If you want to get out of this in one piece you had better be quiet – and I mean quiet. Move back down there, your friends are coming up the street. Get down behind the dustbins.'

Chris seemed to understand and together they crouched behind a line of foul-smelling bins full of a nearby café's food waste. Fear kept Chris low while Anita's professionalism kept her alert, and she pressed herself between the bins and listened.

Footsteps, voices, deep gruff voices speaking Russian.

She held her breath, praying that Crypto would not give them away, and as the men passed the passage entrance she finally relaxed.

'Phew, they've gone. Wait here while I look.'

Chris was shaking and had no intention of going anywhere. He couldn't anyway: fear had turned his legs to jelly.

'Okay, they have gone. Right, we need to get you out of here and quickly. Get up and I'll think what I can do with you.'

That was as far as she got, for Chris Kent, though not quite Superman, had regained enough of his faculties to pick up a dustbin lid and smash it down hard on Anita's head. When she finally came round, Superman had thrown off the kryptonite and flown.

Things were moving fast for Jimi. The ninety-minute flight from Battersea Heliport had him on the ground in Scarborough not long after midday. His first task was to speak with Anita, but when he finally found her she was at the accident and emergency department of the local hospital.

'What happened to you, are you alright?'

'I'm fine, just a bit painful that's all. Nothing I can't handle.'

Jimi looked at her, relieved to see her injuries were superficial. She had taken a nasty blow to the back of her head but had survived with nothing more than mild concussion and a few stitches.

'Can you carry on? I can take you off the case. Let me know what you have found out and I'll take over.'

'You bloody well will not. I owe that scrag one and I've almost cracked the case. You don't think I will let you take all the glory, do you?'

'I must admit you do sound like your old self. I understand the doctor is reasonably happy with you?'

'Yes, I'm just feeling a bit sore, that's all.'

'How did Crypto jump you? I thought he wasn't particularly physical.'

'I found him staggering along an alleyway where I was hiding from Tom and Jerry. He looked like he was on the run – out of breath and helpless, I thought, but he must have recovered and jumped me when I was looking out for the Russians. I have no idea where he is, but that gallery owner will tell us, I'm sure. We need to pay a visit and quiz the people there.'

'Back to work it is, then. I have a car waiting, we can talk on the way.'

'That's reassuring,' she said, standing up.

Jimi watched her, concerned, but managing to get herself into the car unaided left him feeling that she could carry on.

'Right, let's see what we can find. Driver, take us to the Blands Cliff gallery, will you?'

It was late-afternoon by the time the unmarked police car dropped them off at the bottom of the hill and Jimi wondered if it was still open. As they approached the gallery entrance their attention was taken by the picture in the window.

'So that is what they were so interested in,' said Anita, seeing the portrait for the first time. 'It's him alright, and a damn good likeness.'

'Place looks deserted, I hope we're not too late.' said Jimi, pushing the door open. 'We're in look,' he said entering, stopping short and exclaiming, 'Jesus, what a mess. Anita, speak with your friend at the police station, it looks likely we will need their help.'

Jimi proceeded to fully enter the gallery and Anita followed, stepping over broken pottery littering the floor. The two amphorae guarding the door were lying face down, a painting sat at an awkward angle on one wall, and there was blood on the white-painted countertop.

'Crikey when did this happen,' she said, turning her head towards the sound of banging coming from the rear of the gallery.

'I'll have a look back there. Call the police and your CCTV operator, ask if she's seen anything,' said Jimi, making his way towards the source of the noise.

'Leave it with me,' said Anita, taking out her mobile first to call the police and then the town hall.

'Victoria, we have a problem. I need you to have a look at Blands Cliff, or as near as you can. Remember the woman with Clark? Can you do a facial recognition on her as well as Clark, and start looking around the Blands Cliff area from midday? There has been some violence. I suspect two men who were in the vicinity just a short time ago. If either of them shows up, maybe we can get a lead on them,' she said, her attention diverted by Jimi coming back into the main area, helping an injured woman along.

'Baaastards,' said the Australian, touching a tender spot on her face.

'What happened?' Jimi asked.

'Who the hell are you?'

'Police – well, sort of. Was it two men, big men with foreign accents?'

'Yes, but only one spoke. They were after Jade but roughed me up first, the baaastards. They wanted to know who had painted the portrait in the window and where they lived. I told 'em a pack of lies earlier but they came back and tried to frighten the shit outta me.'

'How did they know this Jade was the artist?'

''Cause we were the only two in the gallery. Jade went looking for her boyfriend and then came back a couple of hours later.'

'Did she find him?'

'Naw, he disappeared. She was quite upset; said she couldn't understand what was wrong. I thought they would just quiz her and leave and then I could call the police. They did leave, but they took Jade with them.'

'Where does she live?'

'Up on the cliff above Cornelian Bay, a bungalow at the far end of the row.'

Anita's phone rang. It was Victoria, her voice agitated and anxious.

'The CCTV camera at the south end of the foreshore road picked up the woman less than an hour ago. She is with two men, they bundled her into a car. An onlooker tried to intervene but one of the thugs knocked him to the ground and the car sped off. I have the registration number and I will pass it on to the police. In the meantime, I have it heading out of town along the coast road towards Filey. I'll ring you when I have more information.'

'Thanks, Victoria, that's good work. What about Clark, have you found him?'

'No, but I will keep looking.'

'Is this Cornelian Bay near Filey?' she asked Sherilee.

'No, but it's on the way.'

Hilly walks and the town's steep roads had improved Chris's stamina, made him noticeably stronger than when he was a city dweller. It stood him in good stead as he walked at a brisk pace along the cliff-top path. He had run from the scene of his attack on the woman, wandered aimlessly for a time until he thought to get to Jade's place, find sanctuary. He was almost there another hundred yards and he would be safe. If he could stay with her for a while and then move on he felt he had a chance, but to linger meant the two thugs would find him for certain.

The bungalow came into sight and he breathed a sigh of relief. 'Just a few more metres,' he told himself, and then he could relax.

He had no idea if Jade was at home, only that he had left the gallery in a hurry and not told her why. He was worried. If she wasn't in there was nothing he could do except wait for her return home.

He reached the bungalow and went to the rear, feeling on the windowsill where he knew she kept the key. With fumbling fingers he managed to open the door.

Surely the two thugs would not be able to connect Jade with him. He had left the gallery in a hurry, before the Russians had a chance to enter.

But the woman in the alley – who was she?

Slumping on a kitchen chair, he tried to gather his thoughts. In horror it dawned upon him that if they learned Jade was the portrait artist then they might make the connection.

'Bugger,' he said out loud, putting his head in his hands. He was in that same position ten minutes later when the door burst open.

'Aha... Charles Clark, accountant, late of London. Well, how are you, Mr Clark? You have led us a merry dance but now we have you.'

Charles – Chris, even: he wasn't sure just who he was any more – groaned, his stamina all but evaporated. He had always found Sergei intimidating. Feeling cornered, he did not know which way to turn. Then Markov appeared, dragging Jade through the doorway.

'Oh Chris,' she said, her face smeared with blood. 'Who are these people?'

'Let her go,' Chris said in an uncharacteristically authoritative voice. For a moment Sergei paused.

'Ha, the brave boyfriend, is it? Well now, Mr Clark, there will be no running away this time,' he said with a sneer – and suddenly Chris understood, the words striking like a hammer blow.

He felt physically sick. The tone, the accent... It was him, wasn't it? It was them. He had felt all along, had somehow known, that the men restraining him on the London street were Potanin's men. At the time their features had been unknown to him. They must have been Sergei and Markov, but how?

'You... How?' he managed to say.

Sergei laughed. 'Let's just say we have a good make-up artist. Now, down to business. You know what we want: the letter addressed to Comrade Potanin, which you stole.'

'What letter?'

'Come now, you know what I am talking about. You are the only one to have seen it. Where is it?' he said, nodding to Markov who grabbed Jade's hair and pulled her head back, eliciting a scream of terror. 'Tell me. She is dispensable. If you want her to live, I need that letter.'

Chris really wasn't a Superman, far from it, and under the Russian's threats he wilted.

'Safety deposit box, I put it in a safety deposit box.'

'Where?'

'Hatton Garden.'

'Domonic Give me the number.'

'I can't.'

Sergei nodded at Markov and again a piercing scream filled the small kitchen. 'Yes you can, tell me now,' he shouted.

'It's not as simple as that. To get past security you need a fingerprint.'

'Which finger?'

Unthinking, Chris held up the index finger of his right hand.

'Cut it off, Markov.'

The big man grinned and Chris's face turned white. At the same time Jade fainted, slipping from Markov's grasp to lay slumped at his feet. He simply looked down at her and then reached around to his back for his knife. Charles Clark had glimpsed that knife once before, but this time it was Chris Kent's eyes that widened with fear.

'N-n-no, you can't. It isn't enough. Eyes, eyes,' he repeated.

'Eyes what?'

'The security machine reads irises as well, and they must match the fingerprint before you can gain access to the vault. I must look at the camera.'

'Take his eye out as well, Markov.'

'Noooo... You can't. If you do, you will never get in.'

Sergei thought for a moment. 'If you can't get to the safety deposit box then no one can. Perhaps it is easier to just kill you both here.'

'You can kill me but not her, she knows nothing.'

'She knows us.'

'You won't say anything, will you, Jade?' he said to the barely conscious woman.

'Oh Jade,' he said as she started to come round. 'Are you alright? You can't harm her, you mustn't,' he said, glancing at Sergei.

Looking down again, his eyes softened and she looked back at him, the fear in hers suddenly dissipating.

'Oh Chris, you are so brave.'

'Fuck brave, he's an idiot,' said Markov from between gritted teeth. 'So, we kill her and we hire a car to take you back to London. You will open that box, my friend.'

'Not if you kill her.'

'We take her to London as well then.'

Chris felt bewildered, though not as bewildered as Jade. She was about to lose her life and had half believed Superman was coming to her rescue. Angels were singing and she felt the earth move – well, not quite. The earth didn't move but the door did.

It burst open and Jimi crashed into the room, his bulk finding the flimsy door no obstacle. With his gun gripped in both hands, he barked an order.

'Hold it right there!'

The Russians, quick to adapt, took no notice. Markov grabbed Jade, hauling her to her feet, and held his knife at her throat while Sergei produced a hidden gun.

'Not so fast. I don't know who you are, but just back off or I will shoot,' he said menacingly.

Jimi relented, pointing his gun skywards. Everyone in the room froze – everyone except Chris who, unnoticed for the second time during a confrontation with these men, swung his arm at Markov's face and knocked him off balance. In surprise, he let go of Jade and filled the room with Russian expletives. Chris lunged again, less successfully this time, and the knife sliced through his jacket and into his shoulder muscles.

Sergei on the other hand, riddled with the conflicting obligations to find the letter, keep the big black man at bay, and above all to get out of the house in one piece failed on all counts. Anita appeared in the doorway, her Beretta pointing straight at him. Before he could react, Jimi leaped forward to smash him in the face with a well-aimed blow and Anita switched her attention to Markov.

'Hands up!' she screamed at him. He had little choice; his human shield was gone and Sergei was prostrate on the floor. 'Police are here, Jimi, I hear the sirens.'

Jimi said nothing, turning Sergei face down on the floor and pinning his arms behind his back as he took several electrical wire wraps from his pocket to bind the Russian's wrists.

'You next,' he said to Markov.

As he bound the second Russian, Anita turned her attention to Crypto. He had slumped to the floor, his face ashen. He was losing blood, his jacket already stained red. Quickly, she slid it off his body. Jade offered her first aid kit and between the two of them they managed to stem the flow of blood.

'Looks like we made it just in time,' said the Superintendent, following two of his officers into the now-overcrowded kitchen.

'Yeah, just about,' said Jimi, slipping his gun into his waistband.

'An ambulance is on its way,' said the Superintendent, looking sympathetically at the stabbing victim who's eyes flickered open every few seconds as shock overtook him.

-

The light of the half-moon was just enough for the casual observer to pick out the converted fishing boat as it crossed the invisible line separating the Atlantic Ocean from temporarily tranquil Scottish waters. But tonight there were no observers, casual or otherwise. Captain Kucherov had made sure of that.

Standing with his legs apart, he grasped the ship's binnacle and looked out into the empty black night. His bridge, bathed in dull red light, foretold of the secrecy of the mission. Beside him, the officer of the watch held a pair of binoculars to his eyes and scanned the seascape on the lookout for telltale lights, but there were none. They were alone.

'Nothing to report, Captain.'

Captain Kucherov nodded and leaned forward to examine the large navigation screen, studying for several minutes the coloured lines and symbols that defined their position on the planet.

'We are closing in on the waypoint, I see. Tell the men to get ready, number one.'

The officer picked up a short-wave radio on the desk and spoke briefly. He had plotted the course from their base at Severomorsk in the Murmansk Oblast, a meandering route designed to obscure the vessel's true destination. From leaving Murmansk Fjord until they cleared the North Cape, the captain had ordered that the ship's identification system should remain switched off. Now, as they entered Scottish waters, he ordered it turned off once more.

Legally, the transmitter should transmit their position every three minutes but there was an overarching need to mask the boat's position for a few hours, at least. If challenged at a later date they could always say they had suffered an electrical failure, yet they could still show up on any passing ship's radar and have their position logged. But tonight they were alone.

Chapter 11

Jimi's work was far from done. The prisoners were secure enough in the cells at the local police station, but he needed to interrogate them, find out everything they knew, find the elusive letter. It seemed certain the two Russians didn't have it; it would be pointless them going to all that trouble to locate Crypto if it was already in their possession.

'Superintendent Lester, I need the prisoners transferred south for interrogation. I have informed my department of the situation up here and they are organising a military vehicle and guards. Until they get here, please keep a good watch. These are dangerous men.'

'I can see that, sir. Don't worry, we will keep them secure until the prison van arrives. Can I ask, are they terrorists or organised crime?'

'You can ask, Superintendent. All I can tell you right now is that we believe they are a threat to national security. Now if you will excuse me, I need to visit the hospital.'

Anita looked up from her seat outside the private ward as Jimi walked along the corridor towards her. Her head still throbbed from the blow she had taken from the dustbin lid, and gingerly she touched the dressing over her stitches. The excitement engendered in the cliff-top bungalow incident was still with her, and she was glad that no one other than Crypto had sustained injuries. For him to receive a stab wound was unfortunate but Jimi had decided shock tactics were in order – best to burst in and confront the two thugs before they knew what had hit them. It had almost worked, and Jimi's forethought to use her as backup was the decider. Without her intervention, the outcome could have been truly horrendous.

'How's the patient?'

'Okay so far. He's sleeping right now and his friend is with him. She won't let go after his show of bravery. She reckons he saved her life.'

'And you didn't?'

'It's my job.'

'What did the doctor say, when can we talk to Crypto?'

'The doctor who attended to him when we first arrived says he needs to sleep, the transfusion will help. If we wait until the morning, he thinks he will be fit enough to answer questions.'

'I could do with some answers now. Never mind, I have spoken with Raul Martínez and he, I must say, is more than pleased. To lose an agent is bad enough but to lose two was disastrous. I think the whole of the embassy staff felt it, so for us to have apprehended their killers and find Crypto has come as some relief. At least we have the suspects locked up, and with a bit of legal manoeuvring I expect they will be off to the States to stand trial.'

'Good luck there, the Americans don't stand any nonsense.'

'No, and now we need to decide how to handle Crypto. I will look in on him, then when the prison van arrives I will need to coordinate the transfer with the local police.'

Anita nodded and sat back in her chair.

Although Crypto's injuries were serious, the woman's injuries were superficial; cuts and bruises easily attended to by the paramedic. She would be a comfort to Crypto when he came round, and as Jimi entered the private room Jade turned towards the doorway, her expression one of worry. Jimi smiled and looked down at the forlorn figure of Crypto lying in the bed, plasma bottle hanging beside him, oxygen mask obscuring his features.

'How is he?'

'Sleeping, he seems okay,' said Jade, still unaware of who Jimi was.

'And how are you? It must have been an ordeal.'

'I'm okay, just bruising and a small cut on my hand. Chris is the one who suffered. It's a good job you turned up when you did. How did you know, who are you?'

'When this is all over you may learn why I am here, but it's not over yet. I must go now. I'm glad you are on the mend, so I'll leave Crypto in your capable hands for now.'

'Crypto?'

'Ah... Just a nickname in case we confused him with someone else.'

An hour before dawn on a flat empty ocean, the ship hove to and the captain gave the order to begin the operation, the first officer in turn relayed the command to the deck party. Captain Kucherov pursed his lips and left his seat to walk to the aft of the bridge. He looked through the reinforced glass window to the deck below, where the silhouetted figures of sailors and technicians busied themselves. One operated a deck crane, its hawser vanishing into the modified fish hold, and as the captain watched a sleek object slowly rose from the darkness below. Eight metres long and torpedo-shaped, the object emerged to swing above the men's heads, gradually coming to rest a metre or so above the sea.

It was the best of its type that Russian engineers could produce; an undersea autonomous vehicle essential for the surveillance of Russia's enemies. Most of its hull had been produced by a three-dimensional printer in a top-secret material whose specification Russian hackers had stolen from the American navy. The propulsion system remained aligned, ridged, yet in just a few minutes that stiff mechanical fin would articulate and become a thing of beauty, oscillating, mimicking the tail-fin of a dolphin. It would silently propel the autonomous submarine twelve miles to its destination on the island of Fudensey to begin its mission between the Outer Hebrides and the mainland of Scotland. The machine could stay at sea for many days, unobserved, patrolling the Minch as far south as Rathlin Island and right up to the Butt of Lewis, an area rich in both British and American submarines.

The rout of the Russian army and the ineffectual use of air power had left the navy as the only capable force of the Russian Federation, but even they were finding it difficult to patrol the high seas without a challenge from NATO. The only real success was the submarine fleet, a mixture of nuclear-powered ballistic vessels, and others capable of guided missile attack. Around forty of them were based in the Murmansk Oblast, and Captain Kucherov's mission was to deliver the drone to the waters of Scotland's west coast for intelligence gathering. If the operation proved successful; he would return several times more to deliver a whole secret fleet of robots.

Lifting his binoculars, he scanned the horizon.

'Nothing, Yuri?'

'No, Captain. All clear,' said the sailor with eyes on the ship's instruments.

With a grunt of satisfaction Captain Kucherov turned his attention back to the operation taking place below. The dark torpedo shape was clear of the hull now and hovering above the sea, the crew guiding its movements with lines. After a hand signal from the leading officer, the black shape settled onto the surface of the sea. A diver slipped the dark body from its restraints, leaving the submarine to begin its journey towards the Scottish coast.

The sky over the capital was clear, with just a hint of cloud to the west as the helicopter sank gently onto the helipad. The journey had taken just over an hour and Chris, lying on a stretcher, could do no more than stare up at the machine's interior. Beside him a male nurse sat in silence, and opposite, Jimi looked out of the window with plenty on his mind. He had left Anita to tie up loose ends with the local police after he had supervised the transfer of the prisoners. Markov, sullen and uncooperative had climbed in to the secure van first, Sergei following, his head drooping from the pain of a broken jaw. He was a far more subdued sight in handcuffs and standard-issue prison uniform than when he was threatening violence.

'Quite an eventful twenty-four hours, Ms Simms.

Let's hope you don't visit us too often, eh?'
Superintendent Lester had said, watching the prisoner
transfer.

'I'm sorry, Superintendent?' she had replied, her
mind on other things.

'I was saying that the events of the past day or so are
something I wouldn't like to have to deal with too often.'

'I'm sure.'

'So, what happens now? You will be taking the
prisoners to a secure place, no doubt. And you – will you
be leaving us?'

'I will shortly, as soon as I have made a phone call.'

'I must write a report and advice from above is to
keep it confidential. Apparently, your department will
use it for evidence. That's not our normal way of doing
things.'

'No, but this isn't a normal case, Superintendent. The
fewer people who know about it, the better. Please have
a word with any of your officers who were privy to
events – remind them of the Official Secrets Act and the
consequences of divulging confidential information, and
incidentally, the CCTV personnel. Have a word with
those two women from the art gallery as well. I'm sure
they are still upset, but they mustn't talk about what
they endured. This case is of national importance and
should not become common knowledge. Do I make
myself clear?'

'Of course.'

'Good. If you will excuse me then I will be on my
way.'

The policeman nodded and did not offer his hand to
shake. The woman was formidable but he was glad to
see her leaving his patch. When it came to the matter of
national security, he knew she had an advantage over

him. It would be wise to acquiesce.

The guards climbed into the armoured prison van and Anita watched it leave before walking to her car. She wanted to get away from the place as quickly as she could.

'Jimi, everything okay?'

'Yes, just about. The prisoners are on their way, so we can be on ours.'

'Yes, so far so good. Just one thing, though. I mentioned that I suspect someone from Islington police station is passing on information, and these two must have had inside intel to be in Scarborough when they were. We only received that information a few days ago. I'm not sure who, but someone is leaking.'

'I'll have a think about it and catch up with you when you get back.'

'What time is it now? Ten thirty: I should be back in London by mid-afternoon. I expect you will be briefing Commander Pearson.'

'Yes, I'm seeing him as soon as the chopper gets me back to London. How's your head?'

'I'll survive.'

In his condition Charles hadn't known much of the bright private room in Scarborough hospital. If he had; it would seem a long way from the military hospital he was in now. The room was austere, containing only the bare minimum, the small window and low ceiling instilling a feeling of confinement.

'Where is this? Am I in prison?' he said to the nurse checking his blood pressure.

'No, you're not in prison.'

'Where are we?'

'North London, but I can't say any more than that,

I'm afraid.'

'So I am in prison?'

'No, just a secure hospital where you are safe.'

Charles, his pseudonym now useless, lay back in his bed. The stitches holding his wound suddenly tightened, and he groaned. 'Oh... God.'

'Take it easy. Do you want the pillow moving?'

'No, I'm okay,' said Charles, resigned to his fate. 'How is Jade?'

'Sorry, I don't know any Jade. Try to get some rest, and if you want a sedative just say. Someone will be along to see you soon; they'll explain things better than I can. Do you want some water?'

'Oh, yes please.'

Commander Pearson replaced his desk telephone and sat back in his chair. His visitor had arrived and would be with him in a few minutes; just time for him to order a pot of coffee and two cups. He expected Agent Russet would be ready for a strong coffee, and as he replaced the receiver, he heard a tap on the office door.

'Come.'

The door opened and a sombre-looking Jimi Russet walked in.

'Jimi, good to have you back. I've ordered coffee. You can give me a resumé of the operation until it arrives. What happened?'

'We nearly lost him, and nearly lost me, in fact. Agent Simms's quick thinking saved us both. She did particularly well, her injury no obstacle.'

'Injury how? Is it serious?'

'She's tough, she's okay. In a panic Crypto hit her with a dustbin lid, a metal one, and knocked her out for a time.'

'Ouch, sounds serious, but she *is* okay?'

'Seems to be, she doesn't give up easily.'

'So Crypto is now in the Chelmsford secure hospital for observation and a debrief. This business about a letter is a puzzle, the catalyst for this whole situation.'

'Yes, I think so. My opposite number at the U.S. Embassy told me Crypto was an informant, that he had called the number they said to ring in case of emergency. The operator detected panic in his voice when he said that he had seen the contents of a confidential letter from the Russian Embassy. He said his life was in danger.'

'They were bringing him in?'

'Yes, to take him to a safe house and get to the bottom of why he had broken cover. But as you know, two Russian thugs turned up and took out their agents.'

'A bad situation.'

'Yes, the Americans are still reeling, angry. They will want to carry out an interrogation and no doubt have the suspects extradited for trial in the States.'

'That could be a problem in the short term. We've had a couple of extradition cases and if the papers get hold of this one, they will have a field day. Salisbury, you know. I will have to inform the PM. In the meantime, see what Crypto knows and find out if there is a problem on British soil. If there is, we are responsible for dealing with it. The Americans will have to wait.'

Always happy behind the wheel of her powerful car, Anita raced through the gears, threading her way through the slow-moving traffic and towards the M11 turnoff. Her orders were to meet Jimi at the secure hospital and together they would debrief Crypto. The mission outcome so far was positive and the Russian hitmen were behind bars, but still there was the nagging question of how they had known where to look for Crypto.

The search for Crypto had begun in Islington police station. Was it someone in that building, in CID? Who could have leaked details – someone running the case? She had spoken with some of the officers there and was none too impressed by their sense of urgency. Were they trying to slow the investigation?

And what about the analyst, Tabz Belafonte – she had worked on the case at the police station *and* for the Secret Service at Vauxhall. She was the one who had discovered Crypto's whereabouts, someone who had intimate details of the case. As a judge of character Anita had her down as loyal and honest, but others in the police department who encountered her might have learned something. What about her superior officer? He would have been privy to information about Crypto, or perhaps it was someone else in the chain of command. Careless office talk was another possibility; an unguarded conversation, a note on a pad. She had no real idea of where to look, but the analyst would be a good starting point. For the rest of her journey she turned over every possibility, only relenting when she passed through the gate of the secure hospital and found Jimi waiting for her.

'That was quick, Anita, almost as fast as I was by helicopter,' said Jimi, surprised by her timely arrival.

'Well, I was flying too,' she said with a twinkle in her eye.

'No problem speeding? You must have been speeding...'

'Yes, I was pulled over near Nottingham but once he saw my warrant card and I explained that I was on urgent government business, the cop radioed ahead and I wasn't bothered again.'

'Okay, I have spoken with Commander Pearson and he wants us to conduct Crypto's debrief. He says we know as much as anyone about him, and after his rescue he expects him to be cooperative. We need to find out what the hell it was that scared him so much. Pearson will advise the Americans as the situation develops; he expects them to push us to hand over Tom and Jerry and, in all probability, they will want to talk to Crypto too as he was working for them. Right, let's have a look at him. Down here on the left,' he said, leading her along the corridor.

'How's he doing?'

'The doctor says he's on the mend,' he said, opening the door.

Charles was lying flat on his back, staring at the ceiling and still very much aware of his stab wound. He recounted the incident repeatedly. Events had moved fast after he had caught Sergei peering through the gallery window at his portrait, seeing recognition dawn. At that moment his heart had stopped. Jade was unaware of his dark secret; how could she know? He'd been in no position to explain, and he was wondering what she must have thought when the door opened.

'Bloody hell, what have I done? Oh... it's you. Am I in trouble?'

Jimi looked at him and shook his head. 'No, Mr Clark, you're not in trouble but we do need to talk to you. My name is Alan Donovan and this is Ms Simms; we work for the Ministry of Defence and we are here to try to find out exactly why you were on the run. We know about the murders you witnessed – the culprits are in a military prison and are not going anywhere soon. You are quite safe here, Mr Clark.'

'Mr Clark... It's a relief to get my real name back, at least.'

'Yes, we presumed you were travelling on an assumed name. You took some finding, I can tell you.'

Charles looked at the end of the bed and winced.

'Are you alright? I can ask a nurse to make you more comfortable, a painkiller, perhaps.'

'I'm okay,' said Charles, adjusting his position. 'It stings a bit, that's all. They have told me I will live.'

'Let's hope so. Now, why were you on the run? The Americans said you called them prior to your disappearance. They said you sounded agitated, that you mentioned you had information.'

'Yes, that's what started all this. I work – past tense now, I suppose – for a Russian oligarch. With the situation as precarious as it is, he managed to hang on and run his businesses for quite a long time, but just a few days ago the authorities told him to leave the country. When he left, that thug Sergei and his henchman Markov took charge of his affairs in London. I never liked Sergei, and I liked him even less when he took over the running of the operation. A thug, a dangerous man.'

'Yes, indeed. So, you knew them?'

'They ran security for Potanin's businesses.'

'What was it that caused you to run? The letter?'

'Yes, the letter. Well, a sort-of letter. It was on Russian Embassy headed paper, just a few lines in Russian.'

'And you can read Russian?'

'Nope, haven't a clue.'

'Explain, please.'

'I copied the text into Google Translate.'

'What did it say?'

'Not much, just that the Kremlin was awarding Andrei the "Merit to the Fatherland" medal for his work.'

'His work on what?'

'I don't know exactly. The translation was not great but it mentioned an island and a military operation.'

'What island? What is the connection, Mr Clark? I cannot see how the bestowing of an award would cause you to run, or why the Russians pursued you as they did. Is there something I am missing?'

Charles looked up at his interrogator and said, 'I suppose it's not obvious without some background knowledge. Just over two years ago, before Potanin knew he would have to leave the country, he asked a surveyor to find an uninhabited island somewhere off the west coast of Scotland. He had learned that there were lots of islands that were once the home of local farmers – crofters, you know – and sometimes one would come on the market.'

'So, you purchased an island on behalf of Potanin?' said Anita.

'Yes, in the Hebrides. I took care of the paperwork. The owner was another Russian who had just dabbled with the place, I don't think he ever set foot on the island. Just a speculative deal, I suppose.'

'And who is this Russian?'

'Boris Scarperov.'

'Where can we find him?' said Jimi.

'I have no idea. Sorry, can't help you with that one.'

'So, again, what caused you to run?' pressed Anita.

'I overheard a conversation; they were discussing the purchase.'

'Who was discussing the purchase?'

'Mr Potanin and Sergei. I was about to get the papers signed to complete the deal. They were speaking English, not their normal modus operandi. Mr Potanin had to speak with me in English because I can't speak Russian, but when he was dealing with his associates, he would more often than not speak in Russian. Easier for them, I suppose, and it cut me out of the conversation. A lot went on during the time I worked for him and his companies. Some of it went over my head, I didn't need to know, though I suspected some transactions were not quite legal. Well, one day they were talking inside Sergei's office and the door was open. It was just as the deal to buy the island was ready to finalise, I had the papers for Potanin to sign in my hand. I heard him say to Sergei that the Russian military were pleased, that they would be taking over in the not-too-distant future. They didn't see me, and hearing about the Russian military encouraged me to make myself scarce.'

'So, what did you do?'

'I crept back to my office. A few minutes later Sergei came and summoned me to see his boss.'

'About the purchase of the island?'

'Yes.'

'And what happened?'

'I took the papers back to Potanin's office for signing and that was all.'

'The purchase was completed and they had no idea you had eavesdropped?'

'I suppose so.'

'What can you tell us about this island?' asked Anita. 'Can you identify it?'

'I don't know where it is, just that it is somewhere in the Hebrides.'

'We need to pinpoint it. What's it called?'

'Fludsey, Blindsey, Fodsey... something like that.'

'So, what's its significance?'

'If my translation was correct and the Russian military are involved, I can only think that something untoward is about to happen on that island. It worried me. I was dealing with powerful and dangerous people and I reasoned, rightly or wrongly, that if they suspected I had linked the Russian military to the island, however tenuously, then I was in trouble. When Sergei came bursting into my office looking for the letter, I just about wet my pants.'

'I can imagine.'

'Fudensey, I think it's called Fudensey.'

'Did you never go there?' asked Jimi.

'No, why would I? I just looked after the paperwork. The surveyors we used would be the ones to advise us.'

'Who would that be?'

'Murry and Murry, I think.'

'And where can we find them if we need to talk to them?'

'Er... They were from out of town, I think somewhere in Woking,' he said, beginning to worry.

What if these people dig deeper? he thought. What if they discover I siphoned off some of the purchase money?

Cutting short his concern, Anita, scrolling over a map of the Western Isles on her smartphone, said, 'I think I have found it. It's just off the coast of North Uist.'

Jimi took his mobile phone from his pocket, said 'Fudensey' to it in a precise manner, and a few seconds later the screen filled with text and a photograph of a large house.

'According to this, Fudensey was the home of one

Angus MacRae, a famous powerboat racer in the thirties. As you say, it's between Harris and Uist.'

'That would be right,' said Charles.

'Where is this letter now? Presumably you didn't have it on you when Tom and Jerry tried to kill you.'

'Tom and Jerry?'

'Codenames for the two Russians.'

'Oh. No, it's in a safety deposit box in Hatton Garden.'

'We will need to know where. What's the name of the depository?'

'Hardy and Company.'

'I'll get on to that,' Anita said, looking up the number on her telephone. 'I'll make the call outside.'

Jimi nodded and turned back to a visibly relieved Charles Clark. He had just unloaded the problem that had been weighing him down, and no one had mentioned anything about missing funds.

Chapter 12

Dr Herman Schultz was an expert on the Bronze Age, an academic celebrated in Scottish archaeological circles for his discoveries on Orkney, and he had recently come to the attention of the Russian navy. The top-secret project conceived at Olenya Guba, the secretive submarine base of the Northern Fleet, was well advanced with just a few details left to finalise, and Dr Schultz was one of them.

A chance meeting between Andrei Potanin and Admiral Anatoly Semenov, the officer in charge of clandestine operations at the Northern Fleet's submarine base, had given the admiral an idea.

'Comrade Potanin, you enjoyed your tour of the base? I must say you have good connections; it's not every day we allow a civilian in here.'

'Yes, Comrade Admiral, impressive. I was always interested in the Soviet Navy and had ambitions of joining when I was younger.'

'Instead you became a billionaire. Not much of a choice, I would say.'

Andrei laughed. Being a billionaire in Russia had its perks as well as its downsides, and with time on his hands he had requested a visit to the Northern Fleet to play out a boyhood dream.

'The new submarines are particularly interesting, so big.'

'Without giving too much away, I can say that quite soon a new type of missile is coming into service. Those two submarines are the first in a class that can carry upwards of forty-eight of them. NATO will not know what has hit them. Tell me, Andrei, what effect has the West's sanctions had on you? I see you are returning to the Motherland.'

'I hardly feel them. My businesses are non-military, property mostly, and I am investing a lot of resources in Dubai.'

'So, the United Kingdom is unprofitable now.'

'Not unprofitable, just difficult. I have people in place to look after my affairs.'

'Perhaps you could build a decent hotel here in Severomorsk. Even a dog would complain about the accommodation allotted to me when I visit. I have seen some of these modern places.'

'I'm not sure I will be investing in Russia just yet. I purchased an island off the west coast of Scotland last year, and that's one investment in Britain I am not sure is worth keeping.'

'An island? Whereabouts, Andrei? I have always been fascinated by the coast around Scotland, particularly the Clyde,' the admiral said with some interest.

'The Western Isles, the Hebrides. You know them?'

'Very well, the NATO submarine base at Faslane in particular.'

Andrei Potanin had paused for a few moments, his entrepreneurial mind working overtime. 'It's in an ideal location for spying on the British and the Americans operating out of Faslane. If you could see them, I suppose?'

'Andrei, you are not a naval man but your foresight impresses me. Describe this island of yours.'

'I have never visited the place, it's just an investment. It is not a large island but it has a substantial main house and a small dock area with an enclosed boathouse built by a previous owner, an enthusiastic powerboat racer before the Great Patriotic War.'

'Interesting... and could we use this island of yours for, shall we say, a recreational facility for retired admirals?'

'Hardly, it is Scotland. Cold and wet at the best of times.'

'I joke with you, my friend. What you have described gives me an idea. I presume you will assist the navy in any endeavour we might wish to pursue. I'm sure the Kremlin would be only too happy to reward you with an honour for your services.'

'Of course, I am always happy to help our country.'

'I will be in touch. I need to leave; I have a committee meeting in a few minutes. What is the name of this island again?'

Admiral Semenov could not get the idea of a secret base at the heart of the British sea lanes out of his head, but first he needed to refresh his knowledge of the waters off the west coast of Scotland. Summoning an aide to find a chart of the Western Isles, he was soon spreading it across his desk and tracing a line with his forefinger from the Minch through the sea of the Hebrides and south to Malin Head. To any naval man the possibilities were obvious, and sitting down he looked closer, scanning contours, depths, and lurking dangers.

Could the Special Operations Force create a clandestine base to spy on the Royal Navy? he asked himself, and after perusing the chart for a few more minutes, he decided they could. The undertaking would be dangerous, he knew that, and the project would need thinking through, but from the chart he could see that the island was accessible from several directions. It had a jetty for visiting craft and the old stone-built house was visible from the seaward side. What about the locals? Fishermen no doubt fished the seas around the island, and if Russian fishermen were anything to go by they would be nosey. Any activity on a long-abandoned island would draw their attention, speculation would be rife, and there was the possibility of unwanted visitors. A diversion needed devising, a cover for the real work.

The admiralty warmed to the idea and gave Semenov the go-ahead, allowing him to pull together a small team of experts. After much discussion the team put a plan together. The admiral asked for and received the latest equipment to perform the tasks laid out in the plan, and a cover story of an archaeological dig to disguise the operation was born. So long as the people involved in the archaeology did not mix directly with the team running the clandestine operation, there seemed little chance of discovery. Attention would be on the dig and not the Russian navy personnel.

Admiral Semenov had permission to begin operations, he had money, he had equipment, and the selection of the team to run the base was well underway. All he required to complete preparations was for Potanin to approach Dr Schultz.

The bus from Tarbert to the Caledonian MacBrayne ferry terminal at Leverburgh arrived with time to spare. Most passengers were for the connection to Berneray on North Uist, but disembarking with them was a group of three women and a young man. A woman in her late thirties appeared to oversee the group, a woman used to authority. She was dressed in an anorak, with a military-looking rucksack on her back and a holdall in one hand. She turned to speak with two younger people, a male and a female equally burdened, and the three of them, followed by a third woman, began to walk towards the ferry terminal where a line of cars had already formed. Foot passengers huddled round a van selling tea and bacon sandwiches, and amongst them a man put down his half-empty cup and walked to meet the group. They were the first volunteers making their way to the island of Fudensey to take part in an archaeological dig.

'Professor Stock?' the man asked, looking for a response.

'Yes,' said the woman at the forefront of the group, 'I am Professor Stock.'

'Welcome, I am Stewart (not his real name). I look after Fudensey island for the owner. You are the first to arrive,' he said, producing a small notebook. 'Molly Harrington?' he said, looking over the group.

'That's me,' said a pretty freckle-faced young woman.

'Alice Springhorn?'

'Here,' said Anita, raising her hand.

'And you must be Samuel Kennedy.'

The young man returned a weak smile in acknowledgement.

'Good, you are all here. I have our launch waiting just over there,' he said, pointing. 'If you will follow me.'

The party of volunteers, laden down with their luggage, backpacks and sleeping bags, followed Stewart towards a sleek-looking launch moored between two local fishing boats. As they approached a second man appeared, offering his hand to help them aboard.

'This is David, (not his real name) he oversees the launch, our only connection with the outside world. You will be staying in the house; we have made two of the larger bedrooms available, one for the women and one for the men. Dr Schultz is arriving tomorrow with the rest of his people and he will talk to you about your responsibilities when he arrives. No doubt he will speak about the dig site and advise you of a few ground rules. Ready, David?' he said to the boatman, who nodded, taking the shore lines, and slowly pushed the boat away from the dock.

The passengers sat where they could, their bags stowed below, and as the boatman steered towards the open sea David pointed out Fudensey: a dark, low-lying shape on the horizon.

Anita found herself a place on the hull, sitting with her back against the wheelhouse. As the island grew bigger, she wondered what was in store for her. She could see a house set close above a small cove, and as the launch neared the island, she could see the jetty and running from it a short canal leading to a stone-built shed. The boathouse, built by the powerboat-racing laird, no doubt. Stretching away, the topography undulated towards higher ground in the distance. From her limited knowledge of the island, she knew it was no more than two miles long and less than a mile wide, but from this perspective it looked larger. Turning to look at the house and then the jetty, she noticed two men appear. Within just a few minutes they were taking lines to secure the launch.

'If you will step ashore and wait over there, just off the jetty, I will then escort you to the house,' said Stewart, casting an eye over his charges.

'Not quite what I expected,' said Anita to the others, glancing back at the sea. 'How are you all feeling? No one seemed to be up for conversation out there.'

'No, I felt a bit seasick, I must admit,' said Helen Stock. 'But at least we are here. I hope the dig turns out to be as productive as Dr Schultz thinks it could be. Do you know him, Alice?'

'Er... No, I heard about the dig at work.'

'What's your discipline? I am interested in the Picts of Bronze Age Britain and I find the chance to excavate a site from that period very exciting.'

'Oh... Yes, I am a newcomer, I don't have a lot of experience. I work in the archaeological department of Glasgow City Council. I'm not really qualified, more admin, but after starting my new job I liked the idea of pursuing archaeology and that's why I'm here.'

'What exactly do you do?'

Before she could answer, their host began telling them to gather their possessions and follow him to the house, a sturdy two-storey stone-built construction. It was much larger than Anita had expected, with the upper rooms' arched window frames peering down like wise owls. She noted the layout of those windows and the entrance doorway, and wondered if there were other doors leading to the outside. Then she remembered her conversation with the analyst from the Met.

'There is an island, Fudensey, off the coast of Harris in the Hebrides,' Anita had said to Tabz. 'I need you to find out all you can about the place. Give me a call when you find something.'

Just a few hours later she'd had a result: a call back from Tabz.

'The McDougall clan owned the place until the early nineteen eighties when the last laird, Malcolm McDougall, died and his daughter decided to sell. It was his great-grandfather who built the large house and the jetty, but his father was the one to put the island on the map. He was a speedboat enthusiast and built a short canal and boathouse to accommodate his speedboat. For several years he was prominent in offshore powerboat-racing circles until the outbreak of the Second World War put an end to his activities. Since the daughter sold up, the island has changed hands several times and from what I understand, it fell into a state of disrepair. An obscure company registered in the Bahamas is the present owner, and I am pretty sure Andrei Potanin controls the company. This might interest you: there's currently an advert in *British Archaeology* magazine for a dig organised by a Dr Schultz, an academic working at the University of the Highlands and Islands. He is looking for volunteers to carry out a dig on the island. Something about a roundhouse.'

'That sounds a little strange,' said Anita. 'When is this dig taking place?'

'Well, from what I can gather they plan to begin the dig on the twelfth.'

Anita's ears pricked up. 'Thanks, Tabz, that's helpful.'

How helpful, she wasn't quite sure. It was the third of the month already and Anita knew she needed to be part of that dig if she was to discover anything. Why was an archaeological dig taking place there? It didn't add up. Then, suddenly, her eyes narrowed.

'Was it a cover for something?'

'What?' said Tabz at the other end of the phone.

'Oh sorry, talking to myself. Well, thanks for that, let me know if you find out any more,' she had said, ending the call and sitting back in her chair.

If her calculation was correct, the people running the island were opening the place up after it had lain dormant for years, and they wanted the outside world to believe they had nothing to hide. What was really going on? Anita wondered as she looked up at the house. And the men who had ferried them to the island: who were they really? They sounded more southern than Scottish, with rounded accents – accents that did not ring true. She was still turning possibilities over in her mind when Stewart reached the porch and opened the door to the house.

'In here, ladies and gentlemen. There are two rooms upstairs which we have turned into dormitories for the duration of your excavations. Please use these stairs only. There is another staircase at the other end of the house but the steps are not safe and we cannot afford an accident. Bad publicity and maybe a claim. That reminds me, you will need to sign a disclaimer. If you will follow me, the rooms are up here,' he said, beginning to climb the staircase. On reaching the top he opened the first door he came to. 'Ladies,' he said, gesturing for them to enter.

With inquisitive eyes, the women looked at their new home.

'I'll have the bed by the window,' said Helen, not standing on ceremony and throwing her rucksack onto the camp bed to make her claim.

'Fine, I'll stay by the door,' said Anita, as Molly chose one of the remaining camp beds. Dumping her bag, she said, 'Shall we explore downstairs? I'm dying for a cuppa.'

Jimi had briefed Commander Pearson on Agent Simms's involvement earlier, as she was preparing to take the train to join the archaeologists, explaining how they had substituted her for a woman expecting to join the excavation team. It was then that the commander made the decision to go to Scotland. As her controller he should watch over her.

'You think there is more to this operation than meets the eye?' Pearson said. 'Isn't it just a case of this fella Crypto seeing too much into things and getting carried away?'

'Well, it appears so, but the catalyst for him to run was the letter and in it there was an oblique reference to some island. Agent Simms has spent the past few days with Crypto getting him to run repeatedly through everything that has happened, just in case we have missed something. She says he has strong suspicions about the place; he's convinced the Russians are turning it into some sort of military base.'

'Hardly, we would soon know if a Russian warship turned up,' said Commander Pearson. 'I saw a lot of what went on in Scarborough. It was just a couple of thugs chasing an ex-employee who had probably stolen a lot of money. We never considered the Russian military, did we?'

'No, sir, not really – though we had our suspicions. He was witness to a murder and that could cause anyone to run. But then we need to ask ourselves, what was the motive for the murders in the first place?'

'The Americans say he was one of their informers, passing on information about his employer's dodgy deals. Crypto was closely involved in handling the money side of things, Bitcoin, the dark web. Was that the real reason, that he was involved in money laundering, that he knew too much? I'll bet he was not only moving money about for the Russian but that he also had his finger in the pie.'

'Quite possibly, sir, but Agent Simms thinks there is something sinister going on and she wants to have a closer look. We know the Russian army isn't all it's cracked up to be and their navy is in some state of disrepair, but they still have a lot of assets they can deploy and I know that in certain areas they are as good if not better than us. I think we should not underestimate them, leave no stone unturned. If they are trying to create some sort of base it will not be the first time. Look at Säkkiluoto, that was an island base the Russians were building right under the noses of the Finns.'

Commander Pearson nodded his head. 'Can't trust them with anything. It's possible they are attempting to set up a base, and I must add that on the diplomatic front things are extremely delicate. We could send in the Special Boat squadron, a full-blown commando raid even, but the island is not so far from civilisation. If the press hears of a raid on home soil there could be ramifications for some of the big diplomatic initiatives. We can't risk barging in only to find there is a simple explanation. We don't want egg on our faces; the Americans think we are a diminishing force in the world of espionage and to make a fool of ourselves will not help. Okay, I say let Agent Simms have her way.'

The call to go ahead had been welcome. Anita had her suspicions, instinctively not believing this was a closed case, and on replacing the secure telephone receiver back in its cradle she had returned to her report. Writing in chronological order a list of recent events, she pulled together everything she knew to create a clear picture of what had transpired. For an hour she added, altered, and expanded until the report looked something like complete. Deciding to take a break, she left her desk to walk across the corridor to the room where Tabz was still working.

'So, you will be leaving us in a few days, I hear,' she had said to Tabz. 'Thank you for your work, it was important, helped myself and my colleagues track down our friend Crypto. How are you getting back to Islington, will you drive?'

'Oh, I don't own a car, nowhere to park it like.'

'I guess you will want a holiday after all this?'

'Probably.'

'Where's your favourite destination? Bali, the Caribbean?'

'No, I like the west country. Not too far and within my pocket,' said Tabz, taking a sideways glance at her interrogator. She had learned that people working for the Secret Service were suspicious by nature. Was Anita thinking she might be the mole? 'I've been in this business long enough, you know,' Tabz joked. 'It seems everyone is a suspect at one time or another innit.'

Anita smiled. 'It's the nature of the beast.'

Tabz didn't respond. As a young black woman working in the Met, side-swipes and innuendo were not new. She wasn't the mole, but she was beginning to believe she knew who might be.

'Anything new on the archaeological dig?' Anita asked.

'No, not really. I can't find much online other than that which I have already told you like.'

'What about the people they have recruited – have you any information on them, where they live, their college or university?'

'No, if you want to know more you will need to speak with Dr Schultz. He will know everything about the dig and the diggers, if that's what you call them.'

Anita wasn't sure if Tabz was trying to be humorous, but in her present mood she had little desire to respond.

'Where will I find this Dr Schultz?'

'He has an address in Aberdeen. I have no idea if that is where he will be.'

'Any telephone numbers?'

'Yes, his home address and his office at the university.'

'Thanks, can you write them down for me? I'll give him a call.'

Anita had believed Dr Schultz was her chance to get onto the island; she needed to join the dig. How to manage it was a puzzle, she thought, as she punched in his number.

'Dr Schultz?' she said, relieved to hear his voice.

'Yes, vot do you vont?'

'Dr Schultz, I am ringing from the university about the dig you have organised on Fudensey.'

'Yes, it vill start soon. Vot iss your problem and who are you?'

'I am Lucy Buxton, I am working with the accounts department of the university. I need to know the full names and addresses of the people you have engaged for the dig.'

'Vy, isn't there a list in the departmental office?'

Anita swallowed; it was a long shot but it was all she had left. 'They told me you have the only copy, Doctor, and you appear to have taken it with you back to Aberdeen.'

Dr Schultz felt a sense of puzzlement. He was working on a paper analysing the settlement he had discovered on Orkney, and to have his concentration broken was making him more than a little annoyed.

'Just a minute,' he said, turning to his briefcase. 'Pen, paper?'

'Yes, Doctor, fire away.'

Dr Schultz could not understand why the office did not have a copy, but was relieved when he could finally replace the telephone receiver and carry on with his work.

She will do, thought Anita, after a perusal of the list of names on her pad. She drummed her fingers on her desk for a few seconds, checking the rest of the names. Seeing no real alternative, she called Jimi.

'Yes.'

'Can you organise a chopper?'

Alice Springhorn was excited. Her trip to the Hebrides was just two days away and her new fleece had just arrived by courier. Slipping it on, she admired herself in the mirror and looked down at the rest of her clothes laid neatly on her bed, wondering if she had missed anything. She had cleaned her boots, removed the last traces of her previous dig, and was wondering if the weather would be warm enough for shorts. She had two pairs: old denims, and a less antiquated khaki cotton pair. What the hell, she thought, stick them in the rucksack.

After completing her degree at the University of Aberdeen, she had spent some time on a dig with the university's archaeology department and after that had secured employment with the West of Scotland Archaeology Service as an assistant archaeologist. She had learned of the dig on Fudensey just two weeks earlier, and eager to expand her curriculum vitae, she had applied. Not only would she gain experience, but the chance to visit the Western Isles was too good to miss.

She would need her camera to log as much as she could, and taking it from the drawer in the living room, she switched it on, checked the battery and lifted it to her eye. She hadn't used it for some time and for a minute she played with the zoom. She was intending to take a couple of test photographs, play with the settings to refresh her memory of how the thing worked, when a knock at the door stopped her.

Puzzled, she wondered who it might be. John, a friend who wrote occasional articles for the local newspaper, had said he would call by, wanting to hear her thoughts on the closure of the local pub by a developer, causing uproar in the community. She expected to see him but when she opened the door, of the diminutive John Thornton there was no sign. Instead she was confronted by the sight of a large black man and, beside him, a white woman.

'Hello,' said the man. 'We are from a government department and we would like a word with you.'

Jimi could see alarm in the young woman's eyes and held out his warrant card.

'There is no need to worry but we must talk to you. May we come in?'

'Who are you again?' said Alice, stepping away from the threshold.

'I am David English and this is Lucy Buxton. We work for the police and we have a problem.'

'How does that concern me?'

'We believe you are due to visit Fudensey in the Hebrides quite soon.'

'Yes, the day after tomorrow. I have to go to Skye and catch the ferry. Why, what's this all about?'

'I'm afraid we can't tell you that right now, but if you will sign these papers, I can tell you a bit about what is going on.'

'Papers?'

'The Official Secrets Act. You need to sign it otherwise we might have to take you into custody.'

'What!' exclaimed Alice.

'Don't be alarmed. Will you sign these papers?'

The excitement and anticipation of leaving for the dig turned instantly to anxiety, and she did not know quite what to do.

'I need to assume your identity for a while,' said the woman. 'It's a matter of national importance but you must sign the Official Secrets Act for us to move forward. You know too much already.'

Alice felt like protesting – protesting was in her DNA – but the two people confronting her were intimidating.

'I'll get a pen.'

The weather in the Western Isles is notorious for its unpredictability, and what started out as a bright spring morning had now turned gloomy, the sky overcast, threatening rain. The wind had picked up too, a fatal combination for some of the launch's passengers. The remainder of the excavation team had arrived, led by Dr Schultz and Professor Sean O'Grady together with the last of the volunteers, two young men and a woman. Stewart met them at the CalMac ferry terminal and, like their predecessors, confirmed their names, Liam a stocky twenty year old and Angus, a tall blonde haired young man of about the same age and with them, Masie, a pretty girl with freckles who looked even younger.

'I hope you are all good sailors,' said Stweart leading them towards the launch. 'The crossing will be a little rough. If you feel like being sick, please be a touch selfless regarding your fellow passengers and vomit downwind.'

The three younger passengers looked at each other

with some apprehension, while Dr Schultz appeared not to have heard and Professor O'Grady perused his mobile telephone. In the event, the launch's passengers managed to hang on to their previous meal, though there were some white faces as the party stepped ashore on Fudensey Island.

Stewart led them down the jetty and along the path to the house. He looked them over with a wry smile. As a naval man such conditions were a normality, yet it never failed to give amusement to see the distress on a landsman's face.

As with most cases, as soon as both feet touched solid ground a seasickness sufferer felt cured, and today was no exception. The younger members of the team recovered their composure and if the doctor and Professor O'Grady were suffering, they too soon shook off any nausea. After Stewart's direction, they found themselves in a large room that served as both a dining room and a recreation space. Today, though, it was a meeting room where the volunteers made each other's acquaintance and received their instructions from Dr Schultz.

'So, you are from Edinburgh,' said 'Alice', engaging one of the newly arrived young men.

'Aye, Edinburgh Uni, but I hail from the Orkneys. Liam McDougall. And you?'

'Alice, Alice Springhorn.'

'Och, you sound more English than Scottish, Alice.'

Anita smiled. 'Yes, for my sins.'

'What uni are you from?'

'I'm not, I work for the Glasgow City Council archaeology department. I look after local digs, liaise with developers, that sort of stuff,' she said, hoping the few scraps of information she had gleaned from the internet would see her through. She didn't need to know a great deal of detail, no doubt the site would be crawling with experts, but she did need to have some basic knowledge.

'And you?' Liam asked the woman sitting next to Anita.

'Professor Helen Stock, I work in the archaeology department at St Andrews.'

'A venerable university.'

'Yes, the oldest in Scotland.'

'You must be a lecturer,' he said, the r's rolling off his tongue.

'What makes you think that?'

'You are of a lecturer's age,' he said, grinning.

'Thanks for that, I owe you one.'

Anita listened to the chat, wondering that the dig was some sort of cover – were all these people genuine archaeologists? The conversation angled towards the finer points of the Bronze Age; the young man seemed keen, excited and knowledgeable, and as Professor Stock seemed happy to answer his questions, she felt less inclined to believe they were not genuine.

Starshiy Leytenant Vasyli Pavlov grew up in the closed city of his birth. The military was just about all he ever knew and his ambition had always been to join the navy. His father worked with munitions, his friends' fathers were either technicians or sailors with the Northern Fleet, and almost all the boys he knew aspired to join the navy. Subject to restraints outside the city limits, the teenage boys would roam unnoticed, explore, find vantage points high on the cliffs where they would watch the warships passing through the strait. Trying to outguess each other, to demonstrate their superior knowledge, one might say 'That's the *Ivan Kuznetsov* or the *Admiral Lazarev*' and some bright spark might announce his dad was on one particular ship – though, of course, they never really knew.

The closed, secretive world in which they lived might have seemed a prison to some, but for young men who knew no other environment there were opportunities, and at seventeen years old, Vasyli signed on. He was a quick learner, working hard for his promotions. Progressing from his position as a diver, he followed on with service on a nuclear submarine and now he had his own command.

The small Scottish island of Fudensey wasn't exactly a battleship, but with his small team of English speakers he was about to make a significant contribution to his country's defence.

Apart from himself, the lead technician, he had a weapons expert, Dimitri, a competent and thoughtful native of St Petersburg. There were others – two Spetsnaz, Domonic and Fyodor, special forces assigned to security duties, spending their days patrolling the coastline and the muirs covering most of the island.

Uninhabited since the 1950s, the island had come back to life. The launch patrolled the island's coastal waters, ferried supplies and people from Harris or Skye, activity that would certainly draw the attention of the locals. A nosey passenger on the CalMac ferry might connect to the bush telegraph, and then who might come looking? The planners realised that the small, isolated island might not be as secure as they had once believed. The operation could not and must not stand examination; Vasyli and his team needed to keep a low profile or, better still, hide in plain sight.

During the early planning stage, the idea of a cover was born, various schemes to cover the activities discussed, until finally the planners settled on the idea of an archaeological dig and Dr Schultz, a prominent archaeologist working at the University of Aberdeen, seemed the perfect candidate to run the dig and so, after receiving his instructions, Andrei Potanin had approached him.

Dr Schultz had been intrigued by the proposition Potanin had put to him – the chance to excavate a known site that no one had disturbed since the nineteenth century. A lot of the obvious stuff would have gone, but modern archaeology was more to do with learning about the past, not ransacking it for easy gain. But there again, Mr Potanin had made him an offer he could not easily refuse.

It took less than a week for the doctor to make his first visit to the island, arriving almost a month earlier with an assistant to carry out the first survey. Already having a good idea of the site's layout, the ground-penetrating radar made light work of the underlying structure and once he had the results, he began to organise the dig. As instructed by the island's Russian owner, he involved the local newspaper to give credence to the project and at the same time satisfy the locals' inquisitive minds, shifting attention away from the four permanent residents.

Now things were moving: the volunteer archaeologists were on the island and Vasyli could begin preparing for the mission proper.

'Did you manage to bring all the spares across with your passengers, Dimitri?' he asked as the man stepped ashore, a cardboard box in his hands.

'Most, but the electronic modules and a box of bearings are still outstanding. The office told me the next delivery would be on Wednesday.'

'We're going to be busy. Tell Domonic to make sure we have enough diesel aboard the launch, I want him to keep the tank topped up in case we need to move fast. It wouldn't do to find ourselves stranded out there and in need of help,' Vasyli said, a pensive look on his face. 'Make sure you stow all the equipment in the workshop and label everything, in English. I will leave you to it for now, I must go back to the house.'

Vasyli considered their situation. As he strode back towards the house, he turned over everything he had done in his mind. Dr Schultz was aware that he wanted to speak to the archaeological team before the excavations got underway – address security considerations, he had told him. Vasyli needed to impress upon them that they could not simply wander about in a disorganised muddle. They must obey certain rules.

'Good afternoon,' he said as he walked into the room. 'I see you are settling in.'

Anita looked up, sat back in her chair.

'Ladies and gentlemen, I welcome you to Fudensey. As you know my name is Stewart, and I am in charge here,' Vasyli began. 'I look after the island in all its aspects. As well as your excavation, we are carrying out some work in the house and in the boathouse, so I must ask you not to interfere with our activities and that means you must keep well away. Dr Schultz here will supervise the excavations and when he is unavailable, Professor O' Grady will take charge. You have the permission of the owner to excavate the site of what we

238

believe to be a Bronze Age roundhouse. I am no archaeologist, but I understand it has been known about for many years and dates from several thousand years ago. Nobody has ever formally excavated the site and so, over the next four weeks, you people have the privilege of uncovering some of its mysteries. I must make one point, though – the island is the private preserve of the owner, and he has stipulated in the agreement with Dr Schultz that you should confine yourselves to the house and its immediate surroundings, the path to the excavation, and the site of the roundhouse itself. Under no circumstances are you to go near the boathouse or the jetty or to wander freely. If you need to leave the island for any reason, we will escort you and ferry you in the launch. I hope you understand. The owner is very rich and very private, he doesn't want his investment spoiled in any way. Perhaps you can take over, Dr Schultz.'

'Thank you,' said the doctor, rising to his feet. 'Stewart has told you most of vot you need to know. After you settle in, I propose a visit to the site to let you familiarise yourselves with it and I will tell you vot I vont you all to do. I haven't had time to mark out the first trenches, but I have a diagram. You can do that later. Now, I believe a local shepherd discovered the site in the nineteenth century but after an initial investigation it appears the laird of the time simply looked for any valuables he could find and since then the site has remained undisturbed.'

'Are there any implements? I saw some shovels leaning against a wall over there,' said Liam, pointing. 'Are they for us?'

'Yes, that's right. You will have your own trowels and smaller tools, I think,' said Dr Schultz.

'I suppose when it comes to mealtimes, we just fend for ourselves, do we?' asked one of the women.

'Yes, we will provide the food but you need to prepare it yourselves,' said Stewart, joining in. 'We have a well-stocked food locker. Just help yourselves. My people will eat when you are out on the dig so we don't have too much congestion.'

'Thank you, Stewart, and thank all of you for volunteering. These digs would not be possible without your help and enthusiasm. For those of you unfamiliar with the Bronze Age, let me explain a little about the people of that time, of whom we hope to learn something. We believe Bronze Age people inhabited these islands about two and a half millennia ago, around the sixth century BC. There are records of Bronze Age people going back a long vay, the earliest by the Greek historian Diodorus Siculus, who wrote in fifty-five BC of an island called Hyperborea, ...'

Anita listened intently, surprisingly interested in the doctor's talk. To appear at least a little knowledgeable she had spent just a few hours searching the internet for information on the excavation of ancient remains. She had learned a little of Bronze Age peoples, but in the time available she could only scratch the subject's surface. The doctor's description helped fill a few gaps, but detached as she was from the archaeological dig, she found herself mildly excited at the prospect of unearthing important relics. That was secondary, though – she had a more pressing task to consider. Apart from herself, the volunteers appeared to be either academics or students of archaeology and all of them would have a far wider knowledge of the subject. But as she had discovered from reading articles on the internet, not all volunteers were fully paid-up archaeologists.

Some were simply enthusiasts, and she knew her best chance of acceptance would be to place both feet in that camp; ask advice, flatter her fellow excavators about their knowledge.

The doctor finished speaking and Sean O'Grady stood up. A red haired Irishman in his late thirties with piercing blue eyes, slim, wiry and sporting a three-day stubble beard. He began by saying:

'To be sure you're a fine-looking bunch of mud-shifters as I have ever had the pleasure to work whit.'

'Mud-shifters!' snorted Helen.

'If it rains – and it does frequently in these parts – then the dig could prove a bit slippery,' he said, grinning.

'Ah, Sean,' said Dr Schultz. 'I see vot you are up to, your usual blarney. Ladies and gentlemen, for those who have not met him, this is Professor Sean O'Grady, vun of the foremost Bronze Age scholars in Great Britain.'

'Ireland.'

'Of course. Sean and myself have vurked together on and off for many years and it's a pleasure to have him along. The younger ones can learn a lot from the professor. I have to leave for a few days later on and ven I am not here, he vill oversee the dig.'

'We are very lucky to have this opportunity to excavate this site,' said Sean, looking round at the assembled volunteers. 'From what we know, an excavation took place over a hundred years ago to investigate some remains. They didn't do much, no science as we know it, but from the description written by the laird of the time, we believe there is a Bronze Age roundhouse and Dr Schultz's ground survey seems to reinforce that idea. It may even be that there is more than one dwelling. In the Shetland Isles, excavations believed to be of isolated roundhouses have sometimes led to small settlements, and whit luck, that could be the case here. Until we start removing the turf, we will not know. I think you want to organise us into working parties, Doctor?'

'Yes, I do and thank you for your input, Professor O'Grady.'

'Please, Doctor – Sean, you must all call me Sean.'

Grins appeared on the faces of the young archaeologists, warming to the effervescent Irishman's personality.

'I have a list, and I believe vee should divide into three pairs to carry out the first stages of the excavation,' he said. 'In the morning you can get dug in, ha ha, *dug in.*'

No one laughed, just a few knowing smiles.

'So, who vill make the tea?' said the doctor, moving on.

Molly and Masie stood up, said they would, and while they busied themselves the volunteers began chatting, learning the names of their new friends. Anita listened. They really were archaeologists, enthusiastic, and she began to understand why Potanin had given permission for the excavation. To have so many people on the island would be a distraction, give the nosey neighbours something to occupy them, but under the surface she suspected altogether more sinister activities.

'I think I will take some air,' she said.

'Are you alright?' asked Helen. 'You haven't said much, you look rather pensive.'

'Oh, I'm fine,' she said, walking towards the door and emerging into the late spring sunshine.

She looked out across the waters of the sound, still, reflective and finding a place on a low wall, she sat down to look at the house and its settings.

There must be surveillance cameras, she thought, and scanning the surroundings, finally spotting one perched upon a tall pole. Cameras were a problem; how many were there? The doctor had warned them that certain areas were out of bounds, and those were the areas of interest to her.

'What are you looking for?'

Anita whipped round, surprised she hadn't noticed the speaker approach. It was Stewart.

'Just taking in some air, clearing my mind after Dr Schultz's talk. He's an interesting man. Where did you find him?'

'We have contacts. Now if you don't mind, I would prefer if you don't go wandering about. We have work going on, the renovations. We do not want you falling over anything, getting injured.'

'I'm sure I won't.'

'Never say never. We do not want any claims for injury. You have signed the disclaimer and you should have taken out personal injury insurance; I would hate for you to have a mishap.'

Chapter 13

Dampness percolated the air, a thin mist covered everything, and in places the volunteer archaeologists had a need to tread carefully if they did not want to fall foul of hidden hollows. In single file they followed an old sheep trail, trooping across the heather like a huge sea snake to where the dig unfolded. The ground looked flat and uninteresting. The only clue that they had really arrived was a small tent pitched by the side of the trail.

'Doesn't look much,' said Molly, walking in front of Anita. 'At least it's flat, and those hills should give some shelter from the wind. I hear it can be soul-destroying when a storm blows in from the Atlantic.'

'Three thousand miles of nothing to stop it,' said Liam just in front of her.

'I hope there is a kettle in that tent, I will be dying for a cup of tea in a couple of hours.'

Ahead of them Sean raised his hand, a signal to stop, to gather round.

'Well, here we are. Welcome to "*an t-seann taigh*", everyone,' he said in a convincing Gaelic accent. 'It means the old house by the way. I hope our endeavours bear fruit.'

'So do I, I think a month here without finding anything would drive anybody nuts.'

'Come on, Molly, all digs start like this. Once the sun comes out it will be fun,' said Liam.

Anita listened to the banter as she looked over the site of the so-called roundhouse. There wasn't much to see. Further away she caught sight of blue sea and a horseshoe-shaped bay edged with the whitest sand. She had seen a lot in her time but this was a surprise. The air was fresh, the view having a dynamism all its own; it was beautiful. She could understand why those ancient people must have picked the site for their roundhouse.

'Looks lovely, don't you think?'

'Aye, it does,' said the young Orcadian. 'Makes you proud to be a Scot.'

Molly looked at Liam and smiled. 'I have to admit it is a beautiful, peaceful place.'

'Gather round,' said Sean. 'Drop your bags by the tent, t'will keep them dry if a storm blows in.'

Bright-eyed and eager to begin, the volunteers both young and not so young, experienced and those just starting their careers, gathered round the Irishman while Dr Schultz looked on.

'Herman has asked me to direct the dig as he must go back to the mainland for a few days towards the end of the week. He feels that continuity should be an important facet of this dig. We have just a month to uncover as much as we can, because he believes there will be no extension of time and no opportunity to return to complete our work. The owner is Russian, as I think you know, and that makes for a difficult situation. No matter, we are here now and I want ti tell you how we should proceed. To speed the excavation along I propose to split you into pairs to excavate the trenches that myself and Dr Schultz will mark out. These trenches should produce results as the ground-radar plots were particularly clear, undisturbed for thousands of years which provides quite good definition. Helen, you should work with Molly, I have seen some of her work and I believe her interests align with yours. You will start on the first trench the doctor is already marking out...'

For twenty minutes Sean gave the team their instructions, explained how they should work, and at the end Anita found herself teamed up with Maisie and Liam. Their task was to sift through all the spoil from the two trenches, carefully feeling for anything of interest like tools, pottery or bones the others might have missed. Nothing was too small.

'You haven't forgotten to bring knee pads, have you?' said Liam with a grin.

'No, I haven't,' said Anita, evaluating her fellow volunteers.

'It can be hard going without a good pair, believe me.'

'I believe you. Tell me, where are you from, Maisie? You said you are studying at Newcastle University, where do you come from originally?'

'York. I suppose that's why I like archaeology; it surrounded me while I was growing up. Romans, Vikings, the War of the Roses... We have it all in York. Where are you from?'

'London.'

'Plenty of ancient ruins there.'

'Yes, I suppose so.'

'It's the railway lines down there that are the most productive: HS2, Crossrail, and the tall buildings. They need strong foundations and that means a lot of excavation. We archaeologists must have held up half the building projects in London for years.'

Anita couldn't help smiling. The enthusiasm and openness of these young people made a pleasant change from the bad actors she normally dealt with.

'Could be that you did. By the way, I like your tee

shirt: *Liberté, Égalité, Archaeologié...* Cool.'

'We all have them,' said the girl. 'Kind of a uniform, I suppose.'

Anita smiled but her mind soon turned to the overriding problem of how to get a closer look at the boathouse and the parts of the house that were off limits. On their way to the excavation site, Helen had said the path they were walking was an old sheep trail, overgrown, and as it inclined towards higher ground Anita could see in, the distance, the main house set back from the beach. The boathouse stood apart, the short canal and the jetty invisible just the very top of the launch in view. Before it slipped out of sight, she had seen figures moving around, and she wondered what they were doing.

For the next few days, the team knuckled down to their work. It was hard and demanding if you were unused to being on your knees for hours on end, and for Anita it was a trial. But the company was interesting, stimulating, and humorous.

'Know what they call this hill?' said Maisie one day.

'Sorry,' said Anita, a little puzzled. 'The hill?'

'The hill, yes, over there. It's called a Graham, that's what they call a hill around six or eight hundred metres high. Higher than that and they are called Corbetts.'

'You learn something every day.'

'If you are going to become a real archaeologist you need to know these things.'

'I can see why,' said Anita, unsure if the girl was teasing.

'This is a good place for a settlement, I am quite impressed. They knew what they were doing – had to, life was hard in the Bronze Age. The beach down there looks ideal for fishing,' added Maisie.

'Would they have had boats then? There are hardly any trees.'

'There were trees up until about three thousand years ago, I think. Yes, they could build boats, mostly dugouts. The trees began to disappear when agriculture took over, starting about six thousand years ago. How do you think they were able to colonise the islands in the first place if they didn't have some form of boat?'

'Of course,' said Anita, finding herself interested in Maisie's facts and figures.

The real Alice Springhorn had proved a valuable contact in agreeing to provide her own equipment, her trowel and scraper, waterproof over-garments and even her new fleece. Anita had them all in Alice's own rucksack, and each morning and evening as she carried it on her back, she searched the hills and valleys for signs of surveillance.

The house and outbuildings were the most likely sites for cameras. She might have located several using the app on her smartphone that detected wireless signals but she, like everyone else, had parted with her mobile phone when they landed on the island. That alone had made her suspicious. The excuse that they wanted to keep the results of the dig secret until they were ready to tell the press seemed reasonable, but it certainly felt draconian and she needed that phone.

Dr Schultz was thorough; his survey had indicated the location of at least one roundhouse and as the dig entered its second week, wooden piles of the structure's foundations appeared. One afternoon Dr Schultz gathered his team together.

'As you are all aware, the owner of this island

approached me to organise this dig and from what you can see today, vee have not vasted our time. I am now leaving for a few days and Professor O'Grady vill be in charge. I vonted to say a few vords before I go, to thank you for your dedicated vork. It is already known that Neolithic people inhabited the Vestern Isles but I believe it was Bronze Age people who built this dwelling. From vot you have achieved so far I am certain that beneath the ground lies a buried treasure of pottery and objects used by those ancient peoples. Now vee have removed the top covering of heather and moss, you can see typical depressions and mounds associated vith an ancient dwelling. To my mind it confirms the ground radar survey. I have drawn a new plan of the site, showing the trenches and the places I believe vee need to dig to expand the site,' he said, unfolding a large sheet of paper showing a carefully drawn plan of the site and spreading it on the ground. 'So, gather round and I vill point out salient features. Ven I finish, Sean will help you peg out new trenches.'

'I'm working with you now, according to Maisie,' Anita said, turning to Helen. 'We've sifted through all the material from the trenches so until we get some more I think I'm at a loose end.'

'Might as well, Alice. I'm not sure it matters who works with who. Have you brought some string and pegs?'

'Erm, I think so,' said Anita, pulling back the flap of her rucksack.

'You don't seem too sure.'

Anita rummaged in the bag, finding a ball of string. 'Here, I'll dig out the pegs.'

Helen took the ball of string and the pegs as Sean came up to them.

'Hello, ladies, you'll be itching ti get stuck in?'

'Of course, we always are. Where do you want us to begin?'

The Irishman unfolded the chart.

'This, I think, is that mound there and the depression here,' he said, transposing the chart features. 'If we measure three metres from here,' he said, pointing, 'and ten metres from there, we should have one corner of the new trench. Hold the tape, will you?'

Helen took one end of the tape and waited for Sean to find the starting point. From there she began to push the pegs into the earth.

'Okay, I can leave you to finish pegging out now, can I?'

'Yes, I've done it enough times.'

The Irishman nodded to them both and, winding in his tape measure, walked off to the next pair of volunteers.

The day turned out to be interesting but hard work for Anita. The recalcitrant turf was more difficult to remove than the first time she had done it, and by the way Helen looked at her she wondered if she had suspicions.

'You haven't done much of this, have you?'

Anita shook her head. 'No, I just sifted through what everyone else had dug up.'

'Okay, now we have removed the turf we can start digging. put on your knee pads and start on that side, I will start here. You need to scrape away the soil, pile it up on the grass, look for anything solid. If you do find something, you must carefully scrape around the object to identify it. If you are not sure just ask and I will help you.'

Anita put on the knee pads and took the trowel from

the rucksack. Grateful for the pads, she knelt and scraped for the rest of the morning. She found the work interesting enough, particularly when she struck something solid. Unearthing the tiniest shard of Bronze Age pottery, she was surprised at how thrilling it seemed – but in terms of the case, it was getting her nowhere.

She could not leave the dig to explore, because someone would notice. Her only chance had been when they broke off digging for lunch, when she'd managed a walk to the top of the low hill to look at whatever was in view. She had seen the launch cruising past on occasion, the ferry making its way between Harris and the islands, and a few fishing boats. But from her vantage point the boathouse was not in view and that was annoying her. She wondered if there might be another path she could take and still wondering she joined the rest of the group for lunch. Sitting beside Maisie she reached in her rucksack for her lunch.

'Cheese sandwiches every day,' said one of the younger members of the team as they sat down at the edge of the excavation. 'The last dig I was on we had cheese sandwiches and crisps every day. Regulation excavation food, eh?' she said eliciting a laugh from her colleagues.

Anita listened for a minute or two as they discussed the merits of their rations, and taking the opportunity she said, 'Just going to stretch my legs.'

She had to take a chance, get closer to the boathouse, investigate more. They were a mile or more distant from the house, and even from the top of the hill the boathouse was obscured by the headland. She had to get closer, but that would mean leaving the dig for longer than she should. She felt she had no choice, though, and this time she followed the coast. The going was difficult and the sea grass was extensive, thick, the soft sand tiring her legs. Then she reached higher ground. It was firm, and her pace picked up. Then the jetty came into view, a neat, compact set-up with easy access to the sound and the deeper waters beyond.

'That has to be it,' she said to herself. 'What else is there? The boathouse is a perfect place to hide something and they warned everyone that the place is out of bounds.'

Tonight, after dinner, she would locate any surveillance cameras covering the path to the boathouse, find blind spots, and try to get as close to it as she could.

The two young volunteers were no Michelin star chefs, and the dinner they prepared proved it. A simple affair with a plentiful supply of baked beans, but as the archaeologists were hungry from their day's work and in a subdued mood, they soon cleared their plates.

'To be sure that was a foine dinner you two prepared,' said Sean, holding his hands to his chest and letting out a muffled belch. 'An' which of youse lucky people are going to wash up? It's a team effort, you know.'

'We appreciate that, Sean. How about you and me taking care of that?' said Helen, looking him straight in the eye. She liked Sean, and respected his deep knowledge of archaeology, but it annoyed her that he used his Irish blarney to get others to do the work.

'Of course, I will do any'ting for you, dear lady, you only need to ask.'

Helen's eyes narrowed slightly as she looked at the cheeky Irishman. Unable to resist a smile, she said, 'You devil, flattery will get you nowhere with me.'

'Come on then, let's get started. As you seem so willing to take on the task, I tink it only right that you wash and I'll dry.'

Grinning, he rose to his feet and gestured to those sitting nearby to pass their plates. Gathering them into a pile, he took them to the old porcelain sink.

'Have you had a look round the island, Sean?' said Helen, filling the kettle.

'No. As you know, the agreement is that we can do what we like at the site but we have to stay on pre-determined pathways.'

'Don't you think that's a bit odd?' said Helen, remembering seeing Alice come wandering onto the site after everyone else had returned to their post-lunch digging. She would have said something but Sean had called her over to have a look at some pieces he'd just discovered.

'I do, but I don't really care. We have just over two weeks left and I think we will find some interesting artifacts that could enhance all our CVs. Look at today, the pottery we found. If I have material to take back to the lab, to keep me in a job and to be able to produce a paper or two, I'm happy.'

'Aren't you curious?'

'Of course I'm curious, but there are some strange people in this world. The guy who owns this island must be very rich, and whatever the reason for letting us dig, I don't care to know it so long as I can get my hands on a bit of early history. Chances are, we will not get an opportunity like this again so let's just do as they ask.'

'I suppose so, but I do find it a little strange.'

'What are you talking about in such low tones?' asked Molly, bringing her plate for cleaning.

'Oh, nothing really,' Sean replied. 'Helen here thinks the roundhouse might be Neolithic and I still believe it to be Bronze Age. We haven't found anything that dates the site conclusively, but perhaps in the coming days we will.'

'Quite, Sean, I am with you – Bronze Age, I am sure.'

Helen looked aghast. They were ganging up on her and she had not even fully expressed an opinion. As Molly walked away, she glowered at Sean.

'Thanks for that, now she thinks I am misguided, that I don't know my Stone Age from my Bronze Age.'

'Don't you be worrying about dat. Forget how or why the island is run, just get as much out of it as you can and then we'll be on our way back t' civilisation.'

There wasn't much else to say, but Helen was annoyed as she dried her hands and rolled down her sleeves. A few volunteers still sat around the long wooden table but most had retired, and she thought she might do the same, to read awhile. Looking across the room she was curious to see Alice, a mug of tea in her hand, making her way through the exterior door.

The setting sun provided some cover and in the lengthening shadows Anita leaned against the dry-stone wall, her demeanour relaxed as she sipped her tea. But to know agent Simms was to know that the impression she gave was far from reality. Her senses were fully alert, ears and eyes probing everywhere for weaknesses, the security cameras, and a route away from the house.

She needed to know what vulnerabilities there were in the surveillance system if she was to get inside the boathouse. She knew of two cameras and on venturing further had found a third she had not seen before, set in a tree. Anyone leaving the rear of the house to follow the path to the boathouse would be visible to the camera.

What about the front of the house and the beach just metres away? Her present position put her within the spheres of vision of the two cameras she already was aware of, and as she moved a tiny red flash of light emanated from the nearest one.

Careful not to look too closely, she began a circuit of the house, trying not to make it obvious she was looking for cameras. She turned past the end of the building and from one of the few trees there was a red flash. Then further on a second, and as she turned to walk past the end of the building a figure appeared. In the fading light she recognised the imposing figure of the man she knew as Eric – probably not his real name, but she was in no mood to find out what that might be.

'Where you going? This area is out of bounds; you were told not to go on path when you arrived.'

'Oh, sorry, I was just enjoying the sunset and finishing my tea. Sorry. It's a bit cold anyway so I'll go back to the house.'

The big man blocking her path grunted, his eyes watching her, but when she offered to return to the house, he visibly relaxed.

'Yes, bit chilly. Good night.'

'Good night,' she said, turning back and wondering about him.

He was obviously physically very fit – and that accent? His near-perfect English had a slight flaw, one she had experienced during previous conversations with Russians, which was an occasional omission of the demonstrative. If she had harboured doubts before, they were now dispelled. He was Russian, she was sure, and likely a military man. Why have such security if you were not intent on hiding something?

Returning to the kitchen door, she let herself in and went into the dining room, finding it deserted except for the solitary figure of Dr Schultz sat reading.

'Dr Schultz, mind if I sit with you for a while?'

'Of course.'

'How was your trip?'

'Good, though it's better to be back. Sean has told me of the recent finds.'

'Yes, I understand they are significant. I will make a cup of tea. Do you want one?'

'Yes, just vun sugar.'

Anita filled the kettle and waited for it to boil, wondering what questions to ask the doctor without arousing suspicion. She was unsure of his position – was he involved in any of this deception, or was he simply a stooge? The kettle began to whistle, and breaking from her thoughts she filled the teapot and went back to the dining room.

'What's that you're reading, Doctor? Looks interesting,' said Anita, trying to draw him into conversation.

'*Roundhouses of the Scottish Iron Age*, a technical reference I use a lot,' he said, lowering the dog-eared book. 'I often vunder about the connections between the two ages, Bronze und Iron. I vont vun day to excavate the site of one of the tin mines in the mountains overlooking Loch Sunart. The distance from here is not so great. I doubt smelting of the metal took place anywhere near here. They vould have traded goods with metalworkers in Ireland or North Vales, and there is evidence of bronze objects coming from the Baltic and Scandinavia. Vere does your interest lie?'

'Oh, I'm very new to archaeology, I don't know very much really. I thought you might help me.'

'I am always at the service of a pretty voman.'

Feeling a twinge of embarrassment, she smiled and he responded by putting his book down on the table and leaning forward.

'Vell, vot do you vont to know? Shall we start at the beginning? Vot do you know about the Bronze Age?'

This was a real test for Anita. She had let it be known she was a beginner, an enthusiastic one, someone who was on a dig for the first time, and she'd hoped the other volunteers would accept her without too many questions. But now she felt vulnerable.

'My job with the archaeological department at Glasgow City Council brought me into contact with ancient monuments, and although my work is more administrative, I did make site visits on occasion and that convinced me to learn more. I thought that if I joined the dig that would give me a better insight. I had accumulated some leave and thought, why not?'

'You have come to the right person. I vill tell you a little of what I think vee have here on the island and vot vee might find. Vee are vurking on the remains of a Bronze Age settlement. My survey shows at least vun large roundhouse, and I expect there might be more, that's normal, but vun thing at a time. I see you are not vearing a ring: are you a professional lady or is there a story?' he said, and Anita took the opportunity to direct his questioning away from the archaeology.

The next day was dry and bright, the blue sky bringing out the best in the surrounding seas, turning them an almost Mediterranean blue in contrast to the white unspoiled sand of the beach.

'You could almost imagine we are in Benidorm,' said a mischievous Liam.

'Benidorm? I hardly think so,' said Molly, walking beside him. 'It's far better than Benidorm, you twit.'

Liam grinned. He took pleasure in stirring up his

companions, and with their spirits high they left for yet another day of digging up the past.

At the rear of the group Anita recalled her conversation of the previous evening. Lasting a good twenty minutes, it was time enough for her to learn that the island's owner had approached Dr Schultz and offered the chance to excavate the site. He was aware that the remains of a roundhouse existed and that no one had fully explored the site for more than a hundred years, so to an academic like him it was as if he had won the lottery. When he let slip that he was on a retainer, she realised subterfuge was involved.

Grubbing about in the dirt was not her normal occupation, but it gave her opportunities to engage with individual members of the group and ask subtle questions. In the end, she believed they were what they appeared to be. The younger members were keen archaeologists who talked incessantly of their interest in the subject. It was infectious, and after learning the techniques involved, she found the work quite rewarding. Each time she uncovered a shard of pottery, she understood some of the motivation the others felt.

'Beaker people, I think,' said Helen, holding her latest find up to the sunlight. 'We expected we might find some. Good work, Alice.'

Anita felt proud after making her first substantial find, and more than that, it seemed to cement her place in the group. Several of the youngsters came to look, passing learned comments as they turned the artifact over. Then Sean appeared.

'Well, that is indeed an important find, Alice. I agree with Helen that it probably arrived here with the Beaker people, but we need more evidence to be sure. Chances are, any more pieces will have moved downhill.'

'Thanks, I will have a look,' said Anita, adjusting her knee pads. With an appreciative nod of his head, the Irishman walked away.

'For a beginner you seem to have made a good start,' said Liam. 'I think the girls over there have just found some more pottery. Och, you have started something,' he said, smiling. 'Where is it you're from again, Glasgow?'

'Er... Temporarily, yes,' said Anita, trying to avoid his question. 'Have you done any archaeology on your home turf?' she asked. 'I believe some of the earliest settlements are on the Orkneys.'

'Well, perhaps not the earliest but there are quite a few Neolithic sites and the standing stones.'

'Of course, the standing stones. Have you excavated them?' she said rather clumsily, but he seemed not to notice.

'That's where my interest in archaeology came from. To be close to some of these ancient monuments daily and to have a teacher who was passionate about archaeology was important. We used to spend weekends in the summer helping on the various digs. Och just about every university with an archaeology department visited the islands at some time or other and I got the bug.'

'What are your thoughts on this site? Is it Bronze Age?'

'Oh, no doubt about it.'

Anita nodded her head in agreement and slipped to her knees to scrape the earth.

'You will have to excuse me, Liam, but I think I might be catching the bug.'

After a long day of excavating, the volunteers would

tramp back to the house for dinner. Never a fancy affair, the food was nourishing nonetheless, leaving the crew satisfied and subdued. Each evening gave Anita a chance to slip outside for a look around, each time pushing the limit of her search for a way to the boathouse. But each time detection by the surveillance cameras seemed inevitable bringing out one of the Russians to bar her way. If she could determine a regular schedule of the guards' movements – for she now realised that was what they were – she might find a way to bypass them long enough to explore the boathouse.

'Looks ominous, doesn't it?' said a voice behind her. Turning, she saw Sean. 'I see you like an evening stroll, mind if I join you?'

'No, be my guest.'

'Enjoying the dig?'

'Yes, interesting.'

'The sky looks threatening, don't you tink?' he said, turning to look at the western horizon.

'Oh, yes, I hadn't noticed,' said Anita, surprised at the intensity of the black clouds rolling towards them.

'I can tell you haven't done much excavating. Are you really interested in archaeology or did you think it would be some sort of holiday?'

'Er... both. I am interested, but I know I have a lot to learn and the chance to spend time on a Scottish island seemed like a good idea.'

'Ha, you're not the first single lady to tread that path.'

'What do you mean?'

'Well, a single lady with a decent income and time on her hands. I have met quite a few of you.'

'What's that supposed to mean?'

'You're searching for something to fill your drab life. I can't understand why a good-looking woman like you would need to.'

'Are you always so insulting?'

'Usually, I'm afraid. So, tell me, where is it you're from?'

'I don't think I want to.'

'Oh, come on. I'm just trying to be friendly, don't be offended.'

'Well, you do go about chatting a woman up in a strange way.'

'To be sure I'm not chatting you up, just want a bit of female company after the hard work of digging.'

Taken aback for a second or two by his approach, she soon realised it was in her interest to humour him.

'So, are you single?' she asked.

'Yes, once again.'

'Once again?

'I was divorced for the second time just a month ago.'

'I'm sorry.'

'Don't be, we're still friends. She is a prominent archaeologist back in Dublin and she can put in a good word for me when I need it. I like to move on.'

'Move on in work or marriages?'

'Ha ha, work mainly. I don't think I am the marrying kind really.'

'You've taken a while to find out.'

'Never mind me, what about you? Have you been married.'

'No, never met the right man, never felt the need. Anyway, I don't really want to discuss my private life with you, I've only just met you. What brings you here? Dr Schultz seems to think highly of you, though I must confess I don't know why.'

'And so he should, I know just about as much of Bronze and Iron Age settlements in Scotland and

Ireland as he does – more, in some areas. I helped in no small way in re-creating an Iron Age roundhouse on Skye. If I keep buying the lottery tickets maybe I will be able to build one here.'

'They liked their roundhouses, the ancients.'

'Most economic form of building, and to be fair they spent a long time perfecting the design.'

'I suppose.'

'I like a walk, helps me relax. Would you accompany me?'

'So long as you stop flirting, I will.'

The cheeky Irishman bowed graciously. 'I am honoured, ma'am.'

Anita couldn't help but smile at him. After scraping soil all day, she was grateful for a little light relief and Sean was close to Dr Schultz. Perhaps she might learn something.

'There seems to be a lot of surveillance,' she said. 'Is there a reason for that?'

'Dr Schultz told me they simply don't like uninvited guests. The owner is a very rich man, I believe, a foreigner, and he likes his privacy.'

'Not so private with us crawling all over the island.'

'Not crawling all over. We have strict guidelines as to where we can and cannot go. You know that from the induction.'

'So why have we been allowed on the island at all?'

'The doctor says it's because the owner is looking for kudos. He wants to leave a positive mark. He doesn't normally allow anyone on the island but it is necessary if he wants to secure his legacy. I think the dig will only last for the planned month. I am guessing that whatever we find, the island's owner will spin the resulting publicity in his favour. After that they will close the place down again.'

'So it's a sham, just a pretend excavation?'

'It's about kudos – respectability, perhaps. Very rich people do strange things at times, they like to appear altruistic to the uninitiated. I suggest we enjoy it while we can and, as professionals, take as much from this dig as possible.'

Anita nodded as if she agreed, but really, she wasn't much interested in altruism or even the archaeology. More important things were on her mind.

The force of the wind increased with surprising speed; a cold breeze displacing the still, warm air. For hours the storm remained distant, but the wind was changing and when only minutes earlier the sky was clear, black clouds now began to shut out the sun. The volunteers sensed a change was in the air, distant thunder a precursor to the deluge, and with some urgency Sean directed the volunteers to spread tarpaulins over the excavations. Weighing them down with rocks, they hoped it was enough. They could not afford to leave the trenches exposed; a trench full of water would compromise the dig and they only had so much time.

'If they had let us keep our mobiles, we could have seen this coming,' said Helen, looking towards the west.

'I had an inkling the weather was about to change,' said Sean, looking away.

'An inkling?'

'Er... Yes, I have seen these conditions before. We need to head back to the house before we're inundated.'

Helen looked a little puzzled but knew he was right.

Unable to avoid the first of the rain, the volunteers reached the house in a miserable condition and for the rest of the evening could do no more than suffer the banshee scream of the wind and its accompanying downpour of biblical proportions.

'Don't worry, we will be back excavating in a day or so,' said Helen, drinking her tea. 'The site will be unworkable for a while, the mud and collected rainwater will hamper our excavations most definitely. But with luck the tarpaulins will protect most of the dig.'

'It's not ideal, though, is it?' said Anita, laying her knife and fork on her empty plate.

'No, it's not. If the tarpaulins don't do their job we will lose time – the trenches will become waterlogged and we will have to bail them out before we can work. That's the worst, having to bail out. The mud left behind will make us think we're having a Turkish mud bath.'

'Yuck, that doesn't sound very nice,' said Anita, looking out of the window. 'What will we do tomorrow?'

'Depends upon the weather but same as normal, I think, just muddier. It seems daft to waste time sitting around here, doesn't it?'

'I suppose so,' said Anita, her eyes on the storm.

Her mind was examining possibilities, and feeling the building shake, she wondered how the cameras were coping. She had seen debris and vegetation fly past the window and suspected that it was going to be a long night. What if the full force of the wind and rain affected the cameras? What if they became damaged or dislodged? To be blown out of alignment would be a help to her, skewing their permanent stares long enough for her to get inside the boathouse.

On the first floor of the building, away from the volunteers' accommodation, Vasyli gazed at the two large monitors. He did not see the weather as an

264

immediate problem, as the cameras seemed to be working properly and no one in their right mind would venture out in this storm. But still, he was concerned for their functionality.

'How are the cameras holding up, Fyodor, are they secure?' he asked.

Fyodor made an adjustment to one of the screens.

'So far so good. The one on the roof is taking the most punishment; see how it vibrates?'

Vasyli leaned forward to look over the man's shoulder. 'The one near the boathouse, how is that coping?'

Fyodor turned to his second screen. 'So far all seem to be working.'

Vasyli had impressed upon the dig volunteers more than once that the whole of the area around the jetty and the boathouse was out of bounds. Even so, he was concerned that one of them might stray too close once the storm abated.

'You should check them all out once the storm passes. The wind could put any one of them out of action and although I do not believe our "guests" are a threat, we must be vigilant.'

'Are you still planning to launch tomorrow?'

'Yes, the forecast is for the storm to pass by morning. O'Grady has told me that they may not be going to the dig tomorrow because he believes the site could be waterlogged, so we just need to keep an eye on them, make sure nobody wanders off towards the boathouse.'

'Was it a good idea to let them on the island?'

'Necessary, I think. An inconvenience, but it gives us cover. The newspapers have a story and the locals should not be too suspicious of what goes on here. We need the equipment the launch has brought from the mainland but what we don't need are prying eyes. The agreement with Dr Schultz is for the results of the dig to be inconclusive, for him to say that any discoveries, although interesting, are not important enough to excavate the site any further. Once they have left, never to return, we can settle unmolested into our routine.'

'It seems strange he would want to do that as an academic professional.'

'Not so strange when you know how much we are paying him.'

Chapter 14

Without access to their mobile telephones most of the youngsters were at a loss. On a normal day at the dig they had plenty to keep them occupied, but confined to the house and with time on their hands, keeping busy was proving problematic that evening. Reading was an obvious choice, though Liam had brought a pack of playing cards and was busy dealing to Sam and the two girls. Sean sat alone with his nose in a book and the two older women were sitting by the window engaged in conversation.

Sean paused his reading and looked over the top of his book at them. He knew Professor Helen Stock well; she was an academic with whom he had worked before. The other woman he had learned was from Glasgow, not particularly schooled in the science of archaeology and yet she seemed competent. He looked across at the four card players, engrossed in their game, noisy, laughing. They were a good team. Dr Schultz had left him in charge for a second time while he attended to other business, and given a free hand, he had high hopes they would find relics invaluable to the story of the Bronze Age.

'I wonder what tomorrow will bring, Sean. This storm looks as if it will run all night. Listen to that,' said Helen, standing. 'I think I am ready for my bed. I hope I can sleep with this racket going on.'

'Yes, it sounds bad. At least the house must have withstood storms like this for more than a century, and I suspect it will still be standing in the morning,' he said, rising. 'I think I will retire too. Good night.'

Anita watched him go.

'Are you staying?' said Helen.

'For a while longer, I need to write my diary up for today,' she said, holding up a red notebook.

'Okay, good night, Alice.'

'Good night,' said Anita, returning to look through the rain-spattered window and wondering how the surveillance cameras were standing up. For a minute she stared into the rain-lashed night, finally turning to see she was alone in the room, the card players and Maisie all deciding to retire. Instinctively she realised the time for action had arrived.

Her rucksack lay beside her and, opening the zip, she felt for the waterproof oversuit. She would need it if she were not to drown in the torrent, plus its dark green colour would help conceal her in the night. She pricked up her ears and once she was sure no one was nearby, looked towards the outside door. Next she took her red notebook and quickly climbed the first flight of stairs to the dormitory rooms, leaving it propped against the window facing the sea. Returning to the kitchen, she put on the oversuit, pulled up the hood, and noting the key was still in its lock she removed it and hid it behind the curtains. She was ready. Grasping the door handle with both hands, she stepped out into the maelstrom.

The two younger women were soon fast asleep, snoring gently and from the dormitory window Helen pulled the curtain to one side to take a final look at the storm. A roll of thunder crashed and faded in the distance, then there was another flash of lightning and in the bay she could see an angry sea breaking furiously on the shingle-strewn beach. It was a truly awesome sight and she could not help but admire the forces of nature playing out before her. There was another flash far out at sea, bright enough to profile a shadowy figure creeping along the boundary wall. She was sure it was Alice.

'What the hell is she doing out there?' Helen asked herself, straining for a better look. She had noticed from the moment they boarded the launch that there was something different about the woman. Her knowledge of archaeology was so thin, and she seemed so unenthusiastic compared to the rest of the volunteers. Now she was creeping off into the storm. Helen was intrigued, keen to know what her temporary roommate was up to.

'Bugger it,' she said, turning to her rucksack, dragging out her waterproofs and a torch. She would find out.

A glance at the two sleeping girls told her she was unobserved, and donning her waterproofs, she pulled the hood tight around her face before quietly slipping out of the room. Hurrying down the stairs, she went to the kitchen, and finding the door unlocked fought it open and stepped into the storm. The tempest was at its height, shocking her system momentarily, but she closed the door determinedly and, thrusting her hands into the anorak's pockets, followed in the footsteps of Alice Springhorn.

The constant monitoring of the screens was beginning to tell on Domonic. Motion detection was all very well when conditions were benign, when the infra-red could easily distinguish movement, but the ferocious storm was having an effect. It blinded the sensors, causing the surveillance system to fail, and most of the time he little idea of what he was seeing. He felt a headache coming on and decided he needed a short break, a cup of coffee, anything to help his concentration. He also needed to stretch his legs, so rising, he filled the kettle before pacing back and forth, stopping by the window to pull the curtains to one side. The rain was intense, the window simply a blur. He couldn't believe anyone would venture out on such a night.

'Ah... Stop fretting, there is no one there,' he said to himself as the kettle began to boil. Leaving the window, he poured the hot water, stirring the contents of the mug before returning for one last look outside.

He was sure there was nothing out there – until a shadow moved and his heart missed a beat. Was it a tree swaying, a loose tarpaulin flapping, perhaps? He wasn't sure.

'Nah, shadows,' he murmured, sipping his drink.

The coffee was just what he needed, and returning to his desk, he scanned the two screens. He would check the area, first the camera looking at the rear of the building and then the one monitoring the path to the boathouse. He switched each view to full screen and peered into the gloom. The camera observing the path was taking the full force of the storm, the lens a blur, streaked with rainwater and shaken by the ferocity of the storm was practically useless. He switched the view to the rear of the house – nothing – and then back to the vibrating image of the path.

Suddenly the wind dropped and the camera steadied. The water drained from the lens and for an instant he had a clear view.

What was it? What had caught his eye?

He zoomed in and was amazed to see the

unmistakable silhouette of a person. Panning the camera, he zoomed in for a better look but there was nothing to see except swaying vegetation. Screwing his eyes up, he focused again on the screen.

'There is someone out there, I'm sure of it,' he murmured. He looked at his watch; it was almost one, the archaeologists should be fast asleep, but was one of them snooping around outside?

He needed to know, but with the weather against the technology, the only way was go outside and check for himself. Though not wholly convinced, he pulled on his jacket and picked up his gun, tucking it into his waistband and before he left the room, he grabbed his VHF radio. He would not wake Fyodor, but if he needed help, he would call him.

Locking the door behind himself, Domonic descended silently to the ground floor and made his way to the door leading to the rear of the property. Outside, the storm winds were howling, the rain battering the windows. As he turned the door handle he noticed the key was missing, but he had a more pressing engagement and on swinging the door open he felt the full force of the storm.

Half crouching, he managed to close the door and through the turmoil reached the shelter of the boundary wall. Taking stock, he headed for the path leading to the boathouse. It was tough going, he was in the open and taking the full force of the storm. Gripped by a twinge of homesickness, he thought about how this storm-lashed island on the edge of the Atlantic Ocean was different from Nizhny Novgorod. At least the mind-bendingly low temperatures of the Russian winter did not make him feel as miserable as he felt at that moment. He wondered what his wife would be doing. Curled up warm in bed –

alone, he hoped.

Hunching his shoulders, Domonic studied the deserted rainswept path. Save for a few crazily bending trees straining in the wind's embrace, he was alone. But as the clouds parted momentarily, a shaft of moonlight bathed the landscape and he thought he saw a shadow. Not twenty metres along the path, something was moving. Feeling for his gun, he set off in pursuit but the clouds closed in again. As quickly as it had appeared, the figure vanished into the velvet darkness.

Helen used the brief interlude of illumination to see the path ahead, to help balance her body against the wind and rain. Her progress was necessarily slow and she stumbled, leaving the path to grapple with the darkness. Without the guiding flash of lightning, she was blind and unable to gauge in which direction she should go. She felt she couldn't stop, however, and forcing herself across open ground she found herself amongst bushes. Short of breath and unsure as to where she was, she stopped. Another flash of lightning showed the house silhouetted to her right. She had her bearings again and believed she was still on Alice's trail.

Some way ahead, Anita was fighting her own battle. Reaching the boathouse, she pulled her jacket collar tight and felt her way towards the side door until that same flash of lightning showed it padlocked –and briefly silhouetted her against the building's stone wall.

Domonic saw her but was unable to make out any discerning features from twenty metres away and grasping his gun tighter, crept nearer.

Anita touched the padlock and half turned, sensing his presence. Domonic still did not recognise who it was and believed the individual was about to run. He couldn't let him escape and so he ran at him so fast Anita had neither the time nor the space in which to defend herself. Within seconds she found herself face down in the wet grass.

Helen had found the path, followed it, and was close by when she saw movement and heard a commotion – a woman's cry. With her heart in her mouth she inched closer. She heard a grunt of pain, wondered what was happening and concealed herself in the shadows to listen.

'You!' Domonic said in disbelief. You were warned not to come here. What are you doing?'

'*Aaaargh...* Let me go.'

'What are you doing, who are you really? What are you doing out here?'

'I... I... couldn't sleep. I suffer from insomnia; I just came for a walk. It's... it's so dark, I got lost.'

Domonic's training had taken over, perhaps he had overreacted, and he realised too late that he should probably not have been so forceful. But the damage was done.

'Come – on your feet. You must go in here,' he said, pulling her up and pushing her towards the door. He felt for the padlock key. 'In here,' he ordered.

'What if I do not want to?'

Domonic hit her across the face with the back of his hand. 'You will do as I say, now move,' he said, pushing her forward and compounding his mistake.

Shocked at the severity of his reaction, Anita realised her situation was serious and that resistance would be futile. She couldn't hope to take on such a powerful man without the element of surprise, and when he produced a gun, she genuinely feared for her safety. Silence and obedience might be her best course.

Just metres away, Helen listened. Concealed in the shadows and unsure of exactly what was happening, she strained her ears, learning only that Alice was in trouble.

'Fuck,' she said to herself as her brain began to whizz.

With his hands placed firmly on the windowsill Commander Pearson stared out at the turbulent crashing seas, at trees swaying uncontrollably in the wind. They said it was the worst storm in living memory and he could believe it, but what about agent Simms? He had an operative in the field without proper communication, without any sort of backup, and he was beginning to believe she could be in danger. He stood up straight, folded his arms and looked through the rain across the strait towards the invisible island.

'Relax, Commander. She is the best, and if anyone can pull this off, she can,' said Jimi with some sympathy.

'I hope you're right, Jimi, but I worry that there is something we don't know. I mean, who are those people on the island, the ones running things?'

'You know as much as I do, which is very little, but we both believe them to be Russians, do we not? There are seven volunteers, and our agent over there. How many others I'm not sure; we have seen the boat handlers and there will be others, I expect: four, six, ten? I don't know. All I can tell you is that they are supposed to be caretakers restoring part of the building that has fallen into disrepair. The one in charge is Stewart, I believe, according to the local police. They have had only minor dealings with him, a boat licence and a shotgun licence.'

The commander stopped looking out of the window and turned to face Jimi. 'I guess there isn't much we can do tonight. You can never get much sleep on these jobs, so I think a few hours' shuteye and then I will take the early ferry, have a look through the binos. They must have confiscated her mobile otherwise why has there been no communication from agent Simms. Now why would they do that?'

'Why indeed. Do you think we need an extraction team?'

'I don't like it; we have heard nothing in over two weeks. I have seen the launch picking up provisions and some wooden crates. God knows what is in them: shovels, at a guess.'

Jimi scowled. 'Maybe, but I doubt it. I am starting to wonder if this whole charade is some sort of cover.'

'Well, it's time to find out. When I take the ferry, I want you to at least ready a backup team. I feel uneasy. I don't know why, but I feel it in my water and when I do, it usually means trouble.'

Jimi frowned; he was just as uneasy but it had nothing to do with his water.

Domonic felt he had messed up, overreacted in the belief he was dealing with a man he believed was getting too close to the boathouse and its secrets. Realising it was a woman he should have simply talked to her, advised her that she was trespassing and should go, but the Russian way was not always that simple. To compound the error of unwarranted violence, he had produced his gun and from that moment on there was no going back.

Keeping her at arm's length, he felt for the key, only briefly taking his eyes off her as he released the padlock and waved her inside with his gun.

She had little choice and, in the darkness, she stumbled over the threshold to find herself at last in the boathouse. It was not the situation she would have chosen. She was a prisoner, helplessly under the power of the armed man, but at least she was still in one piece.

As she felt a hand push her forward a light came on. She looked around at the bare stone walls, two wooden benches with equipment and tools. Sitting in the small dock, the launch was rocking gently as the movement generated by the storm encroached under the double doors. A yellow generator stood on the floor at the far end: brand new, powerful, unnecessary. Why such a large power plant? It couldn't be for the launch; it would have its own facility, an alternator at most. Then she noticed the batteries – six of them, black and squat with a curved surface, suggesting a particular resting place.

'Over there, that door. Open it,' said Domonic, pushing her forward.

Anita did as he said, reaching for the handle of the storeroom door as her captor's hand gripped her shoulder. She wondered if this was her moment to attempt escape. Her training told her that a captor, believing he was safe, would be at his most relaxed and that was the instant in which to act.

'*Ty russkiy*?' she said to confuse him.

'What? You speak Russian?'

'I am a part-time lecturer in Russian at Glasgow University. I noticed your accent.'

Surprised, Domonic relaxed his grip and Anita took her chance. She had rehearsed the move a hundred times with her trainers, and gripping her hands into tight balls, she kicked back at his shin. As he gasped in pain and surprise, she swung her elbow into his exposed throat. Domonic took a step backwards, his gun loose at his side, and before he could react she turned to kick at his groin, missing the sensitive area by a fraction and allowing him time to recover.

He stepped away from her and raised his gun.

'*Ostanovis' pryamo tam.*'

Anita understood and raised her hands.

'Well, I think we need to get you locked—'

He got no further; a look of disbelief permeated his face and he slumped to his knees, the gun slipping inexorably from his grip. Helen hit him again for good measure with the piece of wood she had found, sending him sprawling face down on the concrete.

'Bloody hell, where did you come from?' Anita said, stunned.

'I don't really know. What's going on, Alice?'

'I'll tell you one day but first I – we – have to secure him. Come on, give me a hand to get him in there,' she said, pointing to the storeroom.

Helen took hold of one arm while Anita took the other and between them they dragged Domonic inside. He was heavy, a dead weight, but they managed. Once he was propped in a sitting position against a wall, Anita took the chance to have a look around.

It seemed more than a simple storeroom, a workshop with shelves full of mechanical parts and complicated-looking circuit boards, an oscilloscope. She also noticed the thin plastic cable ties used for bundling looms of wire together, a favoured method used for restraining captives.

'Here, hold his wrists together on his chest. Should keep him out of mischief, I don't want to kill him.'

Helen stared at the unconscious man and then at Anita, a look of horror on her face.

'Hurry, if he comes round and manages to get out of here, we could be in real trouble. Come on, Helen, shape up.'

Suddenly the seriousness of the situation dawned on

Professor Stock, and with trembling hands she obliged while Anita worked quickly, slipping the ties over the man's wrists and securing them just enough to restrain him.

'Well done. Come on, I have some work to do,' she said, picking up the gun and shepherding Helen from the storeroom.

'What is this all about, Alice? I think I have a right to know.'

'I work for a government agency and we suspect that there is some sort of operation going on here. I have come to find out what it might be.'

'What kind of operation?'

'We don't know.'

'You're not Alice Springhorn, are you?'

'Top marks for observation, Helen. No, I am not Alice Springhorn, I'm afraid. You do not need to worry about the real Alice Springhorn, she's safe enough. But these people are dangerous, Helen, you have seen what that man in there is capable of. They would have no qualms about killing us if we get in their way.'

'And we are, I guess, in their way.'

'Sure. I need to take a good look around. You keep an eye on him.'

'What is it you are looking for?'

'I don't know, but judging by the gear around this place, it's of a highly technical nature,' she said, pausing for a moment. 'Of course, those boxes on the launch must have contained much of this material: the electronics, the components on the shelves, and that over there,' she said, nodding in the direction of a generator.

Helen followed her gaze and seemed to understand.

'These things have little to do with archaeology or

house renovation, and that begs the question, what is this equipment for?' she said, walking towards the launch, which was rhythmically rocking back and forth. 'You know what these are?'

Anita looked at the objects stacked neatly alongside the generator. 'Batteries?'

'I think so. I've seen these things before, in the engineering department at Edinburgh University when I was there about a year ago. They use them in electric cars.'

'So, what are they doing here?'

'I don't know, maybe backup power?'

'Hardly. With that thing in here, I bet it could run a small town.'

Helen looked a little lost and Anita noticed the launch slewing back and forth as the sea surged through the double doors. She touched the boat's gunnels, looked along the deck at the small wheelhouse and then down at the water.

Could it be? Had she watched too many James Bond films?

She could see no alternative, and without another thought Anita stripped to her underwear, dropping her clothes in an untidy pile before she reached out to the boat's safety railing and lowered herself into the water.

'What are you doing?' Helen asked.

The water was so cold she was not inclined to answer, instead gritting her teeth and pushing off into the murk. She dived beneath the surface. Visibility was practically zero, forcing her to feel her way, and once she had the room she swam under the launch, reaching out to eventually grasp a hard, rounded object. The cold was debilitating and she knew she had little time before she must rise to the surface, but with one last effort, she explored the shape. A slender body, smooth but not metallic and having little time left before she must surface, she ran her hand over the what felt a fin.

Unable to hold her breath any longer, she struck out for the surface. Relieved to finally take a breath, she reached out to the concrete floor ready to haul herself from the dock, but as she attempted to pull herself from the water her eyes cleared to reveal the barrel of a gun. It was pointing straight at her.

'Out, get dressed,' said a very angry-looking Vasyli 'Where is Domonic?'

'Domonic?' Anita managed to say as she pulled her clothes on over her wet body. 'Who's he?'

'One of my men. He alerted us, said he was following an intruder. Where is he?'

'He's in there,' said Helen fearfully.

'Open the door, Fyodor. Where's the key?'

'Here,' said Helen, holding out her hand.

With his binoculars hanging from his neck, haversack over one shoulder, Commander Pearson boarded the ferry. It was due to leave in just a few minutes and as the horn sounded above him, he made for the same vantage point he had used on each previous journey. The view of the island from there was good, and up until now there had been little to draw his attention. Each morning and afternoon he would raise his binoculars to observe the island, the launch, the people –archaeologists, probably – making their way to and from the house. He looked at his watch: six thirty. Fudensey would come within sight within the hour, conditions were improving, the wind had dropped to a steady breeze and the sky was clear.

Anita was half soaked from her explorative dive beneath

the waters of the dock. Her bottom was numb from sitting on the concrete floor and her wrists were sore from the cable ties, and although the storm was finally abating, she hardly noticed. She was annoyed, concerned that she and Helen had become prisoners.

She closed her eyes to relive her dive, remembering the shape she had felt, its contours, the protrusions, and most of all the strange fin like shape at one end of the object. It had felt like a torpedo or something very similar, and the only thing resembling a torpedo that wasn't a torpedo was an underwater drone. She had come across one on a previous case, had learned something of their usage. After her discovery earlier on she now believed Fudensey was a Russian military base and that they were using the drone to conduct a serious operation in British waters.

'How are you feeling?' asked Helen.

'Not good.'

'You realise we have got to get out of here?'

Anita looked up. 'Yes, I know.'

'What will they do with us?'

'I don't know, I think they are in a quandary. If it got out that they killed two innocent archaeologists the ensuing publicity could be a problem for them. Until they decide what to do with us, we have a chance.'

'So, what will happen?'

'I don't know, but whatever they are planning I don't intend hanging around to find out.'

'What can we do?'

'First, we need to get free of these handcuffs. At least we have the use of our legs. Now that goon who was keeping watch has disappeared, we can try to make a run for it. I noticed a toolbox earlier, I will have a look inside, see if there is a knife or some pliers.'

'Surely they wouldn't leave something like that lying around.'

'Maybe not, but you never know. Come on, let's see what we can find,' she said, struggling to her feet. 'It's quiet out there. I think they have gone, probably got their hands full with the guard you laid low. The others up at the house will start asking questions, they'll want to know what's happened to us and the problems will start to mount.'

'What can they do?'

'I'm not even going to guess. We need to get out of here. The toolbox on the shelf at the rear of the store — there must be something in there. Come on.'

They found the toolbox but, disappointingly, it was padlocked.

'That's the end of that, I guess,' said Anita, looking deflated.

Helen did not answer. Instead she reached out to the sheet metal lid and began to rub the plastic handcuffs back and forth on its narrow edge. It wasn't sharp, but it had enough of an edge to wear away the plastic and with perseverance she finally cut through her bindings.

'Phew, that's better,' she said, rubbing her wrists back to life.

'Well done,' said Anita, taking her place, and once she too was free, she turned her attention to a possible escape route. 'The only window in here is that small thing over there. I don't think we can get through it, do you?'

'No, the door looks to be the only way out and we don't know what is on the other side,' said Helen.

Anita had found herself in some difficult situations during her career, but for once she felt stumped.

'Got any ideas, Helen? You got us out of the

handcuffs easily enough.'

'Well, I've been thinking. This building is quite old, and it's most definitely suffered extreme weather for a century, at least. I'll have a close look at the mortar, maybe it's crumbled and there is a weakness, a couple of blocks we can shift.'

Molly Harrington was the first to wake, opening her eyes as the early morning sunlight poked its way through the tattered curtains. A native of Birmingham, she did not normally hear the morning chorus and, lying on her camp bed, was delighted to hear the birdsong. Used more to the sound of traffic, she quietly rejoiced before stretching her arms and looking across the room to where Helen slept.

Funny, she thought, her bed doesn't look as if it has been slept in.

Sitting up, she noticed that Alice was not in the dormitory either, and her bed looked the same.

'Hey, Maisie, what do you think?'

'About what?' said a sleepy Maisie.

'It looks as if Helen and Alice haven't been to bed.'

Maisie sat up 'what?'

'Looks like our roommates were up early but their beds don't look slept in.'

'It seems a bit odd,' said Maisie, starting to dress. 'Perhaps they are in the bathroom. I'll have a look while I brush my teeth. We'll see them at breakfast, I expect. You don't think they are...'

'What?' said Molly.

'Perhaps we should have a look round before breakfast, see if they are outside somewhere.'

The dining room was already alive with the volunteers

when Molly and Maisie finally appeared. It was Liam and Sam's day for making the breakfast and they were cheerfully frying eggs and bacon.

'Top o' the marnin' te ye girls,' said a bright and breezy Sean, spooning baked beans onto his plate. 'The weather has cleared up, look at that sky. I bet we find some interesting artifacts once we get back on site.'

'Let's hope so,' said Molly, joining the queue for breakfast. 'Have you seen Helen this morning, Sean?'

'No, not yet. Why?'

'No sign of her or Alice this morning. They don't seem to have slept in their beds, We had a look around outside but they seem to have disappeared. I can't think where they might have gone, can you?'

'Dear girl, I have been married twice and I still don't understand the female mind. Perhaps they were fascinated by the storm last night. Begorah, wasn't it a heck of storm?'

Molly, unconvinced by Sean's assessment, went and filled her plate, returning to sit down opposite him.

'Something isn't right. Where are they?'

'Give it half an hour and if they don't turn up, I'll get the dig a bit of publicity.'

'What do you mean?'

'Local radio station, give them a story about two missing archaeologists. Might make the newspapers, put us on the map.'

'That's not very nice of you, Sean. Anyway, how will you let the radio station know when we have no means of communication?'

The mischievous Irishman smiled and touched the side of his nose with his forefinger.

'What does that mean?'

'It means I will be ringing them in the next half an

hour.'

'How? We don't have any mobiles on us.'

'I wasn't a runner for the Republicans when I was a kid for nothing. Taught me to look ahead and take no notice of authority. I had two phones when I came here an' dey only got one from me.'

'Why would you have two phones?'

'As I said, I have been married twice. Well, there is a turd on the horizon. Wouldn't do for number two to find out now, would it?'

A frown creased Molly's brow and she looked Sean in the eye. 'Are you serious? If you are, then I will never trust you again.'

Sean almost choked on the last of his beans, and sitting back in his chair, the cheeky smile that seemed to constantly accompany him spread even wider.

'Ah, the innocence of youth. You judge me too harshly; I keep a second phone to call my bookie back in Oirland. I like a flutter on the horses – well, maybe more than a flutter, and my wife would be none too pleased to learn how much I gamble on occasion. Of course, she is always pleased when I win big and spoil her.'

'You're insufferable. Are you really going to call the radio station?'

'To be sure I am, and don't you go lettin' anybody know what I'm up to. I tell ye, it will be good publicity, and good publicity costs a lot. Dose girls will turn up, mark my words. I bet when we get to the dig, they will be waiting fer us dere.'

Molly rolled her eyes as she chewed and, after swallowing, said, 'I hope you are right.'

The storm had abated as quickly as it had arrived, and after such a downpour the atmospherics abruptly changed. No morning mist, just clear, crisp morning air. Even though the swell had noticeably reduced, the ship rolled enough for Commander Pearson to need to rest his elbows on the railings. From his vantage point on the upper deck, he trained his binoculars on the low dark shape that was Fudensey. He swept his binoculars slowly from side to side, picking out the house, easily visible through the powerful binoculars. He glimpsed the boathouse roof amongst the dunes, and the jetty. It was all deserted, nothing moving, nothing to draw his attention, and so he swung the powerful binoculars back towards the house.

Almost immediately a group of figures appeared, the archaeologists. Ms Simms should be with them but they were too far away for positive identification, and now the ferry was passing its closest point to the island. He swept the group again, but try as he might he could see no sign of her. Fine-tuning the focus, he scanned the house and each window in turn, and then his heart missed a beat. His eyes were watering and he had to wipe them. The distance was increasing, the ferry beginning to leave the island behind, and in a mild panic he focused again on the window.

'Blast,' he said out loud, drawing the attention of a male passenger. 'Damn binoculars. I thought I had a good deal, but one of the lenses will just not focus at distance.'

'Aye, Chinese crap, no doubt,' the man said. 'Cheap rubbish, I don't know why we don't make the stuff we used to. British was always best.'

'But not as good as Scottish, no doubt,' said the commander, ignoring the rest of the man's comment as for one last time he focused on the window. There was no mistaking it: a red shape, the notebook, propped against the glass.

The man shrugged his shoulders and looked away. The commander moved to a more secluded part of the deck to call Jimi and let him know his worries when his mobile telephone came to life.

'Jimi, I was just about to ring you. Why are you calling me?'

'I have just heard an announcement on the local radio station. Two women archaeologists taking part in the dig on Fudensey appear to have gone missing.'

'Two?'

'That is what they said.'

Commander Pearson became thoughtful.

'Listen, Jimi, it's a code red – literally. Ms Simms left her red notebook in a window, a signal we pre-arranged in case she felt she was in danger, and now you tell me two women have gone missing. I don't know what is going on but I am not prepared to leave my agent unprotected. She must have discovered something. I think the time has come to bust this lot, archaeologists or no archaeologists. How soon can we get 43 Commando up here?'

'By chopper they can be on the job in under an hour, I think.'

'Do it.'

'I will, and I'll make my way to the island. There is a boatman who takes fishermen out for the day. It's early enough for me to get to him before any anglers turn up. I will go and find him, get him to take me across the sound.'

'Keep out of sight. I will get over there as soon as I can. There are a lot of civilians, we don't want any of them hurt.'

That Helen and Alice had gone missing was by now common knowledge amongst the archaeologists, but it was almost everyone's belief that they would miraculously reappear at the site of the roundhouse. The weather had improved dramatically, the storm's turbulence giving way to a gentle breeze and a cloudless blue sky. All were looking forward to returning to their work, in good spirits and as they ate breakfast Molly buttered her toast and turned to Masie.

'What do you make of Helen and Alice? Do you think they will turn up as Sean says?'

'I don't know. It seems strange to have gone out in the storm. What were they thinking of? Perhaps something has happened, an accident maybe.'

'They could have sheltered somewhere.'

'Where? The only place of any use is that boathouse, and we're not supposed to go there.'

'There is the ruined hamlet, a few abandoned crofts we can see from the site; you know, away towards the bay.'

'Oh yes, a possibility, I suppose.'

'Why don't we take a look over there if they are not at the dig?'

'Good idea, Molly. Shall we tell Sean?'

'No, there isn't any point just yet. Maybe later.'

Chapter 15

Helen Stock had studied archaeology for the best part of twenty years, had been on what seemed like a thousand digs, and was a dab hand with a trowel. It was the same trowel she kept in her anorak for that unexpected situation when she might make a startling discovery, only today she was using it to undermine the stone wall of the boathouse.

'I think they didn't have a lot of money to spend on this place when they built it. Look, you can see that here – it's just thrown together, made from surplus stone walling at a guess, maybe even ancient stone, perhaps Roman. You can see the chisel marks there, look. Clumsy.'

'Helen, as much as I appreciate your expertise on the construction of dry-stone walls, I think your time would be better spent in getting us out of here.'

'Sorry, I got carried away.'

'What can I do to help?'

'See if you can lie on your back and use your feet to prise the first stone from the wall. Then it should be simple enough to make a hole big enough for us to get out.'

Vasyli was a worried man. Domonic's impulsive reaction had put the operation in jeopardy, and he had to find a way out of the predicament. He had no idea if the woman had become lost. Her explanation was plausible, he supposed, except who would venture out in such a storm unless they were up to no good? She had been prowling around the boathouse for a reason and the solution was simple enough.

In his mind, unquestionably, the women were spies. Although killing them would be easy enough, he needed a story. Say they had strayed in the storm, accidently stumbled over a cliff, or got too close to the sea and been swept away – nothing too fanciful, but he had to get rid of them.

Summoning Domonic, Fyodor and Dimitri, he explained his plan. From the beginning it was known that using the archaeologists as a diversion was high-risk, but the belief was that a lot of activity without some kind of cover would draw attention. In reality there were always boats out on the sound, some coming too close for comfort, forcing Domonic and Fyodor to discourage any landings. They needed to bring in technical equipment and spare parts without drawing attention, and the cover of an archaeological dig had not seemed like such a bad idea.

'We have a problem; we must move quickly. My orders are that should I find the operation exposed, we are to destroy all evidence and leave as quickly as possible. Domonic, Fyodor, you are to dispose of the two captives; dump them at sea. Dimitri and myself will start taking apart some of the equipment for you to dispose of later, and as a last act I will program the submarine to make its way out into the Atlantic where the trawler can pick it up.'

'And then what?'

'I haven't considered that,' Vasyli said. 'Our duty is to the Motherland, to the operation and not our own salvation. Don't worry, I will think of something. I am a good English speaker and you can travel anywhere you like in this country without permits or passes. We will get home safely, I'm sure, but first we must close the operation down. The archaeologists will be returning to their excavations. They will know that two of their number are missing and they will ask questions when they don't turn up. We took their mobile phones when they arrived, so they have no means of communication, and if they spend the whole day looking for their treasures that should give us time to dispose of any evidence and leave before they finish for the day.'

'What if one of them comes back to the house looking for the missing women?' said Domonic.

'I think one of you should remain in the control room to monitor the cameras. If anybody does come back then get rid of them, without violence if you can, but if they become difficult... We haven't time to argue. Domonic, once you are free of your encumbrance, return to the boathouse and we can start dumping the circuit boards and spares. Then we need to leave. Right, you three go to the boathouse. I will catch you up, but first I should have a word with our friends, convince them to stay at the dig.'

The three Russian naval men nodded tacit salutes and left the house. Vasyli walked to where the archaeologists were congregating, ready to leave for the dig site.

'Professor O' Grady, we are aware two of your number are missing.'

Sean looked at 'Stewart' and nodded. 'Yes, I understand that their beds have not been slept in.'

'We saw them on one of the surveillance cameras around midnight last night.'

'Where?'

'At the back of the house. They seemed to be looking for somewhere private. They... were kissing.'

Sean frowned. 'You're saying they are having an affair?'

'It looks that way. I think they will have found some shelter to make out. They will be back, I am sure. If you don't see them soon, we will keep a look out for them. No need to worry.'

'Oh, right, thank you,' said Sean, a little puzzled.

He would never have believed Helen was gay, and as for the other woman, Alice, he had caught her eye a couple of times. His experience of women discounted her as having lesbian tendencies. It seemed a bit strange, but then he didn't know everything and today his archaeological instincts were telling him they could possibly find something of importance to make the digging season worthwhile. Rules or no rules, he would publish his paper.

'What was that about, Sean?' asked Molly, zipping her rucksack.

'He reckons Alice and Helen are gay, that they went out last night for some canoodling.'

Molly's jaw dropped. 'I don't think so. But if they were, we wondered if they might have gone to the derelict croft just past the dig.'

'We?'

'Masie and me. We were talking about them earlier. Whatever they were out in the storm for, they would need shelter. The only places we could think of are the boathouse and the ruined crofts.'

The dull roar of the outboard engine disturbed the tranquillity of the Gare Loch, and a military-grade rigid inflatable boat suddenly appeared from behind a rocky outcrop. The boat carried eight Royal Marines of the Fleet Protection Group on exercise from their base in the Clyde. From the shoreline Major Charlie I'Anson watched the rib race across the Loch, and as it drew near he raised his VHF radio and ordered an end to the exercise.

'A new job for you, lads,' he said, as the boat skidded up the slipway and the soldiers bundled out. 'Sergeant Jones, two sections for this one. You and Sergeant Barker take the lead, get your men into that lorry,' he said, pointing. 'The chopper is waiting for you with two small RIBs. I will brief you about the job when we're in the air.'

'Sir,' the two tough sergeants said in unison.

'Come on then, let's get moving,' said the major, already planning their arrival on Fudensey.

Anita was mildly amazed at Helen, who was working her small trowel, digging out the mortar holding the boathouse wall together. She dug in short sharp movements, flicking the debris to the floor, and in no time the first stone came loose.

'Here, give it a push while I work the rest of it,' said Helen, scraping at the joint, and as Anita applied pressure with her feet it began to move. 'Push!' Helen repeated, encouraging her to exert more pressure.

As the stone started to slide from the wall early morning sunlight began to stream into their prison.

'Bloody great, now this one,' she said, beginning to dig into a joint. 'Stay flat on your back and push, you will exert more force while I chip away at the mortar.'

Anita willingly obliged, lying flat with her legs together, her feet hard against the next stone, and within minutes it too began to slide from its foundation. The hole was getting larger and after they moved a third block, the hole was big enough for a body to squeeze through.

'You go first,' said Anita, getting to her knees. 'Be careful when you get outside, they might still be around.'

Helen did not need Anita's advice. Sticking her head into the hole, she wriggled like a snake through the opening to emerge into the early morning sunlight. It felt almost miraculous to be free after her ordeal, and when Anita appeared she believed their troubles were at an end.

'We can't be complacent,' Anita said. 'We need to get as far away from here as we can. Over there, look, the trees. There aren't many but they will give us some cover,' she said, tugging at Helen's sleeve. 'Come on, let's get out of here.'

'I can manage, thank you.'

'Yes, of course, Professor,' said Anita, in no mood to argue.

Half running, she led Helen towards the sparse cover, dropping to the ground as soon as they could. On looking back she was horrified to see a group of men entering the boathouse.

'Shit, they're back. We mustn't stay here; they will be looking for us as soon as they realise we have escaped.'

Still unaware of the breakout, Vasyli ordered Fyodor to check on the prisoners.

'Domonic, prepare the launch. I want you two to take them out to sea and dispose of them straight away. Come on, Dimitri, we need to destroy as much evidence as we can.'

Pulling his gun from his waistband, Fyodor unlocked

the storeroom door and stepped inside. He was puzzled that he could not immediately see the women; instead, his eyes rested on a shaft of light illuminating the rear of the room. He looked again, and it dawned on him that they were not there and uttering a string of expletives shouted out. 'They have gone.'

A startled Vasyli looked up. 'Gone? Where, when?'

'I don't know, but they have escaped. There is a hole in the wall,' said Fydor emerging from the store room.

Vasyli dropped his screwdriver and raced into the storeroom to stare aghast at the hole made in the boathouse wall.

'We must find them before they can raise the alarm. Fyodor, Dimitri, you have your guns?'

The two men nodded.

'Fyodor, make your way back to the house. Scan the surveillance cameras, see if you can find them. Dimitri, check the jetty and then make your way to the cove. Domonic, come with me to search the hill over there. Hurry, we can't afford for them to contact anyone. I don't want to have to kill them all.'

Anita was feeling the strain. Gasping for breath, she halted their flight as she crested the low hill and looked back towards the boathouse. What she saw sent a shiver down her spine.

'They've realized we have escaped. I can see two of them looking around and another is running towards the house. They will see us if we stand up. Quick, crawl over there, into the gulley. Once we are over the crest, we can run for it.'

Helen's eyes widened. If the seriousness of the situation had not fully dawned before, it did now. Dropping onto the rough grass, she slid like a snake.

'Right, let's go for it. Over there, not great cover but it will have to do,' said Anita, leading the way.

The fear of discovery and a lack of sleep weakened the women, and the effort expended in their escape left them in need of some respite. Anita was trained and fit, Helen less so, and on reaching a line of stunted trees the professor gripped the first of them like a long-lost friend and began to sob. Anita had some sympathy for her but the situation demanded they did not give in or give the Russians any opportunity.

As an agent of the Secret Service, Anita had experienced many difficult situations. They never got any easier but the one lesson she had learned was to never give up, never stop planning your next move. Looking back, she half expected to see their pursuers but there was nothing, just an empty landscape and a clear blue sky. Relieved, she sat against a large flat rock and took stock of their situation.

The outlook seemed bleak. The windswept island was covered in heather and lacked large areas of vegetation in which they might hide, but away from the coast the land rose. There were gullies and ancient rock protrusions in which they might seek sanctuary.

They could make for the dig site, seek help from the others, but against determined armed men it would be a less than useless move. Involving the rest of the volunteers would complicate the situation and she could not risk their safety. She was aware, however, that the excavation was no more than a mile away and beyond that was the abandoned hamlet. That might offer a safe hiding place for a while. From what she knew, the last crofters had abandoned the island forty or fifty years ago, leaving the buildings to collapse. The few sheep to escape the removals had happily bred at a sustainable rate and the small flock roamed at will. At present she and Helen were the only ones in any real danger and it was up to her to get them both to a place of safety.

'We must find somewhere to hide, to wait and hope we will be picked up.'

'What do you mean "picked up"? What is going on?'

'Sorry. Look, I will be as straight with you as I can. I believe we have stumbled across a covert Russian cell which is using the island as an observation post for what I can only guess at, but from what I found under the launch, I believe there is a strong possibility they are hunting our submarines or maybe surveying undersea cables.'

'What? That's preposterous.'

'Okay... You have experienced their methods; do you still believe they are just innocent builders renovating this place? They are Russian special forces, I think, dangerous men who want us both dead. My controller is out there somewhere keeping an eye on me. If he's seen my signal then there's hope.'

Helen's eyes widened. 'Oh!'

'You must do everything I tell you and do it as quickly as you can. It's our only chance if we are to survive. We must keep out of sight, get as far away from these people as possible for as long as it takes.'

'Why, what is happening?'

'I don't know, I can only trust that my people are watching and understand that we are in trouble.'

Letting out a sigh she got to her feet, gesturing for Helen to follow her. Walking at a fast pace, she made her way towards a rocky outcrop.

'The ruins are too far right now. We'll try and hide out there for the time being,' she said, pointing up the hill. 'We need some time to recover, then I can decide what to do.'

'What *can* we do?' Helen asked. 'Shouldn't we try to find the rest, strength in numbers?'

'I'm not sure that is a good idea right now. These people are ruthless. They will kill us and then the rest of your friends. No, let's keep them out of it and hope the good guys find us first.'

Fyodor left his associates and decided to take a detour over higher ground on his way to the house. He left the path and took the sheep trail inland: the route he guessed a fugitive might take. Most of the island's coastal flora was heather and grassy dunes, not great for hiding in, but inland there were locations offering better concealment and the craggy outcrop was one of them.

It took twenty minutes to reach the high ground, a sprawling accumulation of ancient rocks protruding through a sparse peaty covering. A shadow swept past and, looking up, he noticed a buzzard wheeling high in the sky. It seemed interested in something, so he kept his eye on the bird and its centre of attention: the rocky outcrop. He noticed movement, a shadow, a rabbit maybe. Was that the focus of the bird's eye? Maybe it was something bigger.

'Domonic,' he said quietly into his hand-held radio. 'Don't speak, just depress the send button three times if you can hear me.'

There was silence for just a few seconds until Fyodor heard three clicks; he had made contact.

'I am on my way to the house but I think I might have found our friends,' he said. 'Listen, you know the large outcrop? Meet me there as quickly as you can.'

It wasn't like Fyodor to go on a wild goose chase,

thought Domonic, as he put the radio in his jacket pocket. After checking the screens, he took his gun and locked the control-room door. He knew of the outcrop, a place he had visited on his rounds when checking for unwelcome visitors.

Mostly he spent his time watching the sea for boats coming too close, but he never neglected other avenues. He had seen a boat out on the sound earlier, the *Siobhan*, a blue-hulled fishing boat he had seen before. It was harmless, a fisherman who never came too close.

Helen dozed while Anita lay back against the rock face. The island was too small to hide them for ever, and she was hopeful Commander Pearson had seen her signal. To lie low and wait was their best hope.

A movement caught her eye and she turned her head to see a large bird hovering overhead. Helen opened her eyes.

'I'm starving. What I would give for a plate of those disgusting scrambled eggs the boys made for breakfast the other day.'

'I would take your mind off such thoughts. Survival can be as much about doing without as anything else, I'm afraid.'

'You know a lot about that, don't you?'

'A bit.'

'I was in the Girl Guides, went camping twice, that's about all I know. So, what's the plan? Are we just sitting here until the cavalry arrives?'

'There isn't much else we can do. Get some more sleep if you want. I'll keep a look out.'

'I'm knackered but real sleep is the last thing on my mind. Couldn't we sneak back to the house and hide out there? If they are looking for us then won't the house be deserted?'

Anita half smiled. 'It's an idea, I must admit.'

'So why not?'

Helen had a point. If the Russians were chasing about looking for them and the others had gone to the dig site as planned, the house could well be deserted. That probably meant no one was monitoring the surveillance cameras. On top of that, they would have the chance to try and locate the confiscated mobile telephones. With her phone back in her possession Anita felt sure she could bring the situation to a close.

'Okay, we'll try it. I don't relish stopping out here all day and then probably tonight.'

'So which way is it?' said Helen, getting to her feet, the low sun casting a long shadow

Chapter 16

As the women were squeezing through the hole in the boathouse wall two anglers, burdened with tackle and rods, were looking forward to spending the day on the *Siobhan* fishing the waters of the Little Minch.

'Looks like he's ready for us. The engine's running, Pete.'

'Who's that with Hamish?' said his companion as they approached the angling boat.

'I don't know, but he's a big one.'

'Morning, lads,' said Hamish, appearing from the wheelhouse. 'I'm afraid I have some bad news. I can't take you out today.'

'What!' exclaimed one. 'We've had this trip booked for weeks. Why can't you take us out? Everything seems okay, your engine's running.'

The two men looked at each other and then at Hamish. They were disappointed and angry.

'I'm sorry to have to tell you the skipper is taking me out today instead,' said Jimi, bracing himself for trouble. 'I have hired the boat for the day and you need to find another.'

'Who the fuck do you think you are?' said Pete, the burly Midlander before looking at the skipper again. 'We booked this boat weeks ago for a long-planned fishing trip. What are you going to do about it, Mr McChittenden?'

'Sorry, lads, this man booked me months ago as well. I double booked, a simple mistake, but I tell you what – if you come back tomorrow, same time, same place, I will take you out fishing for the day at no charge.'

The men were still angry but Jimi's formidable bulk was dissuading them from any rash moves. Looking at each other, they relented.

'Okay, but we're not happy about this.'

'I am truly sorry about the mix-up, lads. I will see you tomorrow. Now, it's time we were off,' said Hamish, letting go of a line, and with a gentle movement of the accelerator he guided the boat away from his disappointed clients.

'Thanks for that,' said Jimi, avoiding the angry looks from the dockside.

'Glad to be of service, your warrant card helped.'

Jimi smiled and as the boat made its way across the water, he looked past the pier end.

'Where is it you want to be when we get there?'

301

Hamish asked.

'I was hoping you might help in that department.'

'Mind if I smoke?' said the bearded Scot, picking up a tin resting near the helm. 'If you're wanting to get ashore unseen then we need to avoid the house and the jetty. You can bet someone will be around there,' he said, pausing to expertly roll a thin cigarette. 'There is a cove to the west; the water is shallow there and I can approach out of sight of the house, though I will not be able to get in close. Are you up for getting wet?'

At least his trousers were dry. Hamish McChittenden had told him to take them off, as the water was not shallow enough to allow him to paddle ashore with his trousers simply rolled up. The hairy Scottish boatman had taken *Siobhan* as close to the shore as he dared, instructing Jimi to go forward and look into the clear unpolluted water, and tell him where the dangerous rocks lurked. Once Hamish was satisfied, he spat his dog-end through the wheelhouse window and brought the vessel to a stop.

'This is as good as it gets. Good luck.'

Jimi had nodded, removed his trousers, and wrapped them around his chest. Then, hanging his shoes around his neck, he slipped quietly over the side into cold water.

'Just right, skipper,' he said as the water reached his waist. 'Don't forget Mr Pearson.'

Hamish grinned and felt for his tobacco tin as he slipped the gears into reverse. 'I won't,' he said, leaving Jimi to wade ashore.

Jimi was over the cold-water shock and grateful for the skipper's competency. He negotiated a course towards the white sandy beach, feeling with his bare feet for unseen obstacles.

The secluded horseshoe-shaped cove possessed pristine white sand dunes rising gently up towards a sparse line of stunted bushes, just like on the map he and Commander Pearson had studied the previous evening. Taking his bearings, he estimated the location of the house and the direction of the dig and set off across the nearest dunes. His job was to stay out of sight, locate the missing women, and learn what the Russians were doing.

Domonic could see Fyodor waving at him. Keeping his body hunched, he made his way across the heather.

'I think they are up there somewhere. I saw movement, and that bird has been hovering a long time,' Fyodor said, raising his eyes. 'I don't think it was a wild animal, the shadow was too large.'

'What do you want to do?'

'We need to cover them from both sides in case they make a run for it.'

'You really think it's them?'

'Yes, more than a good chance. We can wait for them to make the first move or we can try to take them now.'

'Take them out, yes. If it's not them or they stay put, we could be here all day.'

'Okay, you take the path and I will go this way. As soon as one of us can get them in our sights, then call the other.'

Domonic nodded, slipping away towards the sheep track that led past the outcrop whilst Fyodor followed his own path, a manoeuvre they had practiced in training. Keeping low, Fyodor used the larger rocks for cover, pausing from time to time to listen, but apart from isolated bird calls there was nothing. Domonic, following the old sheep trail, was more exposed although progress was easier and it was he who first caught sight of the women – two figures huddled together under an overhang. If he had not been so alert he might have missed them, but Anita had seen him first; just the act of turning her head alerting him.

'Hold it right there,' he said, pointing his gun. 'Fyodor, Fyodor!' he shouted. 'I have them.'

Anita's heart sank. There was nothing she could do except raise her hands in defeat.

'I'm sorry, the game's up,' she said, looking at Helen.

Helen looked back, her eyes dark with fatigue. In silence she accepted her fate.

'So, we meet again,' said Domonic, rubbing his groin and grinning. 'You will not have the same luck this time. What does your Shakespeare say? He who laughs last laughs longest?'

'He also said time will out,' said Helen, suddenly coming to life.

'Well, this is more a Greek tragedy, I think. Now, let's move you back to the boathouse where we can keep an eye on you.'

Commander Pearson looked at his watch: almost eight o'clock. The commandos should be on their way by now, and lifting his binoculars, he scanned the entrance to the ferry terminal. The small blue-hulled boat was larger now as it made its way steadily towards him. He lowered his binos, stowed them in his haversack and took out a bottle of water to quench his thirst. Across the harbour the deep baritone ferry horn announced its return to Leverburgh. Once it left, he would find himself stranded unless the blue-hulled boat heading towards him was his taxi to Fudensey. He need not have worried, for just minutes later the *Siobhan* came alongside the harbour wall and he was stepping aboard.

'Where to? Same place as your buddy?'

'Yes, take me to the boathouse jetty. Could be dangerous, but I can see you're a man who doesn't flinch from danger.'

Hamish McChittenden felt his mouth go dry and he took out his tin of tobacco. 'Mind if I smoke?'

'Go ahead, and don't worry too much – we have the situation under control.'

With a bewildered look, Hamish began rolling yet another cigarette. In these situations, a hand-rolled cigarette usually calmed his nerves.

Commander Pearson grinned. The skipper seemed to know what he was doing and to have his feet on the undulating deck of a small boat felt good, something he had not experienced since his days chasing pirates in the Malacca Strait. Looking towards a dark shape squatting on the sea just a few miles away, he retrieved a short-wave radio from his rucksack.

'Snow Goose, Snow Goose, this is Birdwatcher, Birdwatcher. Over.'

The radio crackled into life.

'Birdwatcher, Snow Goose, over.'

'Good morning. Do you have an ETA, over?

'Fifty-five minutes, over.'

'I will call you in forty minutes with further instructions, over.'

'Affirmative, Snow Goose standing by.'

There was an audible click, the transmission ended and Commander Pearson drummed his fingers on the boat's gunwales. 'How long to Fudensey?' he asked.

'About forty minutes,' said a worried-looking Hamish.

From the top of the dunes Jimi could see the roof of the boathouse, but he needed to get closer. Creeping through the dense, spiky tufts of Lyme grass, he reached open ground and had a clearer view but cover was sparse – just a few isolated bushes and a carpet of yellow-topped potentilla standing high enough to offer just partial concealment.

Before making a move, he scanned the area for potential danger and caught sight of a group of four people walking through the heather towards the boathouse. He was shocked to see that two of them were women. Was one of them Agent Simms, had her identity been revealed?

He looked at his watch: eight thirty. The commandos should be well on their way. He was at least a hundred metres from the group, an ineffective position from which he could do nothing to help. He was troubled to see the women being forced to sit back-to-back, one of the men standing guard.

Then a chance presented itself – perhaps a call from inside the boathouse, he couldn't be sure – but the guard left his charges and for a few seconds he disappeared around the corner of the building. Without thinking twice, Jimi rose to a crouching position and ran as fast as he could towards them. There was a flora-covered depression twenty or more metres away and, taking a dive into it, he disappeared.

Anita was worried. She was fighting fatigue and escape seemed impossible. Even Helen, exhausted and frightened as she was, seemed to be in control but they were in a precarious position. From what she could gather, the Russians were abandoning the base and would probably have little choice but to kill them. The guard had now left them unattended and she thought they might have a chance, but he was gone for just a few seconds, returning with a second man.

'I will check the fuel level. Keep an eye on these two, Fyodor,' said Domonic.

'We should tie their hands, wait for Vasyli to return before we do anything.'

'*Da*,' said Domonic, lowering his gun. 'Just keep an eye on them. That one is dangerous,' he said, pointing to Anita.

'Don't worry, she will not get the better of me. You should be more careful in the company of women, Domonic,' he teased.

'Just keep an eye on them while I sort out the launch.'

So, they need instructions from Stewart or whatever he's called, thought Anita. Realising that the launch would be a necessary component in her and Helen's disappearance, she knew there was still time. They were hardly going to kill them and go to the trouble of carrying their bodies when, alive, the women could do it for them.

That gives me a little time, she thought, and looking from the corner of her eye she weighed up the situation. Domonic was going to the boathouse and would be out of sight for a short time. The path was gravel strewn, a useful weapon if she could distract the one left to guard them. Could they get hold of a handful of grape shot?

She raised her head. 'You okay, Helen?'

Helen nodded and the Russian ordered them to be quiet.

'I don't need you to tell me to be quiet,' said Anita in perfect Russian. 'You may not realise it but we have you rumbled. There's no escape.'

'Shut up,' he said, taking a step forward just as Vasyli

and Dimitri appeared.

'You found them,' said Vasyli. 'Where is Domonic?'

'In there, getting the launch ready. This one speaks Russian, she's heard everything.'

'Dimitri, go and get some electrical ties. We should bind their hands,' said Vasyli, walking towards the boathouse.

From his position in the depression Jimi dare not put his head above its edge. The short flowers gave only limited cover, and if he lifted his head he could be seen. Parting the stalks allowed at least a glimpse of the boathouse, and from his new position he could see that Anita was one of the captives. She was looking away from him and he could not draw her attention, but then, should he? His orders were to observe and report, not to intervene and risk a loss of life.

'Damn... Where's Pearson, where's the marines?' he mumbled to himself as two of the Russians stood over the women. It looked as if they were being bound.

Helen was an archaeologist, not a spy, but Anita was. When Dimitri ordered her to present her wrists, she clenched her fists, bending them forward and increasing the perimeter.

'What are you going to do with us?' she said in Russian to distract her captor.

'You don't need to know, and we will do what is necessary,' he said, slipping the tie wraps around her wrists.

'We need to move quickly,' said Vasyli. 'Tell Domonic to bring the launch out to the jetty and we'll finish this.'

Fyodor finished tying the women's wrists and said to Dimitri, 'Watch them while I help Domonic.'

Dimitri nodded and, with his gun resting on the inside of his elbow, he kept the women under surveillance. To him they did not appear a threat. He looked towards the boathouse as the double doors began to swing open. He could see the launch inside and seconds later he heard the roar of its engine as Domonic prepared to bring it out.

'So, we will not be here much longer. Stand up,' he ordered.

Jimi, close enough to hear, felt decidedly impotent. Then the throaty sound of the launch's engine filled the air and it slowly emerged from the boathouse, coming to a halt at the jetty no more than thirty or forty metres from his hiding place. He could do little else but gingerly part the grass, and as the launch came to a stop, he saw a man forcing the women towards it.

He understood, could wait no longer, and with his gun pointing at the lead Russian, he rose to his feet and called out, 'Hold it right there, drop your weapons!'

Dimitri reacted immediately, turning to fire his gun, an automatic with a rate of fire that forced Jimi flat to the ground.

'Keep him pinned down, Dimitri,' shouted Domonic, standing square on the deck of the launch. In his hands he held an SR-3 Vikhr silenced assault rifle and he too began spraying Jimi's position, keeping the big man pinned down. Vasyli and Dimitri took advantage, bundling the women aboard the launch before taking up positions to cover them. As Fyodor opened the throttle, Domonic continued shooting.

Jimi could do nothing. Pinned down as he was, all he could see was the top of the boat's VHF aerial moving at full speed.

Sprawled on the deck of the fast-moving launch, Anita tried to wriggle free of her restraints, her hands held together as if praying – and in a way she was. Slowly she slid one hand over the other and then the reverse, and with some effort she felt the plastic binding slip over her thumb joint. Gritting her teeth, she pulled the hand free. At least she had the use of them, but without a weapon she faced a daunting task if she were to take on the Russians.

She could see Domonic kneeling, a weapon in his hands as he faced the receding shoreline. Beside her Helen lay with her eyes shut tight in fear.

A wave broke against the speeding craft, the induced motion forcing Domonic to put out his arm to steady himself. Anita took her chance. Leaping to her feet, she ran at the Russian, intent on forcing him overboard. But at the last moment he turned, alerted by her footfall and unable to bring the gun to bear, instead taking the full force of her attack. Anita jabbed her elbow at his face as he fell back but he was too strong, recovering quickly to fight back. Letting the weapon drop, he raised his forearms, deflecting his assailant's blows. Hitting Anita hard in the stomach, he gained the upper hand and forced her to the deck.

'You're first,' he snarled, leaning over her, pulling her arm behind her back.

Anita felt her bones were about to break and screamed out, but it was no use. He had her in his grip and she was unable to move.

'Get us into deep water, Fyodor. Let's get rid of this baggage as quickly as we can,' Domonic called out to his colleague, who was watching from the steering position.

The launch had left with the women on board and there was nothing Jimi could do. He feared the worst. The Russians were still shooting at him and he had to deal with them before he could do anything else. The ferocity of the onslaught had diminished now, just an occasional shot in his direction to keep him down. Taking advantage of a lull, he dared to part the flower stalks for a better view. What he saw was just one man looking his way, and of the second there was no sign. His cartridge clip was almost empty and he had little idea of exactly how many of them there were. Two had left on the launch, and from what he could see there were at least two more, enough to outflank him. Was that their plan?

He heard a shout from the direction of the boathouse and dared to look. The one taking pot shots had turned his head and was calling out a reply, but Jimi couldn't hear it properly. From a situation that only moments earlier had seemed dire, he now had a chance to go on the offensive. Taking a further look in the direction of the boathouse, he was surprised to see the other Russian had gone. This was his chance. He rose from the depression and ran towards the stone building, flinging himself into an area of wild grass. As he caught his breath a voice with a broad Geordie accent called out to him.

'It's alright, we've taken them oot, sir. It's okay, we have them.'

Surprised, Jimi raised his head to see a beret-wearing marine at the side of the boathouse double doors. He lowered his weapon with relief, only to lift it again as a swirl of water lapped the canal sides.

'What was that?' he said.

'Dunno, sir. The one inside was destroying equipment, maybe it's to do with that.'

311

'Where's Commander Pearson?'

'Major I'Anson will fill you in, sir. He's inside.'

'Thanks,' said Jimi, getting to his feet and walking past the soldier into the boathouse's gloomy interior. 'Major I'Anson?'

'Yes, and you are?'

Jimi explained as he looked at the destruction spread about. 'They were intent on getting rid of the evidence, I see.'

'Yes, we've got one of them round the back. He was going at this lot like a madman. I don't know what damage he's done, but you can see what a mess he's made.'

To Jimi's eyes the boathouse looked to be some sort of workshop, a technical one judging by the smashed oscilloscope and the circuit boards strewn across the floor.

'Don't touch anything,' Jimi said. 'We need forensics here as soon as possible, see if we can piece together what they were up to. Let's have a look at your prisoner.'

Vasyli's eye was swollen and turning a dark red when Jimi confronted him. Try as he might, the only information he was able to extract was the name Vasyli Pavlov and his serial number, and yet as a man who had been caught red-handed, he had a curiously self-satisfied look on his face.

Hamish McChittenden had done a sterling job getting The Commander to Fudensey and within minutes of arriving the helicopter was landing on the secluded beach. They were still some way from where the Russians and their prisoners but within minutes of touching down the highly trained soldiers were organizing the RIB and picking up Commander Pearson from the *Siobhan*, while the major led the second troop overland towards the boathouse.

The launch had emerged from the canal faster than it had ever done and was on its way to deeper water when the RIB cleared the headland. Commander Pearson hung on as the craft sped across the sound in pursuit barely managing to lift his binoculars.

'There's a fight,' he said.

'Keep down, sir. We will approach from behind,' said the marine sergeant. 'Frank, you go first and then you, Andy. I will make sure they don't try any foolish moves. Ready?'

'Ready,' said the two marines in unison as the gap closed.

Anita saw them coming. She realised that both Domonic and Fyodor were looking the wrong way but she felt helpless to do anything other than insult them, trying to draw their attention, and then a strange thing happened. No one had thought to search Helen, so while the Russian concentrated on Anita, he neglected the professor. She had watched as the thug felled Anita, believing she would be next, but inspired by the woman's fighting spirit she vowed she would not go quietly. Her excavating trowel was sharp, thousands of scrapings turning its edges into a useful weapon. Very carefully she had used it to sever her bonds and now all her frustration and fear exploded.

'Fucking bastard,' she screeched, lunging with her makeshift weapon at Domonic.

Missing with her thrust she at least took him by surprise, forced him backwards and Anita, who used to be Alice, stuck out a foot to topple him. But the big Russian was still dangerous. Growling like an animal, he rolled over and got to his knees, producing a killing knife from his belt.

'Oh...' gasped Helen, realising his intentions.

She tried to get away but there was little space on the deck. Fatigue had sapped her strength and, wide-eyed, she could do little but watch him approach, preparing for his lunge until Anita, aware of other developments, screamed out.

Domonic paused for just a second, but it was enough. He was blindsided, and a moment later felt an unexplained constraint around his neck. At eighteen stone and six feet four inches tall, Royal Marine Frank Donnelly was a man not to be ignored, and Domonic found himself face down on the deck. In the wheelhouse, Fyodor was unaware of the drama taking place until he looked up from the chart plotter and found himself staring down the barrel of a gun. Shocked, he raised his hands.

'Good boy. Now drop the revs before we all finish up in the drink,' said a grinning Andy Volans.

As the launch lost its way, Commander Pearson stepped aboard.

'You okay, any injuries?' he asked Anita, who was sitting with legs drawn up to her chest.

'Yeah, fine. What took you so long?'

The commander didn't answer. Instead he approached Helen standing by the wheelhouse, her hands gripping a guard rail.

'Hello, I'm Commander Pearson. I think you can relax; we seem to have the situation under control.'

Chapter 17

Charles Clark's body was healing, his mind more settled than it had been even though the traumas of the past few months still reverberated. He ran his fingers across his ribs, over the scar he would carry for the rest of his life. The hospital had patched him up and finally recommended his discharge and when he'd stood at the hospital entrance, he'd had little idea of what his future held.

A car had appeared, plain black. He had expected a taxi but the non-descript black saloon with darkened windows was no taxi. Hesitating at first, he simply looked the car over, perplexed until the rear passenger window slowly slid down to reveal a familiar face.

'Mr Clark, let me help you with your bag.'

'Oh, it's you. I don't have a bag. The hospital gave me these clothes.'

'We can help you with a few things. Don't look so concerned, you are not in any trouble but you do need to come with me.'

'What for?'

'We want to talk to you, but not here. My name is Jimi, by the way. I didn't introduce myself the last time we met.'

'No, you could say that,' said Charles, climbing in beside the man who had helped save his life, the sight of him bringing back unpleasant memories.

'You okay?'

Charles nodded; it was all he could do.

The road the saloon car followed was unfamiliar. Even when they took the A12 Charles still had no idea of where they were going. His new-found 'friend' Jimi wasn't at all talkative, his eyes on the road ahead while Charles could do no more than gaze out at the passing streets and wonder, Who was this man who had saved his life? A policeman? If he was, he was no ordinary policeman? He had no idea of the man's true identity and feeling somewhat glum, he resigned himself to his fate.

The Queen Elizabeth Bridge appeared in the distance. He knew this part of London, the South Bank, could it be? No, that was a farfetched idea, yet less than an hour later they were passing the Kennington Oval and he was sure the car was heading for the Albert Embankment and felt little surprise as the car turned off the road to enter an underground car park.

He knew then that it was the Secret Service offices, and was calm enough when Jimi ushered him from the car and into the building. The glass doors were imposing, the peacefulness of the interior unsettling, and that was when his resolve began to crumble. He was way out of his depth; would he ever emerge into the sunlight again? he wondered.

'In here,' said Jimi opening a door, 'take a seat. Would you like a coffee? It's proper coffee here, not that muck they serve at MI5,' he said with a smile.

'Yes, that would be nice.'

Jimi lifted the internal telephone receiver and asked for two cups of coffee.

'Okay. I expect you are wondering why you are here?'

'You could say that.'

'It's simply a debriefing exercise. There are one or two loose ends we need to tie up and we think you may be able to help.'

There was a knock at the door. Jimi went to open it and after receiving the tray of refreshments, he placed it in front of Charles.

'Help yourself, looks like she's added a couple of chocolate digestives.'

Charles took a cup and saucer, added some milk, and helped himself to a biscuit. It was what he needed, a chocolate biscuit, and feeling better he looked across the table at Jimi.

'They were the murderers, weren't they? Sergei and Markov.'

'Yes, you know them as the security at Potanin Estates, but I can tell you that Sergei Kulikov worked first and foremost for the Russian secret service and took his orders from the embassy of the Russian Federation.'

'Oh, I didn't know that.'

'You weren't supposed to,' said Jimi, looking at his watch. 'We will have a couple of visitors in a few minutes. I want to warn you that we know an awful lot about you, especially your bank accounts and the false passport. That is a criminal offence and you could go to jail for that.' He paused, noting Charles's pained expression before saying, 'You must answer all our questions truthfully, don't hold anything back. We will know if you are lying and that could prove a problem for you.'

Jimi's eyes held Charles's gaze for a moment, long enough to see his words had struck home. There was another knock at the door.

'Come.'

It opened, and a man and a woman entered. 'May I introduce Ms Simms and Tom Slazenger (not his real name) from the U.S. Embassy. You have already met Ms Simms.'

'Yes, good to see you again.'

'Okay, take a seat please and let's get down to business. Charles, you worked for Andrei Potanin's organisation for several years.'

'Three, to be exact.'

'In that time, you were privy to a lot of deals and we know some of those deals involved the dark web and cryptocurrency payments. We are aware you used a web of companies to disguise true ownership of assets and property and to avert tax liability. We know about the Al Falda building in Dubai. Fill us in on the details.'

Charles felt his heart miss a beat. He drank the last of his lukewarm coffee and cleared his throat. 'Yes, I paid two hundred million sterling with cryptocurrency. The seller was another Russian.'

'What is the guy's name?' asked the American.

'I don't know. I rarely learned who the real buyers or sellers were, I only knew about the financial transactions, company names, entities. Very rarely who was involved. But I do know where Potanin Estates registered most of their properties, the names, and jurisdictions of the shell companies.'

'Here's a pad and a pen. Let's go through all the deals you were involved in and where the money came from.'

Charles could feel the palms of his hands beginning to sweat, surreptitiously wiping them on his trousers. 'Right,' he said, picking up the pen.

For almost four hours the American and the two British Secret Service agents cross-examined Charles, teasing a goldmine of information from his meticulous mind. When Jimi sensed they had drained as much out of their subject as they could, he called a halt.

'Just one more thing,' said Anita, who had remained mostly passive during the meeting. 'The murders, the connection to Fudensey, your time on the run... I would briefly like to explore that side of things.'

Charles looked tired and Jimi wondered if perhaps they should take a break, but Anita was persistent. 'You never had any contact with the police?' she pressed.

'No, I wanted to get as far away from them and anyone else.'

'There is a suspicion that someone from Islington police station was feeding inside information to Potanin's organisation. Do you know anything about that?'

'Not offhand, no.'

'Think about it. Did you ever overhear a conversation? Was there any sign that someone was feeding confidential information to Potanin or his subordinates?'

'Well, yes, something was going on but I don't have any details. We always knew if we were getting a surprise visit from tax officials or if the police had a warrant to search any of our properties, but I have no idea who it was.'

'No secret payments?'

'There were lots of those.'

'How did you pay informants, bank accounts, cash?'

'Cash mainly.'

'Did you pay anyone personally?

'Just one, he was local I think.'

'Can you describe him, has he a name?'

'We used the name "Woodland", that's all I know.'

'Mister Woodland?'

'No I don't think so, a code name.'

'Local you say.'

'I'm pretty sure because from what I gathered his information was always about the local police or the local tax office. Once the council sent a building inspector to try and close one of our properties.'

'And did they?'

'No, the informant took care of it – for a price.'

Was Tabz right, an informant at the heart of the Islington police force? thought Anita. From a conversation at Vauxhall Bridge Tabz had set her thinking about the possibility of a mole. Interrupting her thoughts Charles said 'Can I ask a question?'.

'Fire away, I'll answer if I can.'

'What was going on at Fudensey that was so important? I heard something on the news, something about archaeologists.'

'They were a cover for a drug-smuggling operation. They were using the island as a transit hub for drugs coming from South America.'

'Well, I'll be... I did wonder about that. Seems so obvious, doesn't it?'

'It does, Mr Clark,' agreed Jimi. 'I think we're done for now. I know you don't have a lot, so I have authorised a payment of five hundred pounds to tide you over and I can arrange for a car to take you anywhere in London. So, if you will follow me,' he said, rising.

Charles Clark was a little bewildered as he left the building to climb into the car, asking the driver to take him to King's Cross station. He had no intention of returning to his London flat. He hadn't paid the rent for several months and, more than that, the future beckoned. He was not going back to his old life.

Almost reading the accountant's mind, Jimi watched him go before returning to the meeting room.

'How was he?' asked Anita.

'He'll survive.'

'Now, what about this drug smuggling?' asked Raul Martínez, chuckling.

'We had to tell him something,' said Jimi with a straight face. 'In reality, the Russians were running a clandestine spying mission from the island, and the archaeological excavation of the Bronze Age settlement really was a cover. They needed to ferry equipment across from the mainland, and to avoid too many questions they let it be known that the boxes they were transporting were for the dig: sandbags, shovels, anything they could think of. But they were bringing in equipment to enable them to service an underwater autonomous drone. To keep the thing operational, they required spare parts and a decent-sized generator. Knowing the locals in that part of the world, they needed a story to keep them occupied. They even hired a prominent archaeologist called Dr Schultz to set up a dig and invited a reporter from the local newspaper to write a story about it. It would have worked, but our friend Charles Clark came along. If we had not heard about the letter, we would not have known anything was amiss.'

'That was what was worrying him when he called us – some goddamn letter,' said the American.

'Yes, and it seems it contained information about Potanin being awarded a medal for his services to the Motherland, for allowing the use of an island he owned.'

'So why would Clark run if it was just a thank-you letter?'

'Because he knew too much, I think. I get the impression he was already looking to jump ship, and interpreting the letter as he did – correctly, it seems – pushed him over the edge. The situation for any Russian businessman working in the West has become precarious, and by association the authorities could sanction their minions. I think Clark believed that could include him.'

Raul stroked his chin in thought. 'What were they trying to do with this drone?'

'Yes, the drone. We are sure the plan was to send it out into the Minch to loiter, collect intelligence on both American and British submarines operating out of the Faslane naval base. These vehicles can remain on station for days, listening for propellor wash, tracking the subs out on patrol. We expect the Russians on the island would relay that information to their own submarines waiting in deep water. If a conflict ever occurred, they would hope to quickly neutralise our underwater nuclear capability using what intelligence they had gathered. It would be a big advantage when you consider their overwhelming nuclear arsenal.'

'And the underwater connection pipelines, I expect.'

'Yes, we are vulnerable to losing internet connectivity, not to say the gas pipes crossing British and continental waters. I understand the more sophisticated drones can cover hundreds of miles. That would bring the whole of the North Sea into range, and just a couple of specialist subs could create havoc.'

'Where is this drone now?'

'We don't know exactly, but we have search aircraft looking for lone ships out in the Atlantic and a type 23 anti-submarine frigate is undertaking a search. We have every confidence it will locate the drone.'

'The U.S. government hopes you are right.'

Tabz spent her days searching data bases, checking facts, delve into current cases and the one case that had dominated her work for the past few months was the search for Mister Clark. She found herself in the company of clever, secretive people, her trip to the American embassy, Simms, an interesting and capable woman. Working alongside her conversation had turned to the possibility of some bent copper selling confidential information. For a fleeting moment she had felt herself under suspicion and that hurt.

Her workload never seemed to diminish but there were times when the urgency of the situation slackened. She took that opportunity to dig a little further, look for evidence to back up her suspicions and have a look at her suspects residences. She had more than one suspect in her sights, and catching sight of an expensive looking BMW car she dug deeper, called Colin her trusty undercover detective.

'Sergeant Forrest, could I have a word wiv you like?'
'I'm busy Tabz, wot's it abaht?'
'You mainly.'

'What do you mean? Been poking that nose of yours where it doesn't belong,' said the sergeant, his hackles rising.

'I fink we should talk, somewhere private like.'

Sergeant Forrest's eyes narrowed. 'Private, wot's this abaht? I ain't having no private conversation with you. Now get off my back.'

The sergeant was old school, threats, and innuendo all part of his playbook but Tabs had worked alongside him long enough.

'There's a problem wiv your car.'

'What d'you mean?'

'I turned up a sales record, you didn't pay for it did you.'

'Strewth, what are you getting at. I did pay for it.'

'I was checking on a rape case, a taxi driver and he happened to mention you were picking your new car up at the same time he was in the sales office talking to his bruvver.'

'Your wrong.'

'His bruvver was puzzled that the car was paid for by a company called Potanin Investment Services. He knew you were a copper like innit.'

'Patel, Broadstreet motors! He's as crooked as they come. I've had dealings with him yes but the car I bought was with my own money.'

'I obtained a copy of the sales receipt like. Potanin investment Company bought it just a year ago. Why was that?'

'What's it got to do with you anyway? I think I need to talk to Inspector Mills about you,' he said trying to throw her off.

Tabz remained steadfast in her pursuit of the truth, even though she wasn't explicitly accusing Detective Sergeant Forrest of taking bribes. Her line of questioning had evidently unsettled him, which indicated that she was onto something.

'You've got a nerve, I'm the detective around here not you,' he said and with thunder written across his face he turned and walked away.

Tabz felt sick, the encounter had been brutal but she had the evidence and sitting back in her chair she proceeded to document every detail of the encounter, even down to the spittle forming at the corner of the sergeant's mouth and then she forwarded it together with a copy of the car's bill of sale to Anita who, in the event Tabz discovered evidence, should contact her first and not her superiors.

Just hours later, after Jimi and his associates had quizzed him, informed him of his responsibilities under the Official Secrets Act, and after he had learned the true nature of the plot in which he had unwittingly become embroiled, Charles Clark was back in Scarborough.

The seasons had changed, the sun was shining and warm, and the train was full of excited passengers quietly chatting as the train entered the station. A signal rang out and almost as one the passengers collected their belongings, the train shuddering to a halt. The doors slid open and the scene became one not unlike a migrating herd of Serengeti wildebeest as eager passengers spilled onto the platform. But the rush was soon over leaving Charles alone as he walked slowly towards the exit. The idea that history was repeating itself occurred to him, but at least this time he had some notion of where he was going.

'Where to?' asked the grumpy taxi driver. 'No luggage?'

'No, just me and this bag, thanks.'

'So, where to?' he repeated.

Charles gave the address and climbed into the rear passenger seat and as the taxi left the station precinct he glanced out at the now-familiar streets. He found it hard to believe it was just four months since he had first arrived here. Such a short time since that fateful taxi ride to the South Cliff hotel.

The journey comprised just two miles through light

traffic and then along the coast road, past familiar landmarks and, not far off, the sea. Strange, he reflected, how a city dweller could miss the sea's changing mood. Tranquil one day, angry the next, dangerous and foreboding. But today it was fair, with breaks in the clouds that let the sun dance across the watery surface. Charles had experienced its greyness many times, its aloofness as he cast into its depths for fish, but today it was in contrast, the sun giving its surface a pleasant blueish sheen.

Was it real, or was it a reflection of his mood? Contrasts, maybe, and feeling the urge to take up his fishing rod again, he looked out towards the horizon. Fishing for fish would have to wait. He had more important matters to attend to, and as the metalled surface ended abruptly, replaced by the crunch of gravel, he wondered if he was doing the right thing.

'Eight pounds,' announced the taxi driver, bringing his car to a halt.

'Thanks, keep the change,' said Charles, handing over a ten-pound note.

There was no reply, simply an outstretched palm. He was back in the north.

What if she wasn't at home? What if she had moved back to London? He could feel anxiety rising and forced himself to take a deep breath.

With his bag clasped to his chest, he put one foot in front of the other. He looked at the little house. It hadn't changed; the same corrugated tin roof, the small unkempt garden with its low brown fence, and just poking round the side of the building was the workshop, or was it a studio? He still could not decide.

Was she at home? He pushed open the little gate and, with his heart in his mouth, walked up to the front door.

She said she always used her back door, but after all the trouble he had put her to, he felt that she might see him using it as an intrusion. He worried about the reception he might receive. Would she hate him? He just did not know, believing that the formality of the front door was the better choice.

'Bugger it,' he said, rapping hard on the door and taking a pace back.

Nothing happened. She wasn't at home, he decided. Or maybe she was. Should he knock again? He had made enough noise to wake the dead so she probably wasn't at home. Maybe he should ring for a taxi, or better still, why not walk the shoreline and then take the cliff path back to his own little house?

He had a choice, but the growing feeling of disappointment seemed to suggest the latter course. A walk, a chance to reflect maybe, and as he began to turn towards the path an indeterminate thump from within drew his attention.

Half turning, he noticed the door move. Slowly at first, and then abruptly as the tight frame released its grip and the door swung fully open to reveal a perplexed face, an expression that turned into a smile of recognition.

'Jade.'

'Superman! Would you like a cup of tea?'

THE END

Printed in Great Britain
by Amazon